Elizabeth Ferrars and The Murder Room

>>> This title is part of The Murder Room, our series dedicated to making available out-of-print or hard-to-find titles by classic crime writers.

Crime fiction has always held up a mirror to society. The Victorians were fascinated by sensational murder and the emerging science of detection; now we are obsessed with the forensic detail of violent death. And no other genre has so captivated and enthralled readers.

Vast troves of classic crime writing have for a long time been unavailable to all but the most dedicated frequenters of second-hand bookshops. The advent of digital publishing means that we are now able to bring you the backlists of a huge range of titles by classic and contemporary crime writers, some of which have been out of print for decades.

From the genteel amateur private eyes of the Golden Age and the femmes fatales of pulp fiction, to the morally ambiguous hard-boiled detectives of mid twentieth-century America and their descendants who walk our twenty-first century streets, The Murder Room has it all. **>>>**

The Murder Room
Where Criminal Minds Meet

themurderroom.com

T0352205

Elizabeth Ferrars (1907–1995)

One of the most distinguished crime writers of her generation, Elizabeth Ferrars was born Morna Doris MacTaggart in Rangoon and came to Britain at the age of six. She was a pupil at Bedales school between 1918 and 1924, studied journalism at London University and published her first crime novel, *Give a Corpse a Bad Name*, in 1940, the year that she met her second husband, academic Robert Brown. Highly praised by critics, her brand of intelligent, gripping mysteries was also beloved by readers. She wrote over seventy novels and was also published (as E. X. Ferrars) in the States, where she was equally popular. *Ellery Queen Mystery Magazine* described her as 'the writer who may be the closest of all to Christie in style, plotting and general milieu', and the *Washington Post* called her 'a consummate professional in clever plotting, characterization and atmosphere'. She was a founding member of the Crime Writers Association, who, in the early 1980s, gave her a lifetime achievement award.

By Elizabeth Ferrars
(published in The Murder Room)

Toby Dyke
Murder of a Suicide (1941)
  aka *Death in Botanist's Bay*

Police Chief Raposo
Skeleton Staff (1969)
Witness Before the Fact (1979)

Superintendent Ditteridge
A Stranger and Afraid (1971)
Breath of Suspicion (1972)
Alive and Dead (1974)

Virginia Freer
Last Will and Testament (1978)
Frog in the Throat (1980)
I Met Murder (1985)
Beware of the Dog (1992)

Andrew Basnett
The Crime and the Crystal (1985)
The Other Devil's Name (1986)
A Murder Too Many (1988)
A Hobby of Murder (1994)
A Choice of Evils (1995)

Other novels
The Clock That Wouldn't
  Stop (1952)

Murder in Time (1953)
The Lying Voices (1954)
Enough to Kill a Horse (1955)
Murder Moves In (1956)
  aka *Kill or Cure*
We Haven't Seen Her Lately
  (1956)
  aka *Always Say Die*
Furnished for Murder (1957)
Unreasonable Doubt (1958)
  aka *Count the Cost*
Fear the Light (1960)
The Sleeping Dogs (1960)
The Doubly Dead (1963)
A Legal Fiction (1964)
  aka *The Decayed Gentlewoman*
Ninth Life (1965)
No Peace for the Wicked (1966)
The Swaying Pillars (1968)
Hanged Man's House (1974)
The Cup and the Lip (1975)
Experiment with Death (1981)
Skeleton in Search of a
Cupboard (1982)
Seeing is Believing (1994)
A Thief in the Night (1995)

Murder in Time

Elizabeth Ferrars

An Orion book

Copyright © Peter MacTaggart 1953

The right of Elizabeth Ferrars to be identified as the author of this work has
been asserted in accordance with the Copyright, Designs and Patents Act 1988.

This edition published by
The Orion Publishing Group Ltd
Orion House
5 Upper St Martin's Lane
London WC2H 9EA

An Hachette UK company
A CIP catalogue record for this book is available from the British Library

ISBN 978 1 4719 0696 1

www.orionbooks.co.uk

CHAPTER I

IN THE drawing-room of a big stone house in a suburb of Bradford, an old woman was walking up and down, whistling to herself. She interrupted her whistling only to puff at the cigarette that she held between thin, nicotine-stained fingers, heavily loaded with old-fashioned rings.

When the cigarette was finished, she lighted another from the stub, which she then dropped, still glowing, into a glass ash-tray the size of a soup-plate.

She was a very old woman, but she was slender and upright and her steps back and forth across the Persian carpet that covered the whole floor of the enormous room had a jerky vigour. As she threaded her way without hesitation along what was obviously a familiar route, curving between brocade-covered chairs and little polished tables, loaded with photographs in silver frames and bowls full of beautiful roses, her whistling came tunefully from her pursed, shrivelled lips. They were tinted a pale shade of pink and there was a faint flush to match on her cheeks. She wore a dress of dull mauve satin and over it a knitted cardigan of the same shade. Her skirt reached halfway down her calves, showing slim ankles in good nylon stockings. She had diamonds in her ears.

While she walked and whistled and smoked, the room was growing darker. When presently a man came into the room through french windows opening on to the garden, he said at once, " Can't we have the lights, darling, or will that disturb your mental processes ? "

The old woman stood still, looking towards his shadowy figure.

" No, no, my dear, turn them on," she said.

He pressed the switches and lights sprang on inside a great festoon of crystal.

" Got a cigarette left for me ? " he asked.

She took a crumpled packet from the pocket of her cardigan and held it out.

" You really shouldn't," she said. " It's bad for you."

He corroborated what she said by coughing as soon as he drew in the smoke. He was a short, stout man of about fifty-five with a few wisps of dark hair smoothed across the crown of a bald head, a pale, round face and horn-rimmed glasses. He was dressed in an old blue blazer and flannel trousers and had a canary-coloured silk scarf knotted round his neck. His hands, in one of which he held a small trowel, were dirty from gardening.

" Well," he said, " have you come to any decision ? "

" Yes." As she nodded her head decisively, the diamonds hanging from her ears trembled. " We're going."

" Oh dear," he said. " Must we ? And with the garden just at its best too."

He turned to look out wistfully at the rather sooty lawn and formal flower beds enclosed by a high wall of blackened stone.

" That man's up to something," she said, " and I've got to find out what it is. That's why we're going."

" Mother darling, that isn't your reason at all," the stout little man said. " The fact is, you always liked him in spite of everything and you're looking forward to a frivolous week-end at Nice."

" My dear Hector, I can go to Nice whenever I like."

" But this is at someone else's expense, and that's so nice, isn't it ? "

She cackled a little. " Have your joke, boy. Of course, I admit that this invitation does rather appeal to me. It's so ridiculous, with a sort of pre-war ostentation about it that seems particularly attractive in times like these. I shall have to buy some clothes, I suppose—I've nothing in the least suitable for the Riviera. But still, the important thing is that the man's up to something. Mark Auty——" She emphasised the name oddly and laughed again. " Mark Auty would never have invited us, and apparently all those other people too, without having some peculiar object behind it. And I think it might be rather important to discover what that object is."

The man gazed across the room at her with a sad sort of owlishness.

" You're fascinated by him, darling," he said. " You always were."

" Nonsense, nonsense," she said and began walking up and down the room again. But a trace of a flush had mounted behind the delicate pink tinting of her cheeks and as she started whistling again, her first notes were a little off-key.

" Well, if we must go, we must," the man said with a resignation which showed that he knew from long experience that argument was useless. But there was a deep frown on his face as he strolled back into the twilit garden.

That same evening, in a small hotel on the edge of Dartmoor, a pretty young woman who had been serving in the bar said good-night more hurriedly than usual to the last customer and closed the doors.

Until that moment her face had been animated and she had been laughing and talking with such gaiety to the men gathered in the bar that one or two had asked her if by any chance it was her birthday, or if anyone she knew had just died and left her some money. But as the bolts slipped home her face changed. The excitement left it and her expression became determined and rather defiant.

It was a little oval face, naturally pink and white but with a light summer tan on it. She had wide grey eyes and a small, upturned nose. Her hair had been bleached to an almost silver fairness and fell sleekly to her shoulders. She was a slender creature, dressed in a flowered cotton dress cut very low between her breasts. She wore several strands of pearls round her neck and a pair of big ear-rings of painted china.

Turning from the doors, she walked quickly across the empty bar-room to the small room beyond it. Her shoulders were held back tensely, expressing nervousness or anger, while her full lower lip was sucked in under her upper teeth with a look of fierce preparedness for battle. Throwing open the door of the inner room, she stood there and demanded, " Well now, do you see it my way ? "

" Hell," said the man who was sitting at the table with a number of papers spread out before him, " I tell you there's a catch in it. There's something the matter with it."

" All right, then, there is—how should I know about that ? " the girl said. " But when are you and me going to get another chance like this, will you tell me that ? "

3

" You don't know Auty like I do," the man said. His voice was rather thick and heavy. " I know him too bloody well. He's up to something. Asking you and me to a party in Nice ! Chartering a plane for us ! He's never done anything much for us before, has he ? He's never invited us anywhere before."

" He helped you buy this pub, didn't he ? "

" Conscience money."

" What d'you mean ? "

The man did not reply. He was a thin, dark man of about thirty-five, whose pallid, rectangular face had the kind of handsomeness that vaguely recalls a variety of film-stars. His black hair was cropped short, except for a wavy lock that fell over his forehead. He wore a loose tweed jacket, cut in the American style and a nylon shirt. He suffered badly from hay-fever, which made his fine dark eyes water and had reddened his nose.

The girl gazed at him for a moment, frowning, then changed her tactics. Going behind him, she slipped her arms round his neck and bent over him, rubbing her cheek against his hair.

" Timmy darling, you know what this means to me, don't you ? You know nothing like it's ever happened to me before. And you do love me, don't you ? You do want to please me ? "

" Of course I do," he muttered. " But you don't know Auty."

" All right, I don't. But even if he is up to something, what can that matter to us ? Where could people like us fit into any scheme of his ? "

" That's just it—where ? "

" I think it's just like he said in his letter. He's marrying this girl with pots of money and he wants her to know he thinks that he and his friends are just as good as she is."

" That isn't exactly what he said."

" No, but it's what he meant, isn't it ? "

" And him and me aren't friends any more."

" But you used to be, didn't you ? You were pals when you were in the army. You've always said you taught him everything you knew. Well, now he's had this bit of luck, I daresay he's got around to remembering that."

The man gave an abrupt laugh, stood up and disengaged himself from her arms.

"We're not going," he said. "And I'll tell you why we're not going, then you can stop pestering me about it. Maybe Auty knows a few things about me that he thinks he's going to use in some way, see? Maybe he thinks he's going to put the screws on me to make me do something or other that suits his book. Well, I'm not falling for it. Talking about the army and old friends and all that! I know better than that. The only possible reason he could have for asking me to his blasted party is that he means to make use of me. I don't know how and I don't care how— because I'm not going."

He went out of the room.

The girl made as if to follow him, then stood still, gazing after him thoughtfully, her lower lip flattening itself under her upper teeth in the way that made her small, pretty face look savage and determined.

At a later hour that same evening, in a Soho club, a red-haired woman in a short-skirted, strapless evening dress, with a fur stole bundled carelessly on the table before her, sat waiting restlessly for a man who had not arrived at the time that he had promised.

As her anger mounted because of this, her orders for drinks became more and more frequent, and when at last the man appeared, her quite handsome features had acquired a flushed, set look, dull and brooding.

The man only glanced in her direction, then went to talk to the barman.

"Why d'you let her do it?" he asked. "You know I don't like her like that."

The barman shrugged. "She keeps quiet that way."

"I don't like it, I've told you that before."

"I'd get yourself another girl then."

"And I don't like that sort of talk from you either."

"Suit yourself." The barman turned away to attend to another club member.

The man who had just come in went over to the corner where the woman sat.

He was a slightly built, black-haired man of about forty. High cheekbones and a sharply-pointed chin made his face seem triangular. There were hollows under the cheekbones and his skin had a sallow and unhealthy look. He was dressed in a dark blue pin-stripe suit that had come from a good tailor and his shirt and his shoes had been made for him. But a lace handkerchief, demonstratively displayed in his breast-pocket, spoiled the general impression.

The woman stared up at him with dull, resentful eyes.

" So you got here at last," she said.

" No," he said, " quite a while ago, remember ? " His voice was mellow and agreeable and his accent, in a way that was somehow inappropriate to the rest of him, was perfectly cultured. " Remember when I got here, Myra ? "

" Oh, I remember. And Harry remembers too. . . . Pete, I don't like that Harry. He's getting above himself."

" He's all right, he knows his job," the man said. " Come on now, let's go."

" Aren't you going to have even one drink ? "

" No."

" Well, I want to phone my mother first."

The man turned to the barman with a laugh. " Harry, she wants to phone her mother."

" I know ; they're like that sometimes," Harry said.

" It's too late to phone your mother, she'll be in bed," the dark man said. " But I'll drive you home. You're no use to me in that state."

Tears gathered in the woman's dull eyes. " You aren't kind to me, Pete."

" If I were, you wouldn't know the difference," he said. " Come on."

He picked up her fur and threw it round her shoulders. " What about next week ? " she asked.

" No, next week's off. I'm popping down to Nice for a few days. I'll see you the week after. Then we'll have another quiet evening together like this, won't we ? "

" I hope you fall in the sea and drown," the woman said. But she let him take her arm, and, stumbling a little, went with him docilely to his waiting car.

In an old house in an Oxfordshire village, a man and a

woman sat drinking a last cup of tea together before going to bed. The tea had been poured from a fat-bellied, Georgian silver teapot and the man and the woman were drinking it from blue and gold Queen Charlotte cups.

They had had guests that evening, the vicar and his wife from the village, a professor of Ancient History from Oxford, and a young woman who was just about to marry a peer. It had been a quietly successful evening and should have left the host and hostess gratified and at peace with the world. Yet as they sat drinking their tea in the small, beautiful, white-panelled drawing-room, the faces of both were distraught, and the eyes of the woman were filled with positive terror.

" But I can't understand it ! " she said into the silence that had fallen between them. " I can't imagine what he wants. It's—it's absolutely indecent. It's incredible."

She was a tall woman of about forty-three, wide-shouldered and fairly heavily built, with a dignified deliberateness in her gestures. Her brown hair was tinged with grey, parted in the middle and worn in a small bun. Her face was long, with a high-bridged nose and a firm, pleasant mouth and would have had a certain beauty if the skin had not sagged so that she looked a good deal older than she was. She was wearing a shapeless dress of flowered crêpe that she had been wearing for evening parties for two years.

" All the same, I think we ought to go," the man said in a low voice.

He was about five years older than the woman, not quite as tall as she was, with close-cut, fair hair, a ruddy, clear skin, and the look that never quite leaves a naval man, even years after he has retired from the sea. He wore a double-breasted grey suit, old but still presentable. He was watching the woman thoughtfully, while her frightened eyes roamed about the room, taking in nothing.

" After all," he went on after a pause, " he must want a solution as badly as we do. It's possible that he's had some idea that will help us all out of this difficult situation."

" How can there be any way out ? " she asked in a strangled voice. " For us, perhaps yes, if we can face it. But for him, no. None. And that's what I'm afraid of. What does such a man do when the situation's hopeless ? "

" I don't know. But the whole idea of this party in Nice is so bizarre that it may mean he has some idea and I think at least we ought to go and talk the position over with him."

She shivered. " That sounds reasonable, yet everything in me feels that it's the wrong thing to do. Oh, if only I'd never opened that paper ! "

" You'd have opened another one sooner or later." He put down his tea-cup and went over to her, sitting down on the arm of her chair, laying a strong hand on one of her shoulders. " Vi dear, can't you realise that this thing isn't really important for us. It's been a shock, I admit, and I'd give all I possess to have prevented its happening. But still, we can face it. For all we know, we'll have to face far worse things in our lives—disease, death, the real things."

She gave a deep sigh. " It's easier for you, Denis. You're so much surer of yourself than I am. You know what's important and what isn't. But I've done so much pretending all my life that when something strange happens, that I'm not prepared for, I seem to have nothing to hold on to or to guide me."

" You've got me, anyway," he said, " and you can hold on all you like, even if as a guide I'm not all that remarkable."

She smiled up at him. " But that's part of the trouble. You're all I've got in the world and all I've ever had. Don't you see how frightened that makes me ? You and this house and this life here that I've gradually got to understand— though those things are just part of you and wouldn't be anything without you. But if I were to lose it all——"

" You won't lose it, any of it." He bent and kissed her on the forehead. " Will you leave it to me, Vi ? Will you trust me to look after you ? As a matter of fact . . ."

He got up and went to the window. The scent of stocks was strong on the night air, their white clusters showing up in the darkness. Somewhere in the distance a dog barked and another answered it, but the evening was very quiet.

Standing with his back to the room, he felt for a pipe in his pocket. " As a matter of fact," he said, " I think I know how to deal with the situation."

In a hotel-bedroom in Bloomsbury, a young man, sitting by the open window that looked out over a street noisy with traffic, where the heat of the evening had become stale and exhausted, read and re-read a letter that had reached him that morning.

There was practically no expression on the young man's face as he did so, but only an inward look, as if it were memory that occupied him, rather than the words that he was reading so carefully. Yet he was not merely looking through and beyond the letter in his hand, for now and then his lips actually formed the words on the paper.

Partly because his face was so set, it had a stern look. It was a sensitive face, intelligent and imaginative. Its most marked feature were the eyebrows, which were even darker than his dark hair, unusually level and almost meeting above the straight, narrow nose. His lips were full, his chin pointed. His grey eyes had the slight overbrightness of someone who spends too much time alone, staring emptily before him, dreaming too much.

At last he threw the letter down on the bed and stood up. He seemed tired and his movements were languid but without indecision. Opening the battered suitcase that was on a stand in a corner of the room, he rummaged about in it among crumpled shirts and unwashed socks until he found something that was carefully wrapped in a green knitted pullover.

Removing the wrapping, he looked interestedly but not excitedly at the object he held. It was a small revolver.

Still with the same calm, as if merely to reassure himself of something that he was aware he knew already, he examined the revolver to make sure that it was fully loaded, then he wrapped it up again in the green pullover, replaced it in the suitcase, closed the lid and locked the case.

Then he sat down at the table, took a sheet of hotel note-paper from its drawer and began a letter, " My dear Mark," going on to accept an invitation to a week-end party in Nice.

CHAPTER II

ALSO ON THAT same evening, in a quiet street on the north side of Regent's Park, a young woman, turning the corner blindly, walked straight into a tall man in a light suit who was striding rapidly towards her. He began an automatic apology for her blunder, then his tone changed to one of startled recognition.

" Sarah ! Sarah Wing ! "

The girl returned his look confusedly, seeing in the light of the street-lamps a square, blunt-featured face, blue eyes between thick lids, fringed with thick, pale lashes, sleek fair hair that glinted pale golden in the lamplight, and a wide, confident, good-humoured mouth.

She knew the face at once, yet because her mind was reeling with shock, she had to make an almost desperate effort at concentration before she could fit a name to the face.

" Major Auty."

He was looking at her more closely. " What's wrong ? What's the matter with you, Sarah ? "

" I've just seen someone killed," she said.

She swayed, standing there.

He gripped her by both elbows. Looking round hurriedly, he saw a public house a little way down the street and started to say, " Come on, what you need is a drink." But then he changed it to the question, " Where were you going ? Is your home somewhere near ? "

" Just down this street," Sarah said.

" I'll see you home, then."

He slid an arm through hers and they started walking along the street down which he had come.

It was a street of Victorian houses with small, drab gardens enclosed by iron railings. Lights from the windows fell on clumps of laurel and privet. There was no one else in the street. The tapping of Sarah's heels sounded sharply on the empty pavement.

She was hardly aware of the man or of his supporting arm. She kept her gaze frowningly on the ground before her, still afraid of what she might see if she were to look up. She felt dazed and sick, worse now than when the thing had actually happened.

Mark Auty looked at her curiously. It was five years since they had last seen one another in occupied Germany. She had driven his car for him for a few weeks, a cheerful, rosy-cheeked girl whose curly brown hair had nearly always been untidy and who often forgot her make-up. Now she was thinner, the brown curls were well cut, her cheeks had become paler and the rounded girlish features were more defined. But shock had emptied her face of all expression so that there was no guessing at the kind of woman into which she had grown. Her black suit and small black hat were smart but inexpensive. She had no wedding-ring on her finger.

Suddenly she exclaimed, " He did it on purpose ! "

" Who did ? " Auty asked.

" The driver."

Auty asked nothing more. As he looked at her, a wariness came into his heavy-lidded eyes, as if he were thinking that if this situation should turn out to be more complicated than he had realised, he would take the first chance to escape from it. Yet when Sarah stopped at a half-open gate between two high brick gateposts and said, " Here it is," he did not immediately try to leave.

" D'you live with your family ? " he asked.

" No," she said, " they're still in Bristol. I've a flat of my own."

" Will you be all right alone now ? "

" Oh yes, quite all right. But——" She hesitated. " Would you like to come in ? I can give you a drink."

" Won't your landlady mind ? It's pretty late," he said.

" No, nobody'll mind."

" All right then. I'll come in for a little and you can tell me just what it was you saw. It was a car-accident, was it ? You saw someone run over ? "

" Yes—only it wasn't an accident."

She took a key out of her bag and led him up the broad stone steps to the door.

A dim light was burning in the hall inside.

" Be as quiet as you can," Sarah said in a whisper. " The

man on the ground-floor has to go to work at some godless hour in the morning and always goes to bed early."

They started up the stairs on tiptoe.

Sarah's flat was on the first floor. It consisted of two big rooms with a connecting door between them and a smaller room that was both kitchen and bathroom. The sitting-room had white walls, a plain grey carpet and light modern furniture.

Switching on the lights, Sarah said rather self-consciously, " I'm afraid it's not much of a place to bring you into. But I'm not accustomed to important visitors."

She took off her hat, pushing her fingers through her hair so that it sprang up into the untidy curls that he remembered.

" You've become a very important man, haven't you ? " she went on. " I've often read about you in the papers." Her tone sounded much more normal, as if she had already drawn reassurance from her belongings and the familiar room. " Major Auty, M.P. Is it too late to congratulate you on your election ? "

Auty laughed. " Not major, however. That was strictly war-time."

She drew the curtains.

" What luck for me running into you! It feels much better with someone to talk to. What would you like to drink ? I've got some whisky."

" Wonderful girl."

She went to a cupboard and brought out a bottle and glasses.

" I haven't usually got this about," she said, " but I've had my brother staying with me and he brought it along. The one who was in Singapore, d'you remember ? The one who was a prisoner. And now he's gone out there again. I can't understand it. If I'd gone through something like that in any place, I'd never want to go back there all my life. But he didn't seem able to settle down in England. I suppose a lot of people are like that. But you aren't. You went right through the war and spent quite a while in a prison camp, didn't you ? Yet you've been wonderfully successful since then. Of course, I always thought you would be, only somehow I'd never have thought of you in politics. I'd have expected you to go into business and make an enormous amount of money and marry an awfully rich and beautiful wife and probably end up with a title." The numb phase of shock had passed off and she was growing talkative.

Auty, observing her shrewdly, said, " Well, she *is* very beautiful. And she's awfully rich. But the title, I'm afraid, will have to wait."

" Are you married ? " she asked in surprise. " That's something I haven't read about you in the papers."

" You will shortly. But now tell me about this accident. After that we'll talk about nicer things."

Sarah sat down, leaning back and carefully relaxing her muscles.

" It wasn't an accident," she repeated, staring hard into Auty's blue eyes. " He did it on purpose. He ran him down on purpose. He chased him with his car and ran him down."

" Go on."

" You don't believe me."

" Go on and tell me the rest of it."

He crossed the room to the fireplace and stood with one elbow resting on the mantelpiece, sipping his drink, looking very tall and solid, standing over her. He had grown a good deal heavier than he had been five years before and his face was more florid, but he had the same look of good-tempered, practical intelligence that she remembered.

" I don't know, I may be all wrong about it," she said evasively, her nerves dreading an argument.

" Go on," he said again. He seemed intent and interested.

" Well, I didn't realise it at first," she said. " I thought the car had just got out of control. That's what I told the policeman who took my name and address."

" What made you think differently ? "

" It was when I was coming along the road just now. I suddenly remembered the driver's face. It came back to me quite clearly and I realised that he'd actually meant to kill the man."

" From the look on his face in a car going fast down a dark street ? "

" Yes."

" Come, now," he said.

"I did see it," she insisted. "He looked—oh, it was a terrible look. I've never seen anything like it."

"Don't you think that could have been fright because the car really was out of control?"

"It wasn't a frightened look. It was calculating and determined and quite calm. And he never stopped for a moment to see what had happened, but drove straight on."

"Oh." Auty's square, blunt-featured face became more thoughtful. "That's different. Yet even that doesn't necessarily mean murder."

"Murder!" she said sharply, taking fright at the word.

"That's what you're saying, you know." He swallowed some whisky. "What did he look like, this man? Could you describe him to the police?"

"Well, I'd know him again," she said, "though I don't know how to describe him particularly. He was thin and dark and I think he was about forty and he was clean-shaven and he was wearing a dark suit."

"That isn't much to go on."

"I know. But I'd know him again."

"Let's hope he isn't aware of that fact, then."

"What d'you mean?" she asked uncertainly.

"Never mind," Auty said. "Was he alone in the car?"

"I think so."

"What about the number of the car?"

"I didn't notice it."

"What make of car was it?"

"I'm not sure. I rather think it was a Vauxhall, but I'm not really sure."

Auty smiled wryly. "You aren't the perfect witness, are you? You noticed the look on the man's face, yet you didn't notice the number or make of his car."

She stirred restlessly in her chair. "All the same, Mr. Auty, I did see that look on his face and I know what it meant."

"And what about the other one?"

"What other one?"

"The one who was killed."

She had thought that she had quite recovered from the effects of shock, but at the question she shuddered so convulsively that some of her whisky spilled over her skirt.

Groping for a handkerchief, she rubbed violently at the wet mark, going on after there was not a trace of it left. Then, looking up, she caught what she thought was a gleam of amusement in Auty's eyes. It made her all at once and quite unreasonably lose her temper.

"All right, then," she said, "I'm not tough. I don't pretend to be. I've never seen a man killed before. Perhaps you've seen dozens, and think it's all in the day's work, but I haven't. I've seen men who were dead, in a hospital in France, but I've never seen it happen like that to anyone."

Auty was not smiling now. If there was any particular expression on his face, it was anxiety.

"The man who was killed," he repeated; "what was he like?"

Perversely now, she did not want to tell him any more about it. Though he had cast less doubt on her story than she had expected, she felt uneasy talking to him, as if all the time he had been making something of her story that she had not intended.

"Didn't you see him properly?" Auty asked.

"Oh yes, we passed each other a moment before it happened," she said reluctantly. "I noticed him because he was striding along so fast. He looked as if he were in an awful hurry to get somewhere. He was a small man with a grey felt hat and a rather dirty flannel suit. He had small, sharp features and he was quite bald."

"How d'you know he was bald if he was wearing a hat?"

"Because when I looked back—after it had happened— his hat had rolled off and he was lying there on the pavement with the lamplight shining on his bald head."

He took her up quickly. "Let's get this straight. You say you looked back *after* it had happened. Then you didn't actually see the accident?"

"No-o. I'd just seen the little man go by, then the car came shooting past, going from one side of the road to the other, as if the steering had gone, and then a moment later there were screams behind me and I looked round and it had happened. The car was already disappearing down the street and there were people rushing up and the little man was lying half on the pavement and half in the gutter. I—I saw his legs move, then that stopped. Then a policeman came along and started taking all our names and addresses."

" So you weren't the only person who saw the accident ? "

" Oh no."

" You weren't even the nearest ? "

" No."

Auty swallowed the rest of his whisky. " Thank the Lord for that. You had me worried."

" But why ? " she asked.

" Because myself I'd hate to be in the position of having been the only witness of a murder, with a good chance that the murderer could recognise me again as easily as I could him. Now let's have some more of this excellent whisky and talk about pleasanter things. My marriage, for instance. I told you I was getting married, didn't I ? "

She nodded, grateful for the determined change of subject, though she was not really capable of dragging her thoughts away from the horrible scene which, while she had described it, had come before her again so vividly that she felt that the thin, dark face of the man who had driven the car, barely described by her few words, must be as plain to Auty as it was to her.

Auty filled their glasses again and sat down, his big body filling the small easy-chair he chose, his legs seeming to stretch an astonishing way over the carpet.

" You aren't married, by any chance ? " he asked.

" No," Sarah said.

" Engaged ? "

" No."

" Why not ? "

She laughed. " I can't say I know the right answer to that. But tell me about your engagement. Whom are you marrying ? "

" Her name is Anna Maria Dolores Barbosa."

" What a glorious name ! "

" And she's like it, quite glorious." He looked a little smug about it.

" And rich ? "

He grinned. " Shockingly rich. But if she hadn't a bean, she'd still be as glorious. Do believe me ? You would, if you could see her."

" I'm sure I should. What is she, Spanish ? "

" Brazilian. I met the family last year in France. They've a villa at Nice. I'm flying down there next week, then the engagement's going to be announced. As a matter of fact, we've had a rather marvellous idea about that. I've chartered a plane and I'm taking along a party of my old friends, people who knew me long before I'd got anywhere at all. Of course I've had to tell them what it's all about, but I've asked them not to let the reason for the party leak out. Anna will have some of her old friends there and on the first evening we'll make the announcement. Don't you think it's a grand idea ? "

" Wonderful," Sarah said.

" You see, I've got to show people somehow that this business of marrying a fortune isn't important to me," he said, " and that I'm going to go on being the same as I've always been, when I was scratching for a living up in Bradford before the war, or joining the army as a private, or coming out of it with a medal or two and the rank of a major but without a penny to my name except my measly gratuity. I've had luck since then and I might even claim that I've shown a certain ability and I've got where I am without the help of anyone's fortune and that hasn't changed me to my old friends. So why it should be thought that marrying the sweetest and loveliest girl I've ever met should change me, even if she has got a bank account of her own, I don't understand."

He concluded the oddly passionate speech by finishing his glass again and standing up abruptly.

After a moment he went on, " The fact is, things haven't been as simple as I was trying to make out, and there's a reason for this little party of mine that I haven't mentioned. But with luck, if I succeed in what I want to do, I won't have to mention it at all except to one person."

" One of these old friends of yours ? "

" Really I'm not even sure of that."

" But what's been happening ? Anonymous letters or something ? "

" No, nothing like that. But let's not go on about it. Tell me some more about yourself now. What do you do with yourself ? Are you in a job ? Do you like it ? "

17

He fired off the questions without waiting for answers, then when Sarah started to speak about herself, seemed scarcely to be listening to what she was saying, but to be following some anxious line of thought of his own.

Sarah found herself beginning to wish that he would leave. The feeling of shock had subsided, but had left her with a numb sense of exhaustion.

Yet she had been glad to see Mark Auty again. She had remembered him as a strong, cheerful, generous man, never exacting, careless with his money, lavish with small presents. In a casual way, he had been kind to her, much as he had this evening, and because even at that time he had been a rather spectacular figure, more talked of, for some reason, than other men, even though he had been oddly distrusted by many, she had been proud of her connection with him. It now seemed to her right that his life since the war should have been successful and that he should be about to marry the fabulous-sounding Anna Maria Dolores Barbosa.

Sarah had little to tell him about her own life. She told him about the medical publishers and about her excitement at having a flat of her own. She told him a little about the sort of people she knew, the kind of parties she went to and how she had spent her last summer holiday. But that last theme was perhaps unlucky, for she had spent the holiday driving through France with some friends and remembering the car in which they had driven jerked her thoughts back sharply to the accident.

" About that business to-night, Mr. Auty," she said, then became quite certain that for the last few minutes he had not been listening to her at all. She repeated it. " About that business to-night—what ought I to do about it ? "

He gave her a long look, focusing his thoughts on her again. " Do ? Tell the police what you've told me. That's all you can do," he said.

" But you think they won't believe me."

" You can't help that . . . Sarah, forgive me for going back to my own problems, but I've just had an idea. Why don't you join my party next week ? "

" I ? " she said in astonishment. " Your party in Nice ? "

" Yes."

18

" But good heavens, I couldn't afford it. Besides that, I'm a working girl, remember."

" Couldn't that be arranged ? Couldn't you take some of your summer holiday now ? It'll only be a long week-end, after all. And it won't cost you anything, because the plane's my show and then you'd be the guest of the Barbosas." He leant towards her. " Sarah, I'm not being crazy. I'm asking you for a very special reason. That's why my mind wandered during the last few minutes. I was thinking the thing out. Can't you do it ? Please don't say no before you've begun to think about it."

" The danger is that I'll say yes before I've begun to think about it," she said. She tried to suppress the excitement that had been stirred in her by the thought of such a trip to Nice. " What is this very special reason ? "

" It's just that I trust you."

Her cheeks coloured. " I'm glad. But——"

" I don't want to talk about it now," he went on, " except to say that if I could have someone along with me whom I knew for certain I could trust, it would be an enormous help to me. If you decide to come, I'll tell you more."

She stood up restlessly.

" But I can't just decide like that," she said. " I don't know if there's the faintest chance that I could get the time off."

" At least you'll try ? "

" Yes, I'll—I'll try."

He gripped both her hands and squeezed them. " Wonderful girl."

A few minutes later he said good-night, and Sarah, tiptoeing down to the front door with him, let him out. Then she went softly back to her own room, switching out the lights as she went. The whole house was quiet.

As she reached her own room she was suddenly filled with the conviction that none of the things that had occurred during that evening had really happened.

CHAPTER III

SARAH WING had grown up in Bristol. She had an adoring father who was a professor in the university. Her more detached but understanding mother was always interested in local affairs. When Sarah's father, unable to see any limitations to his daughter's capacities, had sketched out for her a successful career in the university, her mother had come to the rescue. Sarah, in her mother's view, was not really the brilliant individual that the professor imagined. She was a dear girl and reasonably intelligent, quite nice-looking too and liable, without much assistance from her parents, to lead a sufficiently pleasant life, provided she was not so foolish as to attempt to develop an intellect which no one but her father would ever dream she possessed. So Sarah, after leaving the A.T.S., had gone to a secretarial school.

She had agreed entirely on this point with her mother, even if she was rather fonder of her father. Her father was the type of man that she admired. She liked men who were thoughtful, highly educated, extremely sincere and a little slow in their reactions. Also, she understood them, whereas men like Mark Auty, shrewd, forceful men who acted quickly and justified their actions later or not at all, would always bewilder her.

Because of her bewilderment, her attitude to Auty, from the first, had a certain reserve in it. She was wild with excitement at the thought of the bizarre invitation that he had given her. Yet the thought of the man himself and of his real reason for inviting her, she held at some distance from herself, as being, in the nature of things, outside her comprehension.

Mark Auty owned a house in Surrey. His guests had been asked to assemble there on the Friday, to be transported next day, by chartered aeroplane, to Nice.

Sarah did a normal day's work at the office, then went by taxi straight to Waterloo and caught a train at six o'clock. At a little after seven she got out at a small station, where a car was waiting for her. However, it was not for her alone. One other guest, a young man of about her own age, with dark eyebrows ruled straight across a narrow, nervous face and eager, bright, grey eyes, had arrived by the same train. They introduced themselves to one another in the car. The young man's name was Alec Marriner.

The evening was cool and drizzly. While the car took them along a highway, then along a curving, leafy lane, they groped for subjects of conversation.

" Are you a very old friend of Mr. Auty's ? " Sarah asked. " He told me this party was particularly for old friends."

" I've known him since the last year of the war," Marriner answered. " Or rather, during the last year of the war. I haven't seen him since." He spoke in quick little spurts, followed by pauses. " You see, I've been abroad."

" Where ? " she asked.

" In East Africa. I'm in the Colonial Service. This is my first visit home for two years."

" And how do you find it? "

" Cool," he said.

She laughed. " Is that all ? "

" Well, you see, it isn't really home for me any more. I mean, I've no family left. And most of my friends seem to have wandered off to the four corners of the earth. I spent the first couple of weeks wishing I was back where I'd come from. But I'm getting more used to it now."

She thought what a blessing Mark Auty's invitation must have been to the lonely young man, and liked Auty for having included him in his party.

" I suppose you and Mr. Auty were in the army together," she said.

" We were in a prison-camp together," he said.

" Oh, of course."

Looking at Marriner, she thought she could guess what must have happened there. Something about this highly-strung but intelligent-looking and rather attractive young man, or boy, as he would have been then, must have appealed to Auty, who probably had taken him under his wing and, with his own good-humoured toughness, protected him from some of the horrors of the life they had shared.

" I met him after the war," she went on, " in Brunswick.

21

I was his driver for a few weeks and actually I haven't seen him since then either, until—until I met him by chance one evening last week."

Marriner was looking straight before him. " I haven't seen him at all yet." He paused. " Has he changed much ? "

" I don't think so."

" I didn't think he would have. His type doesn't."

She thought his tone odd, but while she was wondering what to say next, he went on, " You know, I like this. I like these damp green hedges and this gentle, cloudy sky. This is what one misses everywhere else. You live in London, I suppose."

" Yes."

" Work there ? "

" Yes, I'm a secretary. I work for a publishing firm."

" Like it ? "

" Oh yes, they're quite nice people."

" I think I'd go off my head, working in an office—even worse off it than I am to begin with." He turned his head to her with a brief smile. " When I was at school, before I went into the army, I thought I'd like to be an architect. I had the idea that there'd be a lot of rebuilding to be done in the world and all that sort of thing. I'm glad I dropped it. Most of it would just have been work in an office, completely shut in with the same people all day. That's a horrible state of affairs."

" Even if you quite like them ? "

"I can't imagine liking anyone I had to see every single day."

At that point the car turned in at a pair of gates, and neither Sarah nor Marriner spoke again until it had stopped before a low doorway in the side of a house that had obviously once been an old farmhouse.

It was of red brick and weather-boarding, with a steep, moss-grown roof. A big cherry tree grew close to the wall, casting its shade over a smooth lawn. The house had leaded windows and the door, which stood half open, was of ancient-looking oak, studded with nails. The door was a little too good to be true, but all the rest looked as if the hand of the restorer had not yet fallen too heavily upon it.

Yet it was not the house that Sarah had been expecting. Mark Auty's talk of aeroplanes and Brazilian heiresses and week-end house-parties in Nice, had made her imagine that his own home would be something far more luxurious than this unpretentious and pleasant old farmhouse.

As she and Alec Marriner got out of the car, she caught a glimpse of Auty through one of the small windows. He was seated at a desk, writing, in a room that looked like a library. Glancing up at the sound of the car, his eyes met hers and he lifted a hand in greeting. Then he got up and came to the door. His big body almost blocked the narrow hall, his head almost touched the low, beamed ceiling.

" Well, this is grand," he said warmly, shaking Sarah's hand. " I don't suppose I need introduce you two to each other. Hallo, Alec." He held out his hand to the young man. " It's good to see you again after all this time. How are things with you ? "

Alec Marriner took the outstretched hand but said nothing at all in reply. He seemed to be wholly engrossed in staring at Auty, with his eager, bright-eyed stare. He might not have heard the words that had been spoken to him.

Auty gave a laugh, and clapped him on the shoulder. " The same old Alec. Never quite on the spot. You and I must get together for a good talk later on this evening, Alec. We'll have a lot to tell each other. Come up to your rooms now. Things are a bit of a squash, I'm afraid, and being the young ones, you've been given the smallest rooms. But it's only for one night, after all."

He turned and led them up the stairs.

In fact, the house was far larger than it had appeared from the garden. Its passages, with uneven floors and odd steps up or down at unexpected places, seemed to reach an incredible length. The bedroom in which Sarah found herself was a room of fair size, though its sloping ceiling and the old and bulky furniture in it, notably a four-poster bed, made it look smaller than it was. Sarah felt rather over-awed by the bed, but noticed that Auty had modernised the place to the extent of installing wash-basins and radiators.

She had a wash and changed out of her office-suit into a dress of dull yellow silk, spotted with white. Returning along the winding passage, she found her way back to the head of the staircase and went downstairs. Through an open door, she saw a large sitting-room, which at first sight she thought to be empty, then she heard a soft sound of whistling issuing from it. Going in, Sarah discovered an old lady sitting in a high-backed chair.

The old lady was dressed in a mauve silk dress and mauve knitted cardigan and had diamond ear-rings glittering in her ears. Sarah was not a judge of diamonds, yet something about the old lady herself made her instantly take for granted that these were real. The old lady was just lighting a cigarette from the stub of another, which she then threw, still glowing, into a small ash-tray that was already overflowing with stubs and ash.

" Ridiculous thing," the old lady said malevolently at the inadequate little bronze dish. " Niggling. Stupid. I like things to be big and useful. Now, my dear, tell me who you are."

Sarah took a chair near the old lady. " I'm Sarah Wing," she said.

" An old friend of that man's, I suppose ? "

" Of Mr. Auty's, yes."

" Only not so very old. Not like some of us. I knew him when he was eighteen. He worked for me. In fact, I think it might be said that I gave him his start in life. My name's Kenny. Myrtle Kenny. I don't suppose he ever mentioned me, did he ? "

" Well, I don't think I remember . . ."

" I thought not." Mrs. Kenny laughed dryly. " People don't spend much time remembering their beginnings, not if they're sensible. Smoke ? "

" Thank you."

Sarah took a cigarette from the huge gold case that Mrs. Kenny held out to her.

" I come from Bradford," Mrs. Kenny went on. " Did he ever mention Bradford ? "

" I know he lived there when he was young," Sarah said.

" Oh, you do ? That's something, I'm very fond of Bradford. I wouldn't live anywhere else for the world. I could leave it and go to live anywhere I chose—Hector's quite old enough to look after the business now without me —but why on earth should I move when I like being where I am ? In a life as long as mine one collects lots of things around one that one becomes very attached to. I don't suppose I could take everything with me if I moved. And where should I move to ? London ? I can't bear it. Somewhere like Nice, perhaps ? Or the Bahamas ? No, I've made up my mind to die in Bradford. In fact I've even bought the plot of ground where I mean to be buried. By the way, Hector's my son—my adopted son."

Sarah made a vague, interested sound in reply and looked round the room.

A low ceiling gave it an appearance of great length. There were a great many chintz-covered sofas and easy-chairs in it, and small, carved tables, settles and cupboards with shiny brass handles. At one end of the room there was a yawning stone fireplace with wrought-iron firedogs. An old post-horn hung above it.

Sarah wondered if Auty had simply taken the whole place over as it was from some former owner, or if he had carefully created the heavy, old English atmosphere. If he had, it had been a mistake. It did not suit him. He would never look like the owner of it, never look at home here.

Mrs. Kenny was continuing.

" I think Hector's in the garden just now. He's very interested in gardens. I encourage it, for the sake of his health. He can't take violent exercise because of his wound, but if he takes none at all he puts on weight too quickly. It was in the first war, of course, he got his wound. A terrible thing. Really it's a wonder that he's here at all. The wound was in his lung, and it left trouble behind for the rest of his life. He's in pain half the time, though you'd never guess it. Hector's a very brave man. In fact, he's a very fine character altogether. That's such a reassuring thing for me to think about, for after all, an adopted son isn't the same as one of one's own, whom one has to put up with, like it or not, however he turns out. I chose Hector because I liked the look of him. He was thirteen already, the son of one of my work-people who'd been killed in an accident in the mill and whose mother didn't want him. So you see, if he'd turned out badly, I should have had to recognise that I didn't know how to judge character. And that wouldn't have been at all agreeable for me."

She took a new cigarette from the gold case and lit it from the stub of the one she had just finished.

Then she gave Sarah a look of sharp inquiry. " I imagine
you think that you're a judge of people," she said. " Everyone does at your age. You take a look into somebody's eyes
and imagine you know enough about them to love them,
admire them, marry them, God knows what—or the reverse,
of course. But at my age you're able to look back and
remember some of the mistakes you've made, and that
makes the other occasions, the times when you weren't
wrong in loving and admiring and helping, seem particularly
precious. . . . Ah, here is Hector."

As she said it, a man came into the room.

He was not the man that Sarah's imagination had created
from the old lady's description. Mrs. Kenny's talk of
wounds and heroism and silent suffering had made Sarah
visualise a tall, emaciated man with a look of dignity and
nobility. Instead she saw a short, plump, bald man with a
podgy, amiable face and horn-rimmed glasses. When his
adopted mother introduced him to Sarah, he gave her a
brisk little nod, then addressed the old woman.

" I just looked in to make sure you were all right, darling,"
he said. " Quite comfortable ? Got everything you want ? "

" Except a sensible ash-tray," Mrs. Kenny said.

" Ah, I'll see what I can do about it," he promised. " But
I must go and wash my hands first. I've just been doing a
little weeding. By the way, I've spotted some very nice
things in this garden that I'd like to steal. Though I don't
know if they'd do so well in Bradford."

He turned to go. But the doorway was blocked by the
big figure of Mark Auty. He had heard what Hector Kenny
had said.

" Well, well, Hector," he said, smiling broadly, " still on
the prowl for what you can pick up unnoticed."

Hector looked a little put out. Dodging round Auty, he
trotted off.

Mrs. Kenny said austerely, " I don't care for that kind
of joke, Mark. You might give Miss Wing a quite mistaken
impression of Hector."

" Far be it from me to do that," Auty said solemnly. " I
assure you, Sarah, stealing plants for his herbaceous border
is the only sin of which I have ever suspected Hector."

" And all gardeners do that," Mrs. Kenny stated.

" Is that so ? " Auty said. " The things one lives to learn. Now what about drinks. Mrs. Kenny ? "

" Sherry, please."

Auty opened a cabinet and started pouring out the drinks. As he brought hers to Sarah, he asked: " I haven't had time yet to ask you if you heard anything more about the other evening."

" A policeman came and asked me a lot more questions," she said.

" A policeman ? " Mrs. Kenny asked with quick interest.

Auty explained, " Sarah had the bad luck to be on the spot when a man was run down by a car and killed." He turned to Sarah again. " So you weren't needed at the inquest ? "

" No, they seemed to have enough witnesses without me," she said.

" Did you tell the policeman your theory ? "

" Yes, but—well, he said the same things that you did." Sarah wished he had not brought the subject up, for memories of the scene in the dark street still disturbed her deeply. " But at least I know now who the man was."

" What," he said, " the driver ? "

" No, the one who was killed."

Mrs. Kenny interrupted, " Where was this accident ? And when ? You're telling me only half the story. Please tell me the rest of it."

" It was at the edge of Regent's Park, where Sarah lives," Auty said, " and it was late in the evening of Wednesday, last week. And it was Sarah's theory that it wasn't an accident."

" Good gracious me ! What was it, then ? "

" Sarah thought it was murder."

Mrs. Kenny drew in her breath so that it whistled. The stare that she now fixed on Sarah was quite different from her smiling gaze of a few moments before. For an instant Sarah thought that the old woman, for some mysterious reason, had become violently angry with her, but then she realised that the emotion expressed by that fierce stare was merely a ravenous curiosity.

" And who was the man who was killed ? " Mrs. Kenny demanded.

"He was a man called Darnborough," Sarah said. "He was a private detective."

"A private detective. Well, well." Mrs. Kenny gulped some of her sherry. "In that case, I shouldn't be at all surprised if you were right. After all, those are just the sort of people who get murdered. But what made you suspect murder, my dear? And why couldn't you make the police listen to you? Perhaps if you told me the whole story, I could help you. In any dealings I've ever had to have with police, I've always found I could make them listen to me quite easily."

"That was in Bradford," Auty said, "where the name of Kenny does things."

"Yes, of course." She seemed to hear no irony in his tone. "But now, Miss Wing, go on. Go on and tell me what aroused your suspicions."

Thankfully Sarah heard footsteps in the passage. They saved her from having to reply to Mrs. Kenny, and even if the respite was only for the moment, it was something.

That day had been the first day since the accident, or whatever it had been, that her mind had not been entirely obsessed with thoughts of it. For the first few days after it had happened she had felt that the picture that she carried in her mind, of the small crumpled man, lying dead in the street and of the thin, dark, murderous face of the man in the car, must have been stamped on her imagination for ever. But to-day, until Auty had begun to speak of it, she had been almost free of the ugly memory.

Pointedly refusing to hear Mrs. Kenny's question, she turned to look at the man who had just come into the room.

For a moment she thought she had gone mad.

Was the memory, that had seemed to be fading, in fact so potent that it was making her imprint its image on what in reality had no relation with it whatever? Was she having actual hallucinations?

But in a moment she knew that this could not be so. The thin, dark, murderous face of the man who stood in the doorway, looking at her, was no hallucination

CHAPTER IV

Auty was saying, " Come in, Pete."

He introduced the newcomer to Sarah and Mrs. Kenny as his old friend, Peter Nock. While Auty was doing this, his eyes, with a question in them, were on Sarah. Yet as soon as she looked at him directly, he looked away. It seemed that he did not want any answer to his question then and there.

Sarah's heart was thumping. She had not been able to remain seated but had had to move, had had to put more space between herself and the man at the door. It happened automatically. Before she had had time to think how strange that short, precipitate flight from him must look to Peter Nock, she found herself standing by a window. That he found it strange and was amused by it, he showed by the tight, three-cornered smile he gave her.

He was a slight, dark man of about forty. He had a sallow, triangular face with the skin drawn into hollows under the high cheekbones. His well-cut suit was a pale dove grey. A lace handkerchief was prominently displayed in his breast-pocket.

" What'll you have to drink, Pete ? " Auty asked him.

" Lime-juice, please."

His voice was extraordinary. Sarah had taken for granted that it would be Soho cockney, perhaps slightly but unconvincingly disguised. Instead it was soft, resonant, and entirely cultured.

Mrs. Kenny was as startled by that voice as Sarah. But when Mrs. Kenny was startled, she made no attempt to disguise the fact.

"Are you on the stage, Mr. Nock ? " she asked, puffing smoke at him.

" Long ago," he said.

" Ah." She settled back in her chair, eyeing him with blatant dislike. There was haughty hostility in her voice. One foot tapped. " Were you a failure ? "

" The life didn't suit me," he said. He smiled at her, apparently enjoying her attitude. " I like to take things quietly."

" It takes courage and devotion to be an actor," she said truculently. " I admire actors. In Bradford I go to the theatre every week, even in the pantomime season."

" That must take courage and devotion," he said.

Sipping his lime-juice, he turned to take another look at Sarah.

She had just realised that the window by which she was standing was in fact a door. As the dark eyes in the thin, dark face rested on her again, her fingers fumbled with the latch. Muttering something that no one could have heard about taking a look at the garden, she stepped hurriedly outside.

. She found herself on a paved path that ran along the side of the house. Walking fast, she had gone some distance along this before she realised that she still had her half-filled glass of sherry in her hand, and that she was holding it out before her, like something in an egg-and-spoon race, that must not be spilled.

Pulling herself up, she drank the rest of the sherry. Then she looked behind her, half-hoping to find that Auty had followed her out. But no one had appeared and as she stood there, she heard the door by which she had emerged being closed from inside the room.

Turning away again, she walked on down the paved path.

It led past the house and across a lawn, then under an arch of clipped yew and into an orchard. Under an apple-tree, laden with unripe fruit, she found a wooden seat. Sitting down there, she gave herself time to think.

She wanted to leave immediately. She wanted to go straight back to London and never see Mark Auty or any of his friends again. For he had deceived her. He had let her believe that he knew nothing about that killing that she had seen. He had let her believe that her description of the killer had meant nothing to him, and that his own presence so near the scene had been accidental. None of these things could have been true. He must have known everything that she had told him before she had told him her story and he must have invited her here, not for the reasons that he had given her in her flat that evening, but on purpose that she might meet Peter Nock.

On purpose, yes. But for what purpose ?

Sarah put her empty glass down on the seat beside her, leant her elbows on her knees and her head in her hands. They felt cold and a little clammy against her forehead and she realised that though the drizzling rain had stopped, the bench on which she was sitting was still damp from it.

She tried to bring together her scraps of knowledge about Mark Auty. In the army he had acquired a mass of decorations. After leaving it, he had made money rapidly. He had begun soon to take part in public life. He had begun to lecture on economics and social reform. He had found his way on to committees. Then a month ago he had stood as an Independent candidate in a by-election, and had defeated a Conservative candidate who had been backed as a certainty by the Press. Reading one or two of Auty's reported speeches, Sarah had thought them commonplace and almost indistinguishable in policy from those of his opponent. But his meetings had gone very well. Something about him, perhaps his air of good-humoured strength, had appealed to people, and with a majority of a little over two thousand he had been returned to Parliament.

But what did it all mean to Auty, Sarah wondered. Were the opinions that he had expressed sincerely held by him or were they merely a means by which he intended to establish himself even better than before in the public eye ? Until this evening, until a few minutes ago, she would have stood up loyally for his sincerity. But what was she to think of a man who had listened to what she had had to tell him in her flat and then had introduced Peter Nock to her as an old friend ? A feeling of cold prickled along her spine as she asked herself that question.

She stood up and with head bent, started walking back towards the house. As she drew near to the yew hedge with the arch in it, voices reached her from the other side of the hedge. Not wanting to have to speak to anyone just then, she paused. Then, because of what the voices were saying, she remained standing where she was, tense and puzzled.

" You're mad, quite mad ! " The voice was Mark Auty's. It was sharp and clear and rather contemptuous. " In God's name, how can you imagine such a thing of me ? What did I ever do to you to make you leap to such a frightful conclusion about me ? "

31

Sarah caught her breath. It was as if the words had been spoken directly to her in protest at the thoughts that she herself had just been entertaining.

A second voice muttered something. It was a man's voice and there was something familiar about it, but at first she did not recognise to whom it belonged. Nor did she catch what it said. But Auty replied to it in the same clear, sharp tones. "No, you don't mean what you're saying. I won't take any notice of what you've said. I'll forget it."

"I won't give you any chance to forget it." This time the words were clear, though they were spoken unevenly, with great tension. "You're going to go on remembering it for the rest of your life—though perhaps that won't be so long."

Sarah recognised the voice now. It was that of the young man with whom she had driven up from the station.

"Good heavens, what on earth's got into you?" Auty exclaimed. "D'you know that you can get into pretty serious trouble for saying things like that? It was little short of a threat."

"It *was* a threat."

That made Auty laugh. "But Alec, my dear chap——"

"Stop that! I told you I meant what I said," Alec Marriner said.

"I see. The condemned man was refused a last request." Auty laughed again. The laugh, this time, was not quite so steady. "But shall I tell you why I don't think you meant what you said, Alec?"

"Go on."

"You see, if you were serious, I don't think you'd waste your time threatening me."

"I've got my reasons."

"Oh yes, people always have. They think they want to see their victim squirm, or give him time to repent. Which is it with you?"

"Both, possibly. And a desire to choose my own time, so that I stand a chance of saving my own skin. I'd hate to die on your account, Mark."

"I'm glad to hear it. In that case perhaps neither of us need die. Because our police are amazingly efficient, you know, and even if you wait till we're in France——"

" D'you mean you still expect me to go with you ? "
There was an odd, somehow innocent amazement in the
voice.

" But my dear chap, why ever not ? I told you, I want
you to meet my fiancée. I want all my old friends to meet
my fiancée . . ."

The two men had started to walk towards the house, and
Auty's voice faded.

Sarah waited for a full minute before she moved.

Curiously enough, as she retraced her steps along the
paved path to the house, she found that out of the whole of
the conversation, the words that remained most disturbingly
in her mind were some spoken by Auty and not by the
apparently crazed young man. They were the last words
that she had heard before Auty's voice had become inaudible.
" I want all my old friends to meet my fiancée. . . ."

There was something about that phrase, " old friends,"
as spoken by him, that was beginning to sound distinctly
sinister to Sarah.

Four more people were shortly introduced to Sarah by
Auty as old friends of his. She had returned reluctantly
to the drawing-room, and noted with interest that Auty
showed no signs of just having had his life threatened. In
fact, he was looking hearty and cheerful, as if his party were
going well. These old friends were Mr. and Mrs. Carver
and Mr. and Mrs. Pointing.

The Carvers were both in the early thirties. The man
was slim, dark and handsome, but with a sulky look on his
face, a red nose and a hoarse voice. When he sneezed
repeatedly, his wife, a very small and lively peroxide
blonde, dressed in scarlet taffeta, with several strings of
pearls round her throat, explained that all through the
summer poor Tim suffered terribly with hay-fever, so no
one need fear that there was any infection. Tim did not
seem to welcome this explanation, but muttered into his
martini something about it's not being his fault that he
was here.

The Pointings were probably ten or fifteen years older
than the Carvers. The man had a naval look. His wife was
a big, dignified, slow-moving woman in a dress of limp,
flowered crêpe. They both looked quiet and well-bred,

with the air about them of a couple who were much attached to one another. Sarah liked the look of them and thought that whatever motives Auty might have had for inviting either Peter Nock or the lunatic Marriner or even the rather raffish-looking Carvers to his party, he could have had no more questionable reason for inviting the Pointings than a desire to impress on the rich and beautiful Miss Barbosa the fact that some of his old friends were nice people.

Yet a few minutes after Sarah had returned to the room, she noticed an odd thing. Old Mrs. Kenny, smoking as hard as ever and whistling to herself whenever control of the conversation escaped her, kept looking at Mrs. Pointing in a frowningly suspicious fashion, keeping her eyes on her face until, apparently hypnotised, Mrs. Pointing returned her gaze. But Mrs. Pointing never returned it for more than an instant and after each occasion she unconsciously jerked her chair an inch or two further back, as if to escape from the old woman's scrutiny.

The person in the room who appeared happiest was Hector Kenny. Already everyone was calling him Hector. He appeared to be one of those people who, from childhood upwards, have their own names treated as if they are nick-names and who are generally called by them, by complete strangers, within a few minutes of meeting. Hector was drinking rather more than anyone else in the room, disposing of one gin after another and, to Sarah's surprise, being smiled on in this by Mrs. Kenny.

Peter Nock was still there and so was Alec Marriner, but each of them sat apart, removed from the rest. Neither was drinking and neither spoke. Nock looked very bored, showing that this was not the kind of company that he had expected. Marriner merely looked unaware that there was anyone in the room but himself.

Presently dinner was announced by a small manservant in a white jacket. It was served in another long, narrow room at a long, refectory table. The food and the wines were good and Mark Auty played host with no sign of any misgiving that his party might not be a success. Yet the company was as ill-assorted as if he had deliberately collected it for the purpose of achieving a social disaster.

Not that this showed too openly yet. Courtesy prevailed

and conversation was kept going. But as the guests took stock of one another, and began to see that the only thing that they had in common with one another was some link in the past with Mark Auty, constraint, instead of diminishing, grew upon them. Only Hector appeared to be free of it. Food and drink, it was evident, meant a great deal to him, and as the meal progressed, with the small man-servant refilling Hector's glass more often than anyone else's, his round, pale face took on a rosy glow, his eyes beamed contentedly and he talked with more and more animation to little Mrs. Carver, who was sitting beside him.

This sight seemed to please Mrs. Kenny and as if in gratitude to Auty for supplying the conditions of Hector's happiness, she laid aside a little of her usual tartness in talking with him, But still her eyes wandered frequently to the reserved, serious face of Mrs. Pointing, whose main preoccupation throughout the meal appeared to be the avoiding of these glances.

This led her to make an effort at conversation with Paul Nock. It amused Sarah to notice that the man was flattered by this. He must have placed Mrs. Pointing as a member of a class that generally had no use for him, so that her sustained interest in him came as a gratifying surprise. Mrs. Pointing, in fact, spoke to him with the exaggerated flattery of a shy person attempting to please someone whom she considers an inferior.

Her husband talked to Sarah about travel. He was one of those Englishmen whom it is difficult to imagine in any but English company, yet who has managed somehow to visit almost every country in the world and who speaks several languages, including Swahili and Chinese. But his comments on each country were restricted to the climate and the kinds of drink consumed by the European inhabitants. This was not sufficiently interesting to stop Sarah thinking about the presence in the room of a man who, she was absolutely certain, was a murderer.

The first thing she must do about it, she thought, was to speak to Mark Auty in private. As soon as the meal was over, she must make him see her alone. Then she would tell him that Nock had been the driver of the car and challenge Auty with having known this fact all along. What happened next would depend on Auty. She would tell him, too, of the scene that she had overheard between him and Marriner.

The problem, she thought, would be how to detach Auty from his other guests.

But this turned out to be no problem. When dinner was over and everyone had just risen from the table, Auty tapped her on the shoulder and whispered, " Wait behind a moment."

She waited while the others filed out through the narrow doorway and returned to the drawing-room.

" Now come in here," Auty said. " We'd better talk."

He opened a door in the panelling beside the fireplace.

Going through, Sarah found herself in the small, book-lined room in which she had seen Auty sitting writing when she and Alec Marriner had driven up from the station.

As soon as he had closed the door, Auty's manner changed.

The cheerfulness that he had shown at dinner disappeared from his face and suddenly it was extremely tired. The mouth was bitter. Before saying anything, he stooped over a small round table that had some decanters and glasses on it and poured out a glass of brandy. He was lifting it to his lips before he remembered to offer some to Sarah.

She shook her head.

He straightened up, swallowed most of the brandy in the glass and said, " Well ? Go on. You've got something to say to me, haven't you ? " His voice was not exactly antagonistic, but it had become brusque, businesslike, impersonal.

Sarah hesitated, then said uncertainly, " You know what I've got to say."

" About Nock ? "

" Of course."

" Well, go on and say it."

" He was the driver of the car that killed that man," she said with a certain defiance, expecting argument.

" Are you sure ? " he asked.

" Of course I'm sure ! " Her voice rose as her excitement overcame her. " I told you I'd know him if I ever saw him again. But you knew who he was as soon as I told you about it, didn't you ? Perhaps you knew it before. Perhaps you'd seen the accident yourself and could have told me all about it. But you pretended not to know anything at all and not to believe me!"

"Steady, steady," he said. "And don't speak so loud. The walls are nice and thick here, but doors have cracks." He sat down in the chair at the big desk. "You're going too fast, you know. Don't you remember how you described the driver?"

"Oh, I know I didn't describe him properly," she said impatiently. "I only said that he was thin and dark. Yet you knew who he was."

He shook his head. "Hasn't something struck you since you've been here? There happen to be three thin, dark men in this house at the moment—Pete Nock, Alec Marriner and Tim Carver."

In her surprise at this, which had not occurred to her all the evening, Sarah sat down so suddenly that her chair knocked against the low table that held the drinks and made the glasses rattle.

"Yes, but—but you yourself said Nock just now," she said. "You knew I was going to say it was Nock."

"Certainly," he said, "since I'd seen your face when he first came into the room, and seen the way you bolted out of it, as if you thought you were straight in line for being murdered yourself. After that I couldn't have much doubt which of those three it was that you'd seen."

"But how did you know it was any of them?" To keep her hands still, she clenched them tightly together in her lap. "What were you doing there that evening? Are you going to tell me?"

"I'd gone there to meet Henry Darnborough, the man who was killed," he said. "Doesn't that explain everything?"

"Darnborough—the private detective!"

He finished his brandy and got up to help himself to some more. "That's right. He was working for me, you see. And that evening we'd arranged to meet for a discussion of certain things that had come up. I was on my way to the meeting-place when I ran into you and you were in such a bad state that I couldn't very well leave you to yourself. So I saw you home and then when you described the accident and talked about the dead man's quite bald head, I realised what had happened. So I was able to narrow down the identity of your thin, dark murderer to one of quite a few people." He sat down again, putting the glass of brandy on the desk before him. " Satisfied ? "

She gave a slow nod, but then exclaimed, " No ! That only explains part of it."

" Oh, I know that," he said. " It doesn't begin to explain what Darnborough was doing for me, what he'd found out, why he was killed. But, Sarah, my dear, for your own good I don't want you to know too much about all that. As you've probably realised, there's considerable danger in this situation, and so it's much better that you shouldn't know too much."

She thought that over, unthinkingly ruffling her curly hair and biting her lower lip, while her forehead puckered deeply.

" I'd sooner know more than just the amount I do," she said.

" That's only human. But not necessarily wise, even so."

" Please tell me more, Mr. Auty," she said. " I'm involved in this now, whether you like it or not. After all, you invited me here, knowing that there was this danger you talk about."

" That's true." Picking up a pencil from the desk, he sketched a faint pattern on a sheet of blotting-paper, frowned at it, then carefully darkened the outlines and cross-hatched it. At last he said, " Are you coming to France to-morrow ? "

That was a point about which she was most uncertain.

" Does that affect it ? " she asked.

" Yes. If you decide that you don't like the position, now that you know rather more about it, and that you don't want to come, then I'd sooner not tell you any more than you know now. Believe me, that'll be best for you. But if you decide to come, then I'll make you a promise. To-morrow evening in Nice, after you've met Anna, I'll tell you everything. Absolutely everything."

" *After* I've met Anna," she said. " What has that to do with it ? "

" I'm afraid that's an important part of it."

She shrugged helplessly. " But I don't understand at all."

" I'm glad." He smiled. " Because at this stage you're not meant to. But I'll tell you one thing, Sarah, and then you can answer my question whether or not you're coming with us. It would mean an awful lot to me if you came. Just to have someone there whom Anna and I can trust. That's what I told you the other evening, isn't it ? That I was asking you because I trust you."

He was looking at her steadily now, the thick lids of his eyes raised farther than usual, so that his lips looked large and anxious.

She stood up, sighing as she did so.

" All right, I'll come. I suppose I never really meant to do anything else. But still . . ."

He stood up also, facing her. He put his big hands on her shoulders.

" I knew that," he said. " I knew you'd come. But bless you, all the same. Really, from my heart, Sarah, I'm grateful. Now let's go and have some coffee with the others."

" I think, if you don't mind, I'll go up to my room," she said. " I've the feeling that there's quite a bit of thinking I'd like to do before settling down to a nice chat with Mr. Nock, or any of your other thin, dark friends."

They went out together through the long, empty dining-room.

" Well, good night, then."

As she started up the stairs, Auty stood at the bottom, looking up at her.

" Sleep well and don't worry," he said.

" But remember your promise when we get to Nice," she said.

" I'll remember. You shall know everything. Every-thing." He smiled.

The smile made her feel better. If Auty was in danger, he, at least, was not much afraid and that had a steadying effect on her own nerves. Reaching the top of the stairs, she went along the twisting passage to her room.

She had reached it and closed the door behind her before she remembered that she had said nothing to Auty about having overheard his conversation with Alec Marriner, nor asked him anything concerning the meaning of it.

CHAPTER V

AT PRECISELY ten o'clock, Mrs. Kenny retired to bed. Hector went with her to her room. It was the best bedroom in the house, near the head of the stairs. Though the evening was not yet dark, Mrs. Kenny immediately drew the curtains to shut out the remains of the evening light. Then she sat down at the dressing-table and took the heavy diamonds out of her ears. In the mirror she could see Hector standing behind her, rosy and smiling, looking affectionately at her reflection.

"Well, I believe you enjoyed yourself this evening," she said.

"Quite well, quite well," he said. His stance was not absolutely steady, but that troubled him no more than the heaving of the deck under his feet troubles an experienced sailor.

"I don't think you ever care what sort of company you find yourself in," Mrs. Kenny said. "You have a very fortunate disposition !"

"Yes, I have, haven't I, darling ? " He beamed into the mirror. "I never see the point of worrying about human problems, which at their best never have any satisfactory solutions, when there's good drink to be had. And whatever else you want to say about that man, he has learnt something about wines."

"I imagine he's learnt many other things as well," she said, "since we last saw him. But how are you feeling, dear ? Do you feel quite well ? "

"Fine, fine," he chuckled.

"No pain ? "

"Not a trace, darling, not a trace."

"I'm so glad." She took the pins out of her thin, white hair and let it unroll on to her shoulders. " Nothing pleases me more than to see you enjoying yourself. But to-morrow perhaps you'd better ask that man if you may work a little in his garden. You know how quickly you get upset if you miss your exercise."

" To be sure. My exercise. I won't forget. But now what about you, darling ? What have you against that quite pleasant but rather dull-looking woman who's married to the gallant sea-captain ? Why did you spend the whole evening deliberately making her unhappy by staring at her ? I thought it most unlike you."

Mrs. Kenny picked up a silver-mounted brush and drew it once or twice through her hair.

" D'you know who that woman is, Hector ? "

" Is she anybody ? " But his own question suddenly amused Hector so much that his short, plump body began to rock with nearly silent laughter. " Oh dear," he managed to say at last, " how one does give away what one thinks when one doesn't mean to. Because that sort of large, flabby, dull woman always strikes me as being nobody, nobody at all."

" You're quite wrong," Mrs. Kenny said. " She has a very strong personality and a great deal of intelligence. And I have nothing against her at all. In fact, the contrary. I found myself admiring her this evening more than anyone I've met for a long time."

" I liked the little blonde ever so much better," Hector said. " There's a lot of fun in her. But that husband of hers looks a surly devil."

" No doubt you also liked the unspeakable Mr. Nock," Mrs. Kenny said.

" Well, I thought he looked a pretty interesting fellow. But go on and tell me about that poor woman who so disliked being stared at. Who is she ? "

" Violet Ardwell."

Hector's chuckles stopped as abruptly as if they had been cut off by a switch.

" *What ?* "

Mrs. Kenny nodded. She laid down the hairbrush and began twisting her hair into two thin plaits.

" I recognised her at once, though it's years since I've seen her," she said.

" I didn't know you'd ever seen her," Hector said soberly.

" Yes, I—I had rather a feeling of responsibility about her, mistakenly perhaps. So when she sent me the news of her husband's death, I went to see her. She was a beautiful girl then. She was a mannequin at Danielson and Gibbs, you remember. She was tall and slender and graceful, though rather shy and serious even then."

"And yet, from the look of her to-night, anyone would have been sure that she'd been born and bred among dogs and horses and the slightly impoverished upper classes and probably been to Roedean at great sacrifice to her parents. Well, well, how wrong one can be about things. Really, people are the most amazing creatures, aren't they, darling?"

Mrs. Kenny replied with an odd sigh. "Yes, amazing. Now say good night to me, boy, and run along. And don't stay up too late, because to-morrow will be a tiring day for you."

Hector did not stir, except to sway slightly, as if the deck had just taken a plunge under his feet.

"But what's she doing here, darling? What's her position?" he asked.

"I should so much like to know that," Mrs. Kenny said, "but without anyone knowing that I know—because knowledge, once you are known to possess it, carries with it certain responsibilities."

"Umm. Yes. I see what you mean," Hector said. Then he kissed the top of her head, murmured good night and left the room.

The rest of the party went to bed, or at least to their rooms, about midnight.

Lorna Carver was in a very gay mood. As her husband closed the door of their bedroom behind them, she began to revolve swiftly on one heel in the middle of the room, so that her full, scarlet skirt rose billowing around her.

"Oh, for God's sake!" Carver said disgustedly, throwing himself down on the bed and clasping his hands under his head. "We've had a whole bloody evening of chatter. Can't you keep quiet now?"

She stood still, but was laughing with excitement.

"You don't mean you still don't like it, Tim! This lovely house and wonderful furniture——"

"All phoney as hell," Carver grunted.

"Oh, it isn't. It's all wonderfully genuine, you can tell quite easily. It's given me some marvellous ideas about what we might do with the lounge bar at home. I told Mr. Auty about it and he said it was obvious I had a flair for that sort of thing, and so then I asked him when he was going to come and stay at our hotel and he said he'd come later in the summer. Tim, I can't see what you've got against Mr. Auty. I think he's ever so nice. He's quite different from what you said. For one thing, he's ever so much more of a gentleman——"

" Gentleman ! " Tim said. " My God, you've got a thing or two to learn still. You'll find out before you're finished. And I told you before and I say it again, we oughtn't to have come."

" But why not ? I think we're going to have a wonderful time. Not that the company's much to my taste, except for Mr. Auty and perhaps that funny little fat chap who soaks up all the drink he can get. That Nock man looks too conceited to live and those Pointing people are just snobs, that's all there is to them. But still, to-morrow we'll be in Nice and I can wear that topless dress with the camellia pattern——"

" I wonder."

She had started to pull her dress off over her head, but at his tone she let it slide down again.

" What d'you mean, Tim ? "

" Haven't I told you all along there's something wrong about this whole business ? " he said. " It's not what you think it is and I know we'd have done much better not to come."

" But why ? " she asked, beginning to get angry. " That's what you keep saying, but you don't say why ? "

" Well, let me tell you, Auty hasn't asked us here because he loves us. He's got no use for little Tim, no use at all."

" I'm quite sure you're wrong. He's been as friendly as can be."

" That makes me all the more certain there's something wrong with the set-up."

" But you were pals in the army, weren't you? And he helped us buy our pub."

" Oh, sure, he helped us buy our pub, but I could tell you a thing or two about that——" A fit of sneezing stopped him. Sitting up, he buried his face in his handkerchief while sneeze after sneeze shook his fine, padded shoulders.

Lorna began tugging at her dress again.

" Damn," she said peevishly into its folds, " you always start that just when I think you're going to say something interesting."

Peter Nock undressed quickly, tidily, putting on a pair of dark red silk pyjamas, hanging the clothes he had been wearing on hangers in the wardrobe, then swallowing a vitamin pill and a spoonful of liquid paraffin. After that he stood at the window and did breathing exercises, then stooped and touched his toes. After that he took out of one of his very smart suitcases, suitable for air-travel, a book called *The Ghost of Greystone Manor*, and getting into bed, arranged a pillow comfortably behind him and began to read.

The book began, " Let no one whose mind is enclosed by a stifling materialism read any farther. Let no one whose imagination has never been stirred by the strangeness behind the appearances of things, waste his time on this tale. For in it I shall have to describe certain events which his common-sense will refuse to allow him to believe. I shall have to tell him of certain things which these eyes of mine have seen . . ."

Peter Nock read on with deep attention. He read on for two hours, until the house around him had become completely silent and no sound of any kind was to be heard but the occasional hoot of an owl in the trees beyond the orchard.

Then, at the point in the story where the writer was describing how he had seen a curious pale mist seep out through a crack in the staircase and begin to form into a strange, unrecognisable yet wholly terrifying shape, something made Nock glance up from the book.

He saw a dimly lit room with dark beams across the low ceiling. He saw a great, dark cupboard in which his clothes were hanging and which was not quite closed. Yet he had closed it when he went to bed. A faulty catch ? With difficulty he dragged his eyes away from it, only to notice the mysterious faint motion of the curtains beside the windows.

44

Slamming the book shut, he jumped out of bed, thrust the book back into his suitcase, locked the case, as if that would help to contain the terrors that the book had released in the room, swallowed two sleeping-pills, went back to bed and eventually fell asleep with the light at his side still burning.

Denis and Violet Pointing went to bed almost in silence. They talked a little of the other guests in the house and of the house itself, speculating about its age and about how much of its furnishings were genuinely old.

" It's all a bit overdone in my opinion," Mrs. Pointing said, as she climbed into the four-poster bed. " I don't really like it at all."

" Our friend seems very pleased with it, nevertheless," her husband said.

" Oh, yes. But if he'd talked to a different decorator he'd have made it all chromium and glass."

Pointing laughed. " Fortunately his ideas in that direction aren't any concern of ours and we've enough on our hands without worrying about the genuineness of his furniture."

He got in beside her in the great canopied bed and reached for the switch to put out the light. For a few minutes they lay side by side in silence.

Then Pointing went on, " That old woman, Vi—why did you let her upset you ? "

" I didn't."

" You did. Anyone could see it."

She gave a sigh. " And I thought I'd managed to hide it, more or less."

" You see, I know your face so well," he said. " It's easy for me to guess certain things about you."

" And she saw it too, I suppose ? "

" I shouldn't be surprised."

" Well, it doesn't really matter. But it was a shock running into her and realising at once that she'd recognised me. Now she'll tell everyone else. And after that, nothing matters, does it ? " Her voice was toneless.

" If only you'd realise that it really doesn't matter ! Let them all know. Face it. It won't be nearly as bad as you think."

" It'll be horrible." She stirred in the big bed. " But d'you know what I can't understand, Denis ? "

" There's a lot I can't understand," he said. " The whole situation here is preposterous."

" What I can't understand," she said, " is how he could take the risk of inviting me and Mrs. Kenny at the same time. He must have known she'd recognise me and that the consequence of that would be even worse for him than for me."

" Unless he's got some way of persuading her to keep silence."

" What way could there be, with her, of all people ? "

" There's some sort of pressure to which almost everyone will yield if you can discover what it is and how to apply it."

" I don't think Mrs. Kenny would ever yield to threats."

" Well, she may have a better nature that can be appealed to."

" Possibly." Mrs. Pointing sounded dubious.

" At any rate, she adores her funny little drunken Hector, doesn't she ? She'd do anything in the world for him."

" Oh, Denis, don't get Hector wrong," she said quickly. " He's probably the shrewdest man you've ever met. He runs that mill of hers in Bradford completely. He's done that for the last thirty years and he's as clever a businessman as you'll find anywhere in the North. Mrs. Kenny insists on signing all the cheques—the mill's hers and the money's hers and she takes care that everyone should know that— but Hector runs the whole show."

He gave a laugh. " That's interesting. I'd never have guessed it. But don't tell me he's married and has a family, because that I couldn't believe."

" Oh, no, he's always lived with Mrs. Kenny. And he always spends every evening at home with her except one, when he goes to his club."

" So it looks as if he's had to pay rather heavily for having been adopted by a rich woman."

" Yes and no. He seems quite satisfied, doesn't he ? "

" That wound of his, is that real ? "

" Oh yes. Funny little drunken Hector was a hero once. He got all sorts of decorations."

" Interesting," Pointing said again. He added after a

moment, " I'd like to be good at seeing through people. It must make life fascinating. Our friend Auty now . . ."

" Let's not talk about him, I'll never get to sleep if I start," she said. " We'll have to have a talk with him in the morning, though when I suggested that to him when we met, he said wait till we get to Nice. Wait till we get to Nice and can discuss the whole situation with Miss Barbosa."

" He said that ! " Pointing exclaimed.

" Yes."

" D'you think he really means it ? D'you think he's actually told that girl the real story ? "

" I don't know. Anyway, I mean to make him have a talk with me to-morrow before we go. But let's not talk about it now."

" No, all right. Good night, my dear."

" Good night."

They lay side by side in silence. But neither slept.

When Alec Marriner went into his bedroom, he made no attempt to go to bed. At first he walked up and down. His head was bent, his hands were clasped behind him. Four steps to the window, four steps back to the door. But after a while, looking round uneasily, it seemed to strike him that the whole house was silent and that perhaps this rhythmic tread of his might be disturbing to other people. Pulling a chair close to the open window, he sat down, leaning his elbows on the sill, gazing out at the night sky.

There were no stars in the dark expanse. There was no point on which to focus thought, but only a shifting of dark masses, with an occasional faint brightening between the banks of cloud. Some tree-tops showed against the sky in a jagged ridge of blacker shadow.

At first the lawn near the house was chequered with patches of light from other windows, but one by one, these disappeared, until, besides his own, only one was left shining. But this other light did not fall brightly on the grass like Marriner's, for the window was curtained. Where Marriner's light fell, the grass looked brilliantly green, with the shadow of his head cut sharply out of it.

While he sat there the expression on his face changed

47

many times. At first it showed anger, resolution and a kind of satisfaction. Later there was bewilderment and uncertainty. Still later, tears came into his eyes and then he folded his arms on the window ledge and hid his face in them. For a long time his shoulders went on shaking. But if anyone had been watching, the shadow on the grass would not have revealed this.

At last he sat back, rubbing the tears from his eyes with the back of his hand, and soon afterwards he got up, went to his suitcase and opened it. Taking out the revolver wrapped in the green knitted pullover, he unrolled it, dropped the pullover back into the case, emptied the six chambers of the revolver, then carried it to the window. Leaning out, he took aim at a patch of bushes he could see dimly at the farther edge of the lawn, and threw the revolver towards them.

As it fell there was a faint thud and a bird fluttered out of the bushes with a sudden, alarmed twittering. Then all became still again.

A few minutes later the only patch of light left on the lawn was the one that fell from the curtained window behind which Peter Nock lay sleeping a drugged sleep, with the light beside him shining to keep the terrors of the night away from him.

CHAPTER VI

BY THE MORNING all the clouds had gone from the sky. It was the soft, hazy blue that means a brilliant day. A film of dew lay on the grass. The air was full of the sweet scents of the flower-filled beds and of the damp earth, warming in the sun.

Sarah came downstairs, dressed in a green and white check blouse and a green linen skirt. As she saw the shafts of sunshine entering the old house through open windows, and smelt the freshness of the garden, she felt cheerfully disinclined to remember the disquiets of the evening before. She had not slept well and the little sleep that had come to her had been charged with unpleasant dreams, but now she did not remember them. Also, for a little while, her memory had completely blotted out the presence of Peter Nock in the house. The morning was too serene to be marked by his dark image.

Seated at breakfast in the dining-room she found no one but Hector Kenny. He was wearing an open-necked shirt, flannel trousers and an old blazer. He was eating a boiled egg and drinking coffee. Showing no signs of suffering for what he had drunk the night before, he greeted her smilingly, rang the bell and told the little manservant to bring her breakfast.

" We're early birds, you and I," he remarked, continuing with his own.

It was a quarter past nine.

" I thought I should be about the last," Sarah said. " Normally I have to get up at seven to be in time at the office."

" So do I," Hector said. " Seven o'clock sharp. Horrible. When I retire I shall always have breakfast in bed. I say, I haven't had a fresh egg like this for months. Or perhaps years. The country's certainly the place to live in these days, isn't it ? When I retire I shall live in the country. I shall just have a small place with room for me and some sort of housekeeper and about an acre of garden and a good trout stream near by. Difficult to improve on that, eh ? "

He beamed at Sarah and proceeded to toast and marmalade.

" After all," he went on, " what's the use of making money when it's all taken away from you ? Of course it's different for ambitious blokes who enjoy a bit of power, but what's the good of it to someone like me ? No, as soon as I can, I'm going."

Sarah supposed he meant that as soon as Mrs. Kenny died, he was going. Or else he was merely talking in this way because the morning was fine and the garden outside was beautiful and his egg had been fresh. By the time that the week-end was over, he would no doubt be pining for Bradford and the woollen industry.

Just then they were joined by Alec Marriner.

There was something different about him this morning,

Sarah thought, though at first she could not have put a name to the difference and was inclined to believe that her memory of him from the evening before had not been accurate. Then she began to feel sure that his face really was looking younger than it had yesterday, that it was smoother and less tense, that his eyes had lost some of their nervous glitter.

Sitting down at the table, he asked, " Have you seen Mark? I want to speak to him."

" No, I've not seen him yet," Hector said. " Like a sensible man, he keeps out of the way of his guests until coffee and eggs have had their civilising effect on them."

" I want to tell him I've changed my mind about going to Nice," Marriner said. " I'm going back to London instead. You don't happen to know anything about the trains, do you ? "

" Not coming to Nice ! " Hector popped a large piece of toast and marmalade into his mouth. " Dear me, I'm so sorry to hear that. I hope it doesn't mean you've had bad news or anything of that sort."

" Oh no, nothing like that."

" I think there's a train to London about every hour," Sarah said.

Watching him as he helped himself to coffee, and remembering that conversation in the garden, she thought that she ought to feel a great relief at his change of plan. Yet what she was most conscious of was disappointment.

Hector went on, " Perhaps you're not well. Is that the trouble ? You've been living in Africa, haven't you ? I expect you've found the change of climate rather a shock. But if that's the trouble, you'll enjoy Nice, you know. It'll do you good. I really shouldn't cancel the trip."

" But that isn't the trouble," Marriner said with a smile. " I'm very well indeed. Never felt better."

" Then I know what it must be." Hector turned to Sarah. " He came here, he took one look at us all and he thought, ' What a menagerie ! I can't stand a week-end of these ! ' " He looked back at Marriner. " Have I hit the nail on the head.

" Well, not the nail, exactly," Marriner said.

" Just his thumb-nail, at most," Sarah said.

Marriner laughed and said, " Is that because of the things I was saying yesterday in the car about the horrors of being shut up with the same people all day ? But what I was talking about then was months and years, not a single week-end. And my change of plan hasn't anything to do with that either. It's just that—well, say I'm a changeable character who isn't very good at knowing my own mind."

" Which reminds me," Hector said, " that you and Auty were shut up together for a good while, weren't you ? Wasn't it in that camp from which those twelve men escaped ? "

Marriner drank some coffee. Ignoring the food that had been placed before him, he lit a cigarette.

" From which they tried to escape," he said.

" Oh yes—that's what I meant," Hector said. " It was a frightful affair. Frightful. You knew them all, I suppose."

" Yes." The word was very quietly spoken.

" Didn't any of them get through ? Were they all shot ? "

" All of them."

Hector was leaning towards Marriner, his eyes gleaming with interest through his spectacles.

" Our friend Auty wasn't in on the affair, was he ? " he said. " I wonder why not. I should have thought it was just his sort of thing. He's got initiative and courage and I should say the right sort of recklessness for a venture like that."

Marriner seemed about to answer something quickly, then stubbing out the cigarette he had started, he picked up a spoon and tapped with it gently on the top of his egg.

" He has other qualities besides these you've mentioned," he said.

" Such as ? "

" Foresight, perhaps."

" Yes, no doubt. What else ? "

Sarah became determined to stop the conversation. " Well, I think you might consider changing that changeable mind of yours just once more," she said, " and come to Nice after all. I'm sure when you actually get back to London, you'll be sorry."

Marriner answered with a slight shake of the head.

" I'm sure I'll be sorry too," he said, " if only because

it means I shan't find out the reason for this whole strange arrangement. But perhaps you'll let me know what it was all about when you get back."

" Ah, then you think it's strange," Hector said. He had kept his owlish gaze on Marriner's face. " Strange in just what way, Mr. Marriner ? "

The young man looked at Sarah. " Isn't it strange ? "

" Oh, I don't know," she said vaguely, not wanting to let herself be led into any discussion of the situation in which she might reveal her half-knowledge of Auty's intentions.

" The trouble is," Hector said, getting up from the table and going towards the door, " it's very difficult for supposedly well-bred people to settle down to a discussion of their host and his peculiar motives in asking them to his house. We're all longing to do it, but we can't. We just can't. All the same, I'm relieved to hear you say that you think it's strange. I was worrying a little in case I was the only one who thought so."

The door closed on him.

A moment later Sarah and Marriner saw him walk past outside the window. His hands were clasped behind him and his head was high as he breathed in the sweet air of the summer morning.

" He's right, of course," Marriner said. " I'd love to ask you what you think we're doing here, but I know you wouldn't answer honestly."

" Would you ? " Sarah asked.

" No," he said.

" I don't think you'd even answer if I asked you . . ."

" What ? " He said it in the same light tone, but she thought there was a change of expression in the bright eyes under the dark, level brows.

" No," she said, " it was a pointless question I was going to ask you."

" Go on," he said.

" Oh, it was just why you ever accepted Mr. Auty's invitation when you hate him so."

He spun round in his seat so that he faced her directly. He looked as if he had never seen her before. For a moment his eyes seemed to be trying to force the answer to some question out of her. Then he turned away again and spoke without looking at her.

" I don't think I do hate him." He said it thoughtfully, discussing the matter with himself rather than with her. " It's true I came here hating him, though I didn't mean it to show as clearly as it seems to have done. But I've discovered it's easier to hate a phantom than a real person. Perhaps that's weakness. I'm inclined to think it may be. Plenty of people exist whom one ought to be able to hate when one's face to face with them and not only when they're phantoms in one's mind. But it seems that I'm not good at it and that trying to screw myself up to be isn't much use. So there it is. I really don't hate him. I'm rather sick with myself about it, but there it is."

Sarah had not the faintest doubt of the sincerity of this curious statement, even if she was not quite sure what he was talking about.

" But why should you feel you ought to hate him ? " she asked. " Don't most of us do more hating than we ought to ? "

" Not really," he said. " Not the hate that leads to anything. We're all pretty good at hating phantoms—that's why we don't mind making war—but someone who's standing quite close to you, looking at you, talking to you, seeming to like you, not threatening you in any way—it's extraordinary what that does to you, even when you've been almost choking with hatred. But I think that's mostly weakness and cowardice."

" It's a pity you've such an awfully low opinion of yourself," she said.

That seemed to surprise him. He started to say something, but as voices reached them from the hall, he stopped. As the Pointings came into the room, he gave Sarah one more of his intent glances, in which he seemed anxious to draw out of her some explanation of this remark that she had just made, then he turned away and began eating rapidly.

A few minutes later the Carvers came in, and soon after them Mark Auty.

As Marriner finished his breakfast, he stood up and walked round the table to where Auty was sitting.

" Mark, I'd like to talk to you for a few minutes, as soon as you can manage it," he said in a low voice.

" Of course. Now, if you like," Auty said.

He had a cheerful, eager look, an air of containing some entirely pleasurable excitement, which reminded Sarah that whatever worries and problems he might have on his mind that day, he was also on his way to see the woman he loved and was shortly to marry.

" No hurry," Marriner said. " Wait till you've had breakfast. I'll be around." He went out.

" Well, anyway, the weather's kind to us," Auty said. " A morning like this makes me feel good. And it ought to cheer up any of you who aren't quite happy about flying. It'll be wonderful, you'll see."

The Pointings murmured polite agreement and Carver growled something inaudible into his coffee. The only one who responded to Auty's enthusiasm was Lorna Carver. She was wearing a white shantung suit with a black and white scarf at her throat. With her pale, shining hair scraped tightly off her face and piled on top of her head, she looked radiant with anticipation and pleasure.

" D'you know, I've never been in an aeroplane ? " she said. " Just think of that. Here am I, free, white and an awful lot over twenty-one and I've never been in an aeroplane ! "

" Plenty of other things you don't know anything about either," Carver muttered.

" You bet there are," she said happily. " The Riviera, for one thing. I've never been to the Riviera. Mr. Auty, I think you're the most wonderful darling to think of an idea like this. I'm sure it's the most wonderful engagement party anyone ever thought of."

" What time do we leave ? " Pointing asked Auty.

" Straight after lunch," Auty said. " It's not a long drive to the air-field. If we can get away from here about one-thirty——" He stopped as the little, white-coated man-servant appeared at the door. " Yes, Joe, what is it ? "

" The telephone, sir. A call from Nice."

" Nice ! " Auty jumped to his feet. There was a conflict in his face between pleasure and a sudden anxiety. " I wasn't expecting that."

He hurried out.

" What's the betting, there goes our trip ? " Carver said, smiling for the first time since he had come into the room, a tight little ill-natured smile. " Miss Barbosa may have thought better about entertaining her future husband's dear old friends. And I can't say I blame her."

" Tim ! " Lorna said furiously. She turned to Mrs. Pointing and spoke with great dignity. " It's his hay fever, you know. It affects his nerves. Poor old Tim's quite another person once all the hay's in."

" Hay ! " her husband said sneeringly. " I tell you, if Miss Barbosa's a smart girl, she's just calling the whole thing off. Not just this visit of ours, but the whole works. You wait and see."

Pointing was looking at him with an interest that he had not yet shown.

" Have you any reason for suggesting that," he asked, " or is it just your normal response to hospitality ? "

Carver returned his look with a hostile stare.

" I've got nothing against hospitality," he said slowly, " when there aren't any strings to it."

" Be quiet ! " Lorna said more angrily than ever. " Please don't take any notice of him, Mr. Pointing. He's always like this in the morning when he's got hay fever."

" Nice for him," Pointing murmured.

" Let me tell you," Carver said belligerently, " I keep a pub. You get hospitality there that hasn't got strings to it. You pay your way and you're all right." He thrust out his long cleft chin at Pointing. " Got anything against that ? "

" Not a thing," Pointing said. " But what I was really interested in was whether or not you had any reason for suggesting that Miss Barbosa might, as you put it, be calling the whole thing off."

His wife put a hand on his arm. He did not seem to feel the touch. He and Carver continued their challenging scrutiny of one another, but before Carver had made up his mind how to reply, Auty came back into the room.

From his expression as he came in, Sarah thought that Carver must have been right and that the call from Nice had in fact been made to cancel the trip. Auty's forehead was creased into tight ridges. His mouth was hard. He looked worried and irritated.

" Of all the damned annoying things ! " he said.

Carver winked at Pointing, then turned his head and smirked at Lorna, who looked ready to hit him in the face.

" Not that it's really serious," Auty went on, but it was plain that he was thinking hard while he was speaking and not of the words that he was saying. " The trouble is an uncle of Anna's who's arriving in London to-day from Paris and leaving from Southampton for America to-morrow. Apparently he's a very special uncle and it's important that I see him and look after him all the time he's in England. And that means that I can't go with you to-day. But that's no reason why the rest of you shouldn't go just as arranged. I'll ring up B.E.A. for a seat for myself in the night plane to-morrow. It's damned irritating, but it won't actually make all that much difference."

There was a short silence after he had spoken.

Then Carver said, " This uncle, is it the first you've heard of him ? "

" No," Auty said. " I've known he was coming to England soon, but I wasn't expecting him for at least a fortnight." He crossed the room to the small door beside the fireplace. " I'm extremely sorry about this change, but as I said, it needn't make any difference to you. All the arrangements can go through and when you get to Nice, Anna will look after you."

While he was speaking his eye held Sarah's for a minute and he made a very slight movement with his head, which she interpreted as being a request for her to follow him.

As he went through into the study, Carver remarked, " I wonder if by any chance this uncle is so mighty special that he doesn't exist."

Sarah got up quickly and went after Auty.

Seeing her come in, he closed the door quickly after her and said softly, " Good girl. I wanted you."

She saw now that his manner in the dining-room had been assumed for the benefit of his other guests, for now that he was alone with her his face had reddened, his breathing had become jerky and his blue eyes looked feverish. Taking hold of one of her arms in a hard grip, he pulled her towards him so that her face was only a few inches from his.

"Sarah, you're the only one in this place I can trust," he whispered. "Are you going to help me?"

CHAPTER VII

HER RESPONSE to the drama of it was a wave of distrust. Every doubt that she had had about him since seeing Peter Nock came back to her. She felt acutely how little she knew of him and how little she would ever be able to understand a man of his type, and that probably she would never have come here at all but for the fact that she had been flattered by the notice of someone so much in the public eye.

Drawing away from him, she said, "Did you hear what Mr. Carver said as we came out?"

Shaking his head, uninterested, too busy with his own thoughts to pay much attention to what she was saying, he threw himself into the chair at the desk.

"He's inclined to doubt the existence of Miss Barbosa's uncle," Sarah said.

Auty laughed harshly.

"That's damned funny. By God, it is. And you—I suppose you think the same. If you do, say so and we'll call the whole thing off. Go on, say it."

"I won't say so yet," she said.

"Listen," Auty said, planting his elbows on the table, peering at her as if he could not see her quite distinctly, "if you want to get out, this is the time to do it, because in a minute I'm going to ask you to do something for me, quite an easy thing to do in itself—that side of it needn't worry you—and I'm asking you rather than any of the others because, as I've told you before, you're the only one here I know I can trust. But if you want to get out, say so now and I won't tell you what it is I was going to ask you to do."

"About this uncle of Miss Barbosa's . . ." She looked at him inquiringly.

He struck the table with his fist.

" For God's sake ! " He gave another short, unwilling laugh. " Anna's Uncle Gilberto is as real and as solid as the spanner in the works, the unforeseen circumstance, always is. And he's the one thing I didn't take into my calculations. He's the one thing I didn't allow for. But I know you've only got my word for it and if that isn't good enough for you, I don't know what to do about it. I only wish I knew, though, what I'd ever done to make you so suspicious of me all of a sudden."

The words sounded familiar to Sarah. They were very like those she had heard him say to Alec Marriner in the garden the evening before.

" Listen," she said, sitting down in the chair that she had occupied during their former talk in this room, " yesterday you promised that as soon as we'd got to Nice and had had a talk with Miss Barbosa, you'd tell me what this is all about. That should have been this evening. But now you aren't coming to Nice to-day. You're sending us all off without you. So I shan't get my explanation until the day after to-morrow at the earliest."

He broke in at that point. " Sarah, I swear to you there's nothing phoney about this business of Uncle Gilberto. If there were any possible way of putting him off and coming with you as I'd arranged, I'd do it. But I see your point, and if you like, I'll tell you at least some of what I'd have told you to-night. But come a bit closer, because I'm not going to shout it, for everyone to overhear."

As he spoke, he hitched his chair towards hers. Sarah moved hers a little forward. Auty dropped his voice and went on.

" During the last month, there've been three attempts on my life. I've been shot at, the steering-column of my car's been damaged and someone tried to push me under an electric train. I went to the police, but unfortunately they didn't take me seriously. I'm afraid they thought I was trying to pull a publicity stunt. So I've had to try to find some way of coping with the situation myself. First, I hired a private detective. You know what happened to him. Also, I planned this party. I collected here all the people who have something against me, or who think they have something against me. In short, with the exception of you, my dear, they aren't my old friends but my old enemies. And I'm transporting them, though they don't know it, to a place where they'll be completely cut off from the world around them. There'll be no running for cover. The Barbosa villa isn't in Nice, but in the mountains some distance away and I've arranged things so that once these people are all there, they'll none of them get away till I'm ready to let them go. And that'll be when I've found out which of them is trying to murder me."

He stopped. Sarah could see that he was watching her acutely for her response. But for the life of her, she could not think of anything to say. She noticed, now that his face was near to hers, that a muscle was twitching in his cheek and that he was in a far greater state of tension than she had realised. In fact, she wondered how she could have failed to notice before the signs of a great strain that she now saw so clearly. Yet she could not really take in what he had told her.

" Well ? " he said at last.

She felt the prickling up her spine that came when she was scared. But she tried hard to clear her thoughts. " But you know who it must have been," she said. " That horrible man——"

" No," he said quickly. " Not Nock. That's to say, it may have been Nock who pulled the trigger and tampered with my car and gave me the push on to the line. I dare say it was, just as it was Nock who was driving the car that killed poor Darnborough. But Nock's got nothing to gain by my death. Rather the reverse, in fact. So if it really was he who tried to do those things to me, then it was because he was acting for someone else. And that's the person I've got to uncover—jolly little Hector, perhaps, or that crazy young Marriner, or any of them."

That reminded Sarah. " Alec Marriner says he isn't going to Nice at all. He's changed his mind. He's going back to London."

" Damnation ! " The muscle in Auty's cheek gave a convulsive twitch. " Is nothing going to go right ? "

" But I'm sure he couldn't have been the person who's been trying to kill you. The way he talked this morning . . ." She stopped. After all, she was not at all sure that the way that Marriner had talked meant that he was incapable of murder by proxy. Perhaps a man who found it so hard to keep up the full power of his antagonism in the presence of his enemy, might find murder by proxy a convenient solution to his problem. " But where do I come in ? " she asked. " What use am I to you ? And what is this thing that you were asking me to do ? "

" You come in," he said, " because of Anna. I did all I could to make her keep clear of the whole business, but she wouldn't hear of that. She insisted on being in on it. I don't know if you can guess what that means to me in the way of anxiety. It's wonderful, but it's frightful for me at the same time. So I thought that if only someone like you was there too, someone whom I knew for certain wasn't mixed up in this vile business, yet who'd seen Darnborough killed and knew that the story I've told you is serious and not just a horrible fantasy—well, that I could ask that person to stay with Anna as much as possible, keep her out of the way sometimes and . . . Oh, I know I'm asking a terrible lot, Sarah. Probably much, much more than anyone in his senses would ask. Much more than I've any right to ask. But just to have you there to be with Anna, if—well, if my scheme goes wrong."

Sarah started. " You mean if——"

" If it's fourth time successful," he said wryly.

Now that that was out, that the fear had been put into words, he seemed to relax and feel at ease. He managed a smile.

" Well, what's the answer ? " he asked. " Going or not going ? "

" Oh, I'm going," she said.

" Wonderful girl."

" I promised you last night I'd go," she said. " But you haven't told me yet what this special job is that you want me to do."

" Just to take something with you and give it to Anna."

" What kind of thing ? "

" This."

He bent and pulled out from under the desk a leather brief-case. Putting it on the desk, he opened it. The

60

brief-case appeared to be full of papers. Those on top looked like letters in a large, sloping feminine handwriting.

" I could keep it with me and take it over to-morrow," he said, " but I want to be dead sure that, whatever happens, Anna gets it. There are two of Darnborough's reports here and certain other things that I want to know will get safely into her hands. That's very important."

" Don't you think it would get safely into her hands if you took it yourself ? " Sarah asked. " Aren't all the dangerous people going on ahead of you ? "

" I can't be quite sure, can I ? Well, will you take it ? "

" Oh yes, I'll take it."

" It's not very heavy and there's nothing you need to declare at the customs. With luck you won't have to open it. But if you do, it doesn't much matter. The main thing is, not to let the others in the party know that it doesn't belong to you. If a certain one of them realised that you were carrying something for me, I don't think it would stay long in your possession."

" All right, I'll do my best," she said. " Is that all ? "

He took a key out of his pocket and locked the case.

" That's all," he said, handing her the key. " Put that in a safe place."

She stood up and lifted the brief case from the desk.

" I don't really know what to say about it all," she said. " I can't take it in."

" Of course you can't. No decent person could take it in easily."

" Are you really afraid, Mr. Auty ? "

" Yes," he said briefly.

She walked towards the door. But he reached it before her.

" Wait," he said. " If some of them are still in the dining-room, I don't want you to go out yet. I don't want them to see you come out of this room, carrying that thing."

He opened the door and looked out. The dining-room was empty.

" All right," he said. " Go ahead."

She reached the door and turned for an instant to look at him. He gave her a cheerful smile and repeated softly his pet phrase, " Wonderful girl."

She smiled back and went out.

As she emerged from the dining-room, crossed the hall and started up the stairs, there was still no one in sight. She reached her room without seeing anybody, or, she thought, being seen. Yet as she went in, she heard a sound in the passage behind her. It was a very soft sound, like that of a door being gently closed. But she did not know from which door it had come. She had not noticed any of them standing open when she passed.

The possibility, however, that she had been seen made her still more nervous. It made her decide that probably she ought to hide the brief case, and looking round the room, she tried to think of some safe place of concealment.

As she did so, a disturbing thought persisted in her mind. The unfortunate fact was that she still did not believe in Uncle Gilberto.

She could not stop thinking about this while she searched for a hiding-place for the brief case and came to the conclusion that there was none in the room that was entirely safe. There was no cupboard or drawer with a stout lock. Finally she climbed on a chair and laid the case down flat on top of the tall wardrobe. The key of the brief case she put into the pocket in her handbag that contained the small amount of French money that she had brought with her.

When she had done this, she lit a cigarette, and went to the window.

As she leant on the sill, the sunshine fell warmly on her face. A chaffinch, perched on a drainpipe near her, chirruped at her and showed no signs of being afraid. Looking out across the garden, she saw Hector Kenny stooping over a flower bed, weeding. He had taken off his blue blazer and dropped it on to one of the garden chairs that someone had put out on the lawn. The seat of his trousers was stretched tight as he bent and pulled and prodded with a little hand-fork at the few stray pieces of groundsel in the bed. From time to time he stood upright, breathing deeply and rubbing the small of his back.

If there was no Uncle Gilberto, Sarah thought, it meant that Auty had never intended to travel to Nice with his guests. That much was obvious. A non-existent Uncle Gilberto could only be a device for keeping Auty behind.

But in that case, why should Auty not have confided that part of his scheme to her. He talked of trusting her, but in fact he had trusted her no farther than was unavoidable.

Sarah was really a good deal annoyed by this. Yet in his place, she supposed, she might have acted in the same way. After all, why should he trust her ? What did he know about her ?

A thought struck her then that brought a sharp frown to her face. He had told her that his presence near to the scene of the so-called accident had not been a coincidence. Was it possible that he could suspect that her presence there had not been a coincidence either ?

But after a moment's consideration, she rejected that possibility. If Auty had any such suspicion of her in his mind, he would not have trusted her even as far as he had.

And perhaps Uncle Gilberto did exist. It would be pleasant to think so.

Just then Hector stood up to ease his back and happened to see her at the window.

He waved his little weeding-fork.

" Why don't you come down and sit in the garden ? " he called. " It's very nice out here and I'd have someone to talk to me while I exert myself."

" All right," she called back. " I'll come down in a moment."

She turned from the window, took one more look round to see if there was any safter hiding-place for the brief case than the one she had found, decided that there was none and went out into the passage.

She found herself face to face with Alec Marriner.

He had apparently just come from the staircase and was on his way to his room.

" Well, have you told Mr. Auty that you aren't going with us ? " she asked.

" No," Marriner said, " because I'm going."

" You've changed your mind again ? "

" Yes. I said I was changeable, didn't I ? "

" At least you seem to know yourself," she said.

" I doubt it rather."

She lingered for a moment. " Is there any special reason this time ? "

" Yes."

" I suppose there's always a special reason."

" So one thinks at the time," he agreed.

CHAPTER VIII

SHE WENT into the garden. Hector heard her come and straightened up once more. As she sat down in one of the chairs on the lawn, he walked towards her and sat down in one of the other chairs. He smiled at her contentedly.

" Are you interested in gardening ? " he asked.

" I dare say I'd become interested if I had a garden," she said. " But I live in a flat on the first floor of a house that hasn't much more than a back-yard anyway."

" You might explore the possibilities of window-boxes," he said seriously. " There's more to them than you'd think."

Leaning back in the garden chair, he rested his earthy hands on his plump knees.

The sun was growing hotter. The haze that had covered the morning sky was melting, its blue growing deeper and brighter. Sarah moved her head a little, blinking at the strong light. Then she closed her eyes, enjoying the sensation of warmth on her eyelids.

" That's how I feel too," Hector murmured. " I could stay here for hours. How nice it would be, wouldn't it, if Miss Barbosa were coming here to see us, instead of us going there to see her ? Getting into an aeroplane seems such a waste of a nice day."

Sarah opened her eyes again. She was about to say something vaguely agreeing with him, when she saw, to her great astonishment, that he was pointing a revolver at her.

At her gasp, he exclaimed, " I'm so sorry ! " and hurriedly jerked the revolver round so that it pointed at a clump of lupins. " It isn't loaded though. There's nothing to worry about."

" But what are you doing with it ? " she asked. " Do you always carry a gun ? "

" Practically never," he said regretfully. " I got this out

of the flower bed. Without exception, it's the oddest weed I've ever found."

" That flower bed there ? " she asked incredulously.

" Just there—under that japonica." He pointed the revolver at the shrub.

At first she doubted that he was serious. From his face, it was difficult to guess what he thought of his discovery. His expression was what it might have been if he had just picked up an unusual shell on the sea-shore or found a rare butterfly sunning itself on the window-pane in mid-winter.

" When did you find it ? " she asked.

" About half an hour ago."

" Is it an old one—old and rusty ? "

" That might have been lying out there for some time, you mean ? " he said. " Oh no, it's in perfect condition, cleaned and oiled."

" What are you going to do with it ? "

He glanced at her sideways. His forehead puckered. " I'm not quite sure. Hand it over to our host, I suppose. What do you suggest ? "

She hesitated. " Yes, I suppose you should do that."

" I should like to keep it," he said, " and if someone threw it away because he simply didn't want it any more, I don't really see why I shouldn't. But there's always the possibility of some mistake." He turned his head and looked at her directly. " Why don't you think I ought to give it to our friend Auty ? "

" But I didn't say that," she said. " I said you should."

" You have your doubts, however."

" No, I haven't," she said, trying to sound convinced of what she was saying. But her impulse was to tell Hector to take the revolver back to the flower bed and bury it there, bury it deep. " I expect it belongs to Mr. Auty."

" I'd be very surprised if that were so," he said.

" Why ? " she asked.

" I feel that any weapons belonging to our friend would always be kept in their proper places—whether for use or for show."

An odd thing struck her then. It was that Hector seemed incapable of referring to Auty simply by his name. It was always " our friend " or " our friend Auty," with what sounded like an undertone of irony in the words.

" Whose d'you think it is ? " she asked.

" I haven't any idea. At any rate, it isn't yours, is it ? "

" Good heavens, no."

" Pistol-packing momma—I was afraid not. Well, I'll give it to our host when he appears. Meanwhile, how would you like to take care of it, while I go back to my weeding ? No ? " For he saw her recoil. " All right then, I'll just conceal it in this for the time being." He picked up his blazer and slipped the revolver into its folds. Walking over to the flower bed, he laid the blazer down on the edge of the lawn, then stooped and renewed his assault on the groundsel.

Sarah thought of going straight into the house to tell Auty about the find. She had an idea that that was what she ought to do. Yet she did not want to. She did not want to move. She was beginning to dread more and more having to participate actively in the situation that Auty had described to her. The reason for this was simple enough. She was frightened. She was horribly frightened. With a part of her mind she still disbelieved the whole story, feeling that it was so unlike anything else that had ever happened to her that it could not be true and this thought was so comforting that she kept returning to it, trying to find arguments for convincing herself that poor Mark Auty must be suffering at the moment from ideas of persecution. But in the intervals of quite seriously considering this idea, which after all offered the most rational explanation of the situation, she was scared. And the longer that she had to think about it, the more scared she was becoming.

But she had committed herself, so that was that.

Sitting in the garden, enjoying the sun, though it was growing so hot that soon it would drive her into the shade, and watching Hector happily slaying weeds, she was still moderately able to cling to the ordinariness of things and to cover up some of her fear from herself. But if she moved, she thought, and went back into the shadowy house, terror would leap upon her.

Anything might happen then. She might turn tail and fly. She might fail Auty completely. So the only thing to do for the present was to stay still and let things take their own course.

She was growing half-drowsy with the heat and the effort to deaden her panic, when she heard behind her a soft, melodious whistling.

Then she heard Mrs. Kenny say, " I suppose you have this modern mania for toasting yourself dark brown. If I sit here, however, I shall get sunstroke. Perhaps you'll be so good as to move a chair for me into the shade of that nice copper beech."

Sarah jumped up. Hector too, at the sound of his mother's voice, looked up from his weeding and catching Sarah's eye, gestured at his blazer and shook his head, meaning that she was to say nothing about his discovery to Mrs. Kenny.

Sarah moved a couple of chairs into the patch of shade under a copper beech at one end of the lawn. Mrs. Kenny, who was smoking as usual, sat down and offered Sarah a cigarette.

" Someone told me," the old woman said, " that you had decided not to come with us this afternoon. Is that so ? "

" No, it was Mr. Marriner who changed his mind," Sarah said. " But he's changed it back again. He's going after all."

" And you're definitely coming with us ? "

" Oh yes."

" I'm so glad. And I'm glad Mr. Marriner intends to accompany us. He's a nervous type and nervous people usually upset me, yet I find him quite agreeable. But certainly there are some members of this party who I wish would experience a change of mind. I know I'm being ill-mannered, referring critically to my fellow-guests, but you'll find as you get to know me better that I always say whatever comes into my mind. I stopped having manners of any kind about twenty years ago. In my opinion, if other people would do the same, they would all live much longer. Do you know, I'm eighty-three ? Would you have guessed that ? "

" No, I certainly shouldn't have," Sarah said perfectly truthfully.

Mrs. Kenny nodded her head so that the diamonds in her ears trembled.

" Eighty-three. It's a very nice age to be. I advise you

to get there too, if you can. But don't coddle yourself, mind, and don't listen to other people's advice, and don't be afraid of age, look forward to it, that's my recipe. But I was talking about that man Nock, wasn't I ? "

" Were you ? " Sarah said.

" Yes, didn't I say I wished he'd change his mind about coming with us ? I could spare his company very easily. An incredibly unpleasant person, don't you agree with me? "

As Sarah hesitated, Mrs. Kenny went on, " Perhaps you don't. Perhaps he strikes you as handsome. One never can tell what the young will think. Do you think he's handsome ? "

" I hadn't thought about it," Sarah said. " Perhaps he is."

" Now I consider Mr. Auty a handsome man," Mrs. Kenny said. " Well, perhaps not strictly speaking handsome. But big, strong-looking, blond men have always appealed to me. My husband was very big and strong and fair-haired. He died more than thirty years ago, you know. What I'd have done all that time without Hector I simply can't imagine. I should have had a very sad life. Of course one can't call Hector exactly handsome—with him it's a case of character. There's a great deal of character in his face, isn't there ? But if you're young, I suppose someone like that man Nock strikes you as romantic. In fact, a generation brought up on Hollywood films probably finds that type irresistible, and you don't stop to think about his very dubious character, or the almost certainly disreputable fashion in which such a man makes his living."

All at once Sarah's interest quickened. She asked, " Just what makes you think that about him, Mrs. Kenny— I mean, about his being dubious and disreputable ? "

" His ears," Mrs. Kenny said promptly.

Sarah found the answer disappointing. She had hoped for some piece of information about Peter Nock.

" I don't think I've noticed his ears particularly," she said.

" They're too flat against his head," Mrs. Kenny said. " That's always a bad sign. It's a sign of viciousness and treachery. Now look at Hector's ears. They don't stick out, there's nothing prominent or absurd about them, but they've none of that look of being laid back like the ears of an angry cur. Hector has nice, honest ears. By the way, has he been working like that all the morning ? "

" I think so," Sarah said.

" I wonder if the sun's too hot for him. Perhaps I ought to call him to come and sit in the shade. He has very little sense about his own welfare, and when he's interested in something, he forgets everything else. Still, I don't like to interfere with his pleasures. It will, of course, be much hotter in the South of France and I shall have to be firm with him then and see that he doesn't try to be too active. He's naturally a very active man, and it's a great hardship to him to remember his poor health . . ."

The saga of Hector's virtues and misfortunes continued.

Sarah's attention wandered. An occasional " yes " or " really " satisfied Mrs. Kenny that she was listening, and Sarah's thoughts were able to return to Auty, to Uncle Gilberto and to the fact that if he or his visit to England were a fiction, then Auty had never intended to travel with his guests. What, in that case, Sarah kept asking herself, did he intend to do with the time after the party had left for France ? Having got them all out of the way in that spectacular fashion, what could he mean to do next ?

There was also the problem of Alec Marriner's changes of plan. Why should Auty's announcement that he was not travelling that day have made Marriner decide after all to go to France with the party ? Not that Sarah had any proof that the two events were connected. One had followed the other, that was all. There could easily be some other reason, of which she knew nothing, for Marriner's second change of plan.

It was Mrs. Kenny cutting a sentence off short, the silence that followed it breaking in upon Sarah's abstraction, where the flow of words had sustained it, that interrupted that line of thought. Hoping that she had not failed to answer some question of importance to Mrs. Kenny and so offended her, Sarah tried hard to recall what had just been said, but then saw that it had not been any lack of response in herself that had stopped Mrs. Kenny talking. She had stopped because someone else was approaching them from the house.

Sarah, with her thoughts full of Alec Marriner and seeing

the newcomer out of the corner of her eye, thought for an instant that it was he who was walking towards them across the lawn. Then she realised that it was Peter Nock.

She was surprised at his seeking the company of Mrs. Kenny and herself. This he appeared to be doing deliberately, for after greeting them briefly, he fetched one of the garden chairs and set it down near them in the shade of the copper beech.

"The little man looks like a hard worker," he remarked, looking amusedly at Hector. " Now that's something I can't understand. Why should anyone fiddle around like that when they could be sitting down in comfort ? "

As always, when he spoke, the attractive quality of his voice was startling. But his face filled Sarah with the same sense of horror as it had the evening before, bringing before her with sickening vividness the picture of a speeding car and a thin, dark profile, set in a ghastly determination.

She would have got up at once and gone into the house but that Mrs. Kenny forestalled her. Looking straight before her and speaking in a voice full of corrosive dislike, Mrs. Kenny said, " I have a few letters here to post. I believe, when we were arriving yesterday, I noticed a letter-box a little way along the lane. If you will excuse me, I shall now attend to the matter."

She began to get up.

Nock stood up quickly. " Let me take them for you, Mrs. Kenny."

" No, thank you," she replied stiffly. " A short walk will suit me very well."

She walked away towards the corner of the house.

Sarah hesitated, wanting to follow her, and as she did so, heard Nock say, " Don't go too, as if I'd brought the plague with me."

His voice was still amused, but when she glanced at him, she found him looking at her with no humour and with an intent speculation in his dark eyes.

" I was just thinking of walking with Mrs. Kenny," she said.

" As you just thought of drinking your sherry in the garden yesterday as soon as I came into the room. What's the matter with me ? I've never done anything to you, have

I ? I may be wrong, but it's my impression that we've never met before."

She did not answer.

" Have we met ? " he asked.

" No," she said.

" You're sure ? "

" Quite sure," she said, a little too loudly.

" If I'd the faintest memory of your face, I'd think. . . . But I'm good at faces. You have to be, in my line of work, It's half the game. If I'd ever met you anywhere, I'd have remembered you."

" What is your line of work ? " she asked, with an irony that she could not keep out of her voice.

" Ever been to a place called the Songbird ? It's a night-club. I own it."

" It must be interesting."

" It is. Very. But you've got to be good at remembering faces. And you've got to be good at sizing people up, knowing the sort of people you're dealing with and handling them just the right way for the kind of people they are. See what I mean ? "

She had a crazy impulse to say, " And the ones you can't handle, you murder, I suppose." Holding it back, she managed to say, " Oh yes, I see."

" But you've got me puzzled, really puzzled," Nock said. " I've been watching you and you don't run away from everyone, like some people do. You don't even run away from all the men in the place. You'd be surprised how many girls do that, you know, nice-looking girls too, who don't look as if they'd anything the matter with them. But you aren't that type at all."

" You seem to be a psychologist."

" That's right." He was complacent about it. " But then I've special opportunities for it in my work. It interests me too. But you've got me really puzzled."

" I'm sorry."

" Look here——" He changed his tone to that of one who was offering intimacy. " What's the trouble really ? You're a nice girl, I can see that with half an eye. So I don't like it when you run out on me the moment you see me."

71

"But I haven't run out on you," Sarah said. "I'm sitting here enjoying our conversation."

"Like hell. You've got your eye on that corner of the house all the time, wondering when the old woman's going to get back from posting her letters to rescue you. Now why don't you tell me what the trouble is ? We're going off to France together, we're going to be seeing a lot of each other during the next few days. It'd be much better to be friends."

"There's no trouble," she said stubbornly.

It seemed to be the only way of answering him. If she were to say more, either to admit the revulsion he caused in her, or to elaborate a lie to explain her attitude towards him, she felt that she would immediately lose control of what she was saying and find herself telling him, in a tone of hysterical accusation, of the occasion when she had seen him. And that surely would be a very unwise and very dangerous thing to tell Peter Nock.

"There's no trouble," she repeated.

But he persisted. "Has Auty been saying anything ? Has he told you something about me you didn't like ? "

"Why should he do that ? " she asked.

"Don't ask me. People have their own reasons for what they do. And he's a subtle one."

"Subtle ? " she said, surprised. "I shouldn't have thought it."

"There you are, then," he said. "It shows you don't know much about people. Auty's subtle, you take it from me."

In spite of herself, she was becoming interested.

"Have you known him a long time ? " she asked.

"What's a long time ? Three or four years. Is that a long time ? "

"Is he a member of your club ? "

"He shows up there now and then. Why ? "

"I was just asking."

"Don't you approve ? "

"Why shouldn't I ? "

"That's right, why shouldn't you ? That's what I'd like to know. What have you got against me ? Why don't you like your friend Auty knowing me ? What's he been saying ?

Or if he hasn't been saying anything, what have I ever done to you to give you the right to look at me like you do ? "

So they had come back to the same question and this time Nock was leaning towards her with anger glinting in his eyes. His hollow cheeks seemed to be drawn in more sharply under his high cheekbones.

" If you'd prefer it," she said, " I'll do my best not to look at you at all."

At that moment, somebody screamed.

CHAPTER IX

WHEN MRS. KENNY left Sarah and Nock sitting under the tree, she walked rapidly as far as the corner of the house, but as soon as she had turned the corner and was invisible to the two people on the lawn, she stood still, putting a hand on her bosom and panting slightly. Then, more slowly, she went on towards the gate. With no one to see her, she allowed herself to walk more like an old woman. Also, she talked to herself, her pink-tinted lips moving rapidly in what looked like an agitated argument with an imaginary companion.

When she reached the gate the argument was broken off and her lips pursed themselves in their usual whistling. Continuing along the lane, she paused now and then to look at a wild flower in the tangled grass of the hedgerow, and seeing some tiny pansies, picked two or three and tucked them through an amethyst brooch at her throat. On reaching the letter-box, she stood still and opened her bag. Hunting about in it, she found an unused postcard and a pencil. Flattening the postcard against the letter-box, she wrote a short and unimportant message on it to her house-keeper, addressed it to her own home in Bradford and dropped it into the letter-box. Then she turned back, and even more slowly than she had come, retraced her steps towards the house.

While Mrs. Kenny was posting her letter, Lorna and Tim Carver were in their bedroom together. Lorna was making additions to her make-up. Carver was lying on the bed, glowering at the ceiling. Lorna was pretending to ignore him, but while she re-shaped her mouth and brushed her eyelashes with more mascara, she kept glancing past her own reflection in the mirror to that of her husband.

At last she could not stand his silence any longer.

" Well, what *did* he say, then ? " she asked, with an exasperation in her voice that suggested that she had already attempted a number of times to get the answer to this question.

Carver did not answer. A fly on the ceiling seemed to hold his disdainful attention.

" What did he say, what did he say ? " Lorna sang out louder, hitting her hairbrush on the top of the dressing-table.

Carver winced at the noise.

" Can that bloody row, can't you ? " he grunted.

" But what did he say ? What did you say ? Why did you go and talk to him ? Why did you rush out suddenly, saying you'd settle with him ? What have you got to settle with him ? "

" For God's sake. . . . Doesn't it ever strike you that one day you'll ask a question too much ? "

" Well, I'm your wife, aren't I ? I've got a right to ask you questions."

" Not about some things, you haven't, and you'd better get that into your head before you drive me too far."

" But what *did* he say ? "

" God Almighty ! He didn't say anything. We just had a drink together."

" And that's why you came up here looking as if you were ready to do murder ? " She hit the dressing-table again with her hairbrush. " I want to know, what did he say to make you look like that ? "

" I wasn't looking like anything," he said. " I was just fed up. Fed up with the whole show. I never wanted to come here and I don't want to stay. And why I went downstairs was that I'd thought of telling Auty that you and me were going back to Devon, but he pushed a drink in my hand and talked me out of it, and that's all there is to it. Now for God's sake, shut up and leave me in peace."

She swung round on her stool, staring at him in amazement.

" *You were going to say we were going back to Devon ?* " she asked on a rising note of incredulous rage.

But something in his face stopped her then.

Turning back to the mirror, she started applying a new coat of red to her lips, holding the lipstick in a hand that was trembling slightly.

The Pointings also were in their bedroom. Violet Pointing was doing a small repair to the flowered crêpe dress that she had been wearing the evening before. Denis Pointing was standing by the window, looking out over the garden.

" So really, Vi, it looks as if that's the only thing to do," he said, after waiting in vain for her to make a reply to the last thing he had said.

Sighing deeply, she lowered her sewing on to her lap.

" I know you're right," she said. " I know there isn't any other way."

" And when it's all over, we can make a new start."

" *When* it's over," she murmured.

" What's that ? " he asked, turning.

" Never mind," she said. " I know you're right."

" You'll let me go ahead then ? "

" Yes, Denis."

" Good girl. You'll see, it won't be nearly as bad as you expect."

" Probably not."

She stood up, shaking out the flowered dress and putting it back on its hanger in the wardrobe.

Seeing her do it, her husband said, " Mightn't you just as well start packing straight away ? "

" Yes," she said. " Yes, I suppose so."

She picked up the little linen hold-all that contained her sewing things and replaced her needle and thimble in it, then tucked it down into a corner of an open suitcase.

Then she walked towards the door.

" Where are you going ? " Pointing asked.

" Only to the bathroom," she said.

She went out and closed the door.

Pointing turned back to the window. As he did so, he

gave a startled exclamation, then he too went to the door. But unlike his wife, he moved rapidly and it was on swift, silent feet that he sped along the passage.

Alec Marriner spent most of the morning reading in his room.

At first he read with apparent interest, his attention concentrating easily on the book. But as time passed he grew increasingly restless and presently he threw the book aside, as if he had done with it. Almost immediately, however, he picked it up again and read a few more pages, but from time to time his eyes became riveted on one sentence for as long as two or three minutes, and when they started moving again they had an empty look, as if they were not conveying to his mind the words that they were seeing. He was like someone who is waiting for something, half hopeful, half in dread. Now and then he glanced at his watch, as if he could not believe that time was passing so slowly.

Walking slowly, Mrs. Kenny returned to the house. Still unobserved, she had her stooping, old woman's walk. But as she came near to the house, she deliberately drew herself more erect, thrusting back her thin shoulders in her mauve knitted cardigan. She had finished her last cigarette as she turned in at the gate and had not yet started another, but she was whistling as usual, a soft, monotonous little trickle of sound pouring out through her shrivelled, pink-tinted lips.

Suddenly the whistling stopped and Mrs. Kenny stood still. She was near the cherry tree and facing the window of Mark Auty's study. For a moment she stood rigid, staring at the window.

Then she screamed.

A single scream is difficult to identify.

It is difficult to be certain that it was a scream. It is difficult to say where it came from.

In her chair in the shade of the copper beech, Sarah sat up with a jerk, feeling a tingling up her spine at the sound, but not even being sure that it had come from a human throat.

Then more screams came.

Nock was soonest on his feet, running towards the corner of the house. Sarah was out of her chair and running after him a moment later. Some distance behind her, very white of face, clutching his little weeding-fork, came Hector.

The screams stopped. But as soon as Nock and Sarah, running, reached the front of the house, someone cried out, " I saw it—in there, I saw it ! "

Mrs. Kenny was leaning against the cherry tree on the lawn. She was clutching its trunk, as if to stop herself falling to the ground, but she had one arm flung out, pointing at the window of Mark Auty's little study. Her face was turned away from it, half-hidden against the tree.

" I saw him do it ! " she cried. " I looked in at the window and I saw him kill him ! "

CHAPTER X

Nock, Sarah and Hector turned to the window. But before Sarah had had more than a glimpse of the room, Hector thrust her away with a gesture of surprising roughness.

" Look after my mother," he said. " Get her away."

Sarah saw the sense of this, though she wanted to see what that shape was that was lying on the floor in the middle of the room.

However, going to Mrs. Kenny and putting an arm round her, she said, " Come, let me take you inside."

" Not into the house ! I won't set foot in it again," Mrs. Kenny said violently.

" Come round to the back then and sit down," Sarah said. " I'm sure there's some mistake."

" I saw him," Mrs. Kenny repeated. " I saw it all as clearly as I see you."

Turning to them from the window, Hector said, " It's Auty. Looks as if he's been knocked out. I'm going inside."

" He's dead," Mrs. Kenny said. " He hit him on the back as he was stooping over the table pouring out a drink. He went down like a stone."

" I'm going inside," Hector repeated. " Nock will keep

an eye on things from here. You two go round to the back again." He put a hand on his mother's arm. " Go along with Miss Wing, darling. I'll come and tell you about things as soon as there's someone responsible on the spot. You'll take care of her, won't you, Miss Wing ? "

Sarah nodded, and Mrs. Kenny said, " Very well, Hector." But she did not move or even let go of the tree.

Hector went rapidly into the house.

As soon as he had gone, Mrs. Kenny said in Sarah's ear, " I don't mean to stir a step while that man's the only person about." She made an unobtrusive gesture towards Nock. " I wouldn't trust him half as far as I can see him. He might get up to anything. For all I know, he was the one who did it."

" I thought you saw who did it," Sarah said.

" No, no, I only saw him doing it, I only saw his arm." Mrs. Kenny's voice was getting back to normal and her face was less ashen. In a moment Sarah thought, she would be quite herself again. " It was the other one I saw as he stooped and then went down. . . . Please get me a cigarette out of my bag, my dear. My hands are shaking so that I don't believe I could do it myself."

Sarah took the bag from the old lady's arm, opened it and brought out her gold cigarette-case. Putting a cigarette between Mrs. Kenny's lips, she lit it for her.

Breathing the smoke in deeply, Mrs. Kenny said, " There, that's better. I apologise for making such an exhibition of myself. I didn't know I was so hysterical. If you'd made the scene I did just now, I'd have criticised you severely. But it was a great shock. I don't suppose you've ever watched a man being killed."

All this time Nock had stood silently by the window, looking in. Now he turned on them.

" What the hell's that little fool got up to ? " he said. " He's had all the time he needed to get round to the door. Why hasn't he shown up ? "

Mrs. Kenny straightened herself immediately. " My son is not a fool, Mr. Nock. He has his wits about him much better than most people. I imagine he's telephoning to the police."

" If he doesn't show in a moment———"

78

Just then Hector came hurrying out of the house. He was followed by Denis Pointing, who looked puzzled and agitated.

" What's happened ? What's the matter ? " Pointing asked.

Hector was saying, " The door of that room's locked. I can't get in."

" What's happened ? " Pointing repeated.

Nock answered, " The party's off. Take a look and see."

Looking in at the window, Pointing gave a start and exclaimed, " Good God—Auty ! "

Sarah suddenly lost the false calm that had held her quiet till then. " Do something ! Do something ! " she shouted at the group round the window. " Get inside. Do something for him. You don't know he's dead."

" Pardon me," Nock said, " I feel fairly sure of it. And I'm not getting in at the window unless someone comes with me. I prefer to have a witness to anything I may do in a room where a man's been murdered."

" Always ? " Sarah asked, then cursed herself for the way that the word had burst from her.

Nock gave no sign of having heard it. He had moved to one side to make room for Pointing, who had put one leg in at the window and was working the rest of himself in after it.

" Damned narrow window," Hector said, watching. " Doubt if I can make it."

Pointing stood upright inside the room.

" There's no key on the inside of the door either," he called out. " Someone went out by the door, locked it and took the key away."

" Bright boy," Nock said, climbing in at the window after Pointing. " You can see what's under your nose, can't you ? " A moment afterwards he added, " He's dead all right."

Sarah had judged that by this time it was safe to leave Mrs. Kenny to look after herself. In fact, to all appearances, the old lady was now the most collected person present. So, letting go of her, Sarah went close up to the window.

She knew that she had to do this. She had to do it for Mark Auty's sake, for she was the one person here, so far as she knew, who was aware that someone in this house had already tried three times to have Auty murdered. Also she knew that the agent who had carried out these attempts had just climbed in at the window of the room where Auty was lying dead.

Not that Nock could have struck this blow. Whoever had hired him before must this time have done his own dirty work. But Nock was still his tool and under his orders and it might be part of his assignment to cover up some traces left behind by the murderer.

If this was so, Nock was in no hurry to get on with the job. He was standing in the middle of the room with his hands in his pockets, while Pointing was calling the police on the telephone.

Mark Auty lay sprawled on the floor at Nock's feet. He was on his face with both arms flung out across the carpet and with the hilt of a knife showing between his shoulders. His coat was darkly stained with blood. Some blood from the wound had trickled on to the floor. Not far from his right hand a glass decanter lay on its side, with the liquid from it spilled across the carpet. A wine-glass also lay on the floor, at the foot of a bookcase, about a yard from Auty's left hand. Another wine-glass, empty, stood on the desk. The low, round table, on which some bottles and glasses stood, seemed undisturbed.

When these details had printed themselves on Sarah's mind, she had had enough of looking in at the window. She was profoundly thankful that she could not see Auty's face. Even so, she found the scene charged with more horror than she could bear. But Peter Nock was still in the room and still had to be watched.

" Miss Wing——" A low voice spoke close behind her. She glanced round. It was Hector. " Miss Wing, I do wish you'd get my mother away from here. She thinks she can stand anything, but she's really very old and she has to pay terribly afterwards for getting over-excited. Don't worry about things here. I'll keep an eye on them. After all, you know I couldn't have had anything to do with it. I was under your own eye all the time."

Sarah nodded and returned to Mrs. Kenny. The old woman was ready now to take her arm and retire from the scene, so together they walked away, going round the house and returning to the chairs under the copper beech. Sitting down there, they both fell silent.

Sarah was thinking of the complicated story that she would have to tell the police and wondering uneasily how much of it she would be able to make them believe. Then all at once she realised that it would not sound so unlikely now as it had sounded to her when Auty had told her of the attempts on his life. For his life had been attempted and taken.

It was very peaceful in the garden. No sound of excited voices reached them. A bee buzzed drowsily in the air over their heads, and a sparrow pecked at the ground only a yard or so from their feet.

Presently Mrs. Kenny spoke. " I suppose the police will be here shortly and we shall all be subjected to a great deal of questioning."

" That's just what I was thinking about," Sarah said.

" I have a feeling that some strange facts will emerge about our friend," Mrs. Kenny went on.

" And about the rest of us here."

" Ah yes, that without question. And very interesting that will be. The real story of that man Nock, for instance. I have no doubt myself that he did the murder."

" I'd like to agree with you," Sarah said, " but I'm afraid that's not possible. He stayed talking to me after you left until the time when we heard you scream."

" Those screams," Mrs. Kenny said, " I'm so ashamed of them. I don't think I've ever realised before, in all my long life, that I was capable of screaming. I really don't believe I've ever done such a thing since my childhood. No doubt I practised it then. . . . Miss Wing, what's the matter ? " She had realised that Sarah was staring across the garden with peculiar fixity.

The matter was that Sarah had just realised that Hector's blazer, which had had the revolver wrapped up in it, was no longer lying in a neat bundle near the flower bed. It was in the middle of the lawn, no longer rolled up but spread-eagled and obviously not wrapping up anything.

With difficulty she brought her attention back to Mrs. Kenny. " Your son was out here too," she said, " so he can vouch for the fact that it couldn't have been Mr. Nock whom you saw."

" So it was one of the others," Mrs. Kenny said thoughtfully. " That man with the hay fever, or that nice Mr. Pointing or Mr. Marriner. . . . Whom would you guess ? "

Sarah had no wish to start a guessing-game, which she found startlingly irresponsible. " Are you sure it was a man ? " she asked.

" Oh yes . . . That's to say . . . Well, I felt sure of it a moment ago, but now that you ask me . . . Really all I saw was an arm in a dark sleeve, and I never thought of its being anything but a man. A hand with a knife. I saw the light flash on the blade of the knife as it came down and went into Mr. Auty's back as he was bending over that little table to pour out a drink. Of course I didn't grasp at first that the flash I'd seen was the glitter of a knife. You know how you can see a thing or hear a thing and not know what it is until you've connected it up with other things. Well, that was how it happened. For a moment I thought I was merely seeing someone slap Mr. Auty on the back and I couldn't imagine why he should collapse on the ground like that. Then I went closer to the window and I understood. I understood the flash I'd seen. . . . Oh dear, I suppose I shall have to tell this story over and over again. But I suppose they'll catch the murderer very quickly. They always do, don't they ? "

She had to repeat the story for the first time a few minutes later when Mrs. Pointing, followed by Marriner and the Carvers, came out of the house. They all knew that something had happened. Mrs. Pointing had had a few hurried words with her husband, had heard that Auty was dead and had told the others. But none of them knew yet, or would admit to knowing, that a murder had taken place.

Sarah told them briefly that Auty had been found stabbed in the back in his study. From a sense of caution she said nothing of Mrs. Kenny's having actually seen the murder. A nervous murderer, she thought, might not believe in the old woman's declaration that she had not been able to see the murderer himself.

This did not suit Mrs. Kenny, however.

" And I saw it happen," she said as soon as Sarah stopped.

" I saw the whole thing and gave the alarm. A most extraordinary situation to find myself in. Nothing in the least like it has ever happened to me."

They all took the news differently.

Lorna Carver became very white and began to tremble, and putting out a hand, groped for her husband's arm. When she found it, she held on so tightly that her hand looked like a claw, the talons of which were digging into his flesh. Tim Carver's handsome, sullen face did not turn pale. For a moment, it showed scarcely any change at all, then all of a sudden it turned a deep red. Muttering something, he tried to turn away, but his wife's hand held him.

Mrs. Pointing had sat down in one of the garden chairs. She seemed to be struggling to contain some intense emotion and though no tears had appeared in her eyes, they had reddened, as if there were tears behind them. She would have been motionless except that her hands, doubled into fists, drummed against one another.

Alec Marriner turned away and stood with his head bent, looking down at the ground.

The curious thing was that not one of them spoke.

Sarah could not bear that silence.

" But Mrs. Kenny didn't see the murderer," she said. " She only saw an arm and the knife. She can't tell us who did it."

" Thank God for that ! " Marriner said softly, without turning round.

" What d'you mean ? " Lorna Carver asked shrilly. " Do *you* know who did it ? Is that it ? Was it you yourself, by any chance, that you're so glad the murderer wasn't seen and all the rest of us now going to be under suspicion ? "

" Be quiet, you damned fool ! " her husband said harshly. " Can't you ever keep your mouth shut ? "

" Not when there's something I want to know." She sounded near hysteria. " What did you mean, Mr. Marriner? Why did you say thank God ? "

He did not answer, but only moved a few steps farther away.

" Well, I know who I think did it," Lorna went on, her voice going high and starting to shake. " It was that man Nock. You can see the sort he is——"

" Shut up ! " her husband shouted at her.

The sound made Mrs. Pointing jerk in her chair and put a hand confusedly to her head. " Mrs. Kenny, would you mind telling us exactly what you saw ? I can't understand it. I can't make out what happened."

Mrs. Kenny gave her one of her direct stares, which made the other woman turn her head away.

" Yet some things must be clear to you, I should have thought, Mrs. Pointing," the old woman said.

" Well, what *did* you see ? " Lorna Carver asked excitedly. " An arm and a knife—it sounds like delusions to me."

" I was inclined to think the same myself," Mrs. Kenny replied evenly, " but when I went closer to the window, I saw what proved that it had not been a delusion. I saw Mr. Auty lying dead on the floor, with a knife in his back."

" How did you know he was dead ? " Lorna sounded angry now, as if she were almost deliberately working herself into a rage. " You must see mighty well. Personally I don't believe a word of it. I think you're just saying you saw a lot of things to attract attention to yourself. As if you could possibly tell he was dead ! "

" You're perfectly right, of course," Mrs. Kenny said. " I couldn't. It was only afterwards that I knew for certain he was dead."

" You see, you can't even tell a straight story ! " Lorna cried. " A lot of notice the police will take of you. But I can tell them who did it. It was that man Nock."

" Mr. Nock, my son Hector and Miss Wing were all here in the garden together at the time of the murder," Mrs. Kenny said. " Even if I wished to agree with you, Mrs. Carver, I'm afraid the testimony of Miss Wing and Hector would prevent my doing so."

" Please go on and tell us what you saw, Mrs. Kenny." Mrs. Pointing said in a low voice.

Mrs. Kenny sighed. " Yes—yes, certainly, but I hope that young woman will not go on interrupting. It makes a difficult task more difficult. What I saw was this. I saw Mr. Auty in his study. I saw him bend down over that little round table on which the drinks stand. I saw him pick up a decanter and start to pour out a drink. Then I saw an arm appear. It belonged to somebody who must have been standing to one side, just inside the window. I saw the hand raised and something flash—that was the light on the blade of the knife. Then the hand came down, stabbing Mr. Auty. He went down without any struggle at all. I don't think he even cried out. I believed I screamed at that point, though I hardly believed in what I'd seen. Then I went right up to the window and I saw him lying there. There was no one else in the room, but the door of the study was just closing."

Behind the copper beech, somebody started swearing.

No one had heard anyone approach and they all turned, startled, towards the sound.

It came from Peter Nock. In a voice as cultured as ever, he poured out the filthiest language that Sarah had ever heard. It seemed to be directed at Mrs. Kenny, yet it might have been at any or all of them. Then he turned on his heel and walked rapidly into the house.

Tim Carver wrenched his arm away from Lorna's grasp.

" He heard you all right and he isn't the kind to forget that sort of thing," he snarled at her. " You're a big help in a time of trouble, aren't you ? "

She looked at him anxiously. " Did he hear me ? Is that why he swore like that ? "

Carver shrugged his shoulders. " Anyway, don't go saying things to the police you've no evidence for. You've no evidence against Nock or anyone else, and you know it."

Just then, perhaps because of the sight of Nock going into the house, Sarah thought of the brief case that Auty had given her. That case was her responsibility, to be handed over intact to the police. Without giving any explanation to the others of what she was doing, she ran into the house after Nock.

He had not gone upstairs. He was standing in the door-way of the dining-room, looking across it towards the locked door of Auty's study. Standing near the locked door were the small manservant who had waited at dinner, another man who looked like a gardener and a woman in an apron. Nock was watching them expressionlessly, his hands in his pockets.

He heard Sarah and turned. Seeing who it was, he took a swift step towards her and gripped her by an arm. Trusting his pale, triangular face close to hers, he whispered, " Are you going to be a good girl and tell the truth about me ? Or are you going to be like that bitch out there and try to put this job on me."

She drew away from him but his grip was hard.

" I'll tell the truth about you," she said. " As much as I know."

" You'll tell them I was out there with you and that fat fool Hector when the thing happened ? "

" Oh yes, I'll certainly tell them that," she said. She knew that that was all she should have said just then. Yet her tongue seemed to go on moving of itself, without her willing it. " And I'll tell them where you were on the evening of Wednesday, last week," she said. " I'll tell them the truth about that too."

He looked puzzled. His hold on her arm slackened a little. " Wednesday ? " he said. " Last week ? You saw me then, did you ? "

" Yes, I saw you then," she said.

" Then why couldn't you say so when I asked you before ? Ashamed to admit you sometimes go to places like the Songbird ? You shouldn't feel like that. It's quite a decent place."

" It wasn't in the Songbird I saw you."

" No ? Where was it, then ? " He seemed not much interested, which was not the reaction to her information that Sarah had expected.

" It was in a street just off Regent's Park, a street where an accident happened," she said.

He shook his head. " Must have been someone else. I spent the whole evening in my club. Plenty of people can tell you that, if you doubt me—just as you can tell where I was this morning."

" But that happens to be true."

" Of course. So does the other." His head turned at a sound from outside the house. " There—that'll be the police, I think. Just you tell them the truth, my dear. That's all I want, the truth."

CHAPTER XI

THE ARRIVAL of the police made Sarah forget for the moment why she had been about to go upstairs. When she remembered it again, she found a young policeman at the foot of the stairs. Barring her way, he told her that the inspector would be wanting to speak to her in a few minutes.

She started trying to explain to the young man that she was anxious about the safety of something in her room, something that had been given to her that morning by Mark Auty, with instructions to take special care of it. The policeman replied that the Inspector would certainly be interested to hear about that, but made no move to let her pass. Reluctantly she returned to the garden.

Hector was busy weeding again. The others, except for Mrs. Kenny, who at that moment was being questioned in the drawing-room by Inspector Hughes, were still sitting in the shade under the copper beech. Sarah would have liked a few private words with Hector, but did not see how this could be managed. She would have liked to ask him if it had been he who had snatched up the revolver and, if so, what he had done with it. But there was no possibility of her speaking to him without being overheard by the others.

She did not want to speak to any of the others. One of them was a murderer, and because she did not know on which of them to focus her sense of horror, it engulfed them all at the same time, making them all seem evil. Walking some distance away from them, she sat down on the grass by herself.

Almost at once Alec Marriner came over to her and sat down beside her. He did not speak. Sitting with his knees drawn up to his chin and his arms clasped round them, he chewed on a short twig that he had stuck into his mouth.

In the group under the tree Lorna Carver talked almost incessantly, but received hardly any answers.

After some minutes, Marriner took the twig from his mouth and threw it away, then said haltingly, " Did you care about Auty ? "

Sarah raised her eyebrows uncertainly.

He added, " I mean, did you know him very well ? Does his—his death mean a great deal to you ? "

" I didn't know him very well," she said. She hoped he would leave it at that.

He went on, " I'm not trying to interrogate you. But I've been puzzled about you, because you don't seem to fit in . . ." He paused as if he were only halfway through a sentence.

" Well, go on," she said.

" You see, I think everyone else here was afraid of Auty," he said. " But you weren't."

" Why should I be ? " she said. " We were friends."

" That's what he called all the rest of us. Only we weren't his friends."

" I know. You were his enemies. He told me so."

" Ah." He seemed interested. " All of us were his enemies—is that so ? "

Shrugging her shoulders, she said, " He didn't go into details about it."

" I didn't imagine he had."

Rather angrily, she said, " I don't know why you should say all these people were afraid of him. What had they to be afraid of ? "

" Naturally, I don't know. But couldn't you see that they were all afraid ? Fear's just about the hardest feeling to hide completely. It comes out in all sorts of odd ways."

" Perhaps it was just you who was afraid. Perhaps it was your own fear you were seeing, reflected in the others."

" Well, perhaps," he agreed. " I was afraid, all right."

" What were you afraid of ? "

" It sounds so hackneyed to say, myself. But that's what I mean."

" Then where did Mr. Auty come in ? "

" He succeeded in generating the feeling. . . . And that, I suppose, only sounds absurd to you."

She traced a pattern on the grass beside her with her finger.

" The fact is, you know," she said, " that Mr. Auty was afraid of all of you."

" Yes, of course."

" Oh, you saw that too ? "

" I told you," he answered, " fear's easy to recognise. And I knew Mark pretty well. Better, from the sound of things, than you did."

" I told you I didn't know him very well."

" I know. And I'm . . ." He hesitated, " I'm glad you didn't know him well." He stood up and walked away from her, then went on walking up and down the length of the lawn.

The time passed slowly. The sun grew hotter and the patch of shade under the rich red leaves of the copper beech grew smaller.

The next to be questioned after Mrs. Kenny was Denis Pointing and after him Peter Nock. Then it was Sarah's turn.

As she went towards the drawing-room, she thought that she had her whole story clear in her mind. She thought that she could give Inspector Hughes a fairly orderly succession of facts, which up to a point made sense. But as soon as she sat down facing him in the long, low-ceilinged room, the story dissolved and she could not think where to begin.

At that moment Hughes said to her, " I'm told there's something you want in your room, Miss Wing. Something you were given by Mr. Auty. Can I have it fetched for you ? "

" Yes," she said hurriedly. " Please. I think it may be important."

" What is it ? " he asked.

" A brief case. It's on top of the wardrobe. That was the best hiding-place I could find, but still, if anyone knew about it . . . It was full of papers, you see, and some of them, I think, were about the people here, and Mr. Auty asked me to take care of them and hand them over to Miss Barbosa to-night. I believe it was very important to him in some way and I've been awfully worried about it."

Hughes spoke to one of the other men in the room. The man went out.

" If the case was still there when we arrived, Miss Wing," Hughes said, " it'll still be there. Nobody's been upstairs. Now tell me some more about this brief case. When did Mr. Auty give it to you ? "

" This morning," she said, " after he'd had the telephone call from Nice and knew that he wouldn't be travelling with us to-day."

" Oh yes. It surprised you, I suppose, that telephone call. You'd expected him to be travelling with you ? "

" Of course."

" Just so. And then Mr. Auty gave you this brief case and asked you to take it to Nice for him ? "

" Yes."

" And you immediately hid it ? "

" Well, it wasn't a very good hiding-place, as I said, but it was the best I could find."

Hughes gave her a smile. It was a grave smile, for he had a grave, inexpressive face. He was about forty, with a chunky, heavily-built body, a short neck, a reddish, slightly-freckled skin, sandy hair that would, no doubt, have been curly if it had not been cropped so short, grey eyes that were intently sizing her up, and an air of taking life seriously because the occasional humour of it was a little beyond him, though he would always do his best to see a joke.

He did not look particularly formidable, Sarah thought, and she wondered for a moment if he would turn out to be equal to the job in front of him.

" It sounds to me," he was saying, " that you may have quite a lot to tell me, Miss Wing. So let's begin at the beginning."

After that he asked her for her full name, her address, how she had become acquainted with Mark Auty, her reason for being in the house at present, precisely where she had been when Mrs. Kenny had started screaming, how long she had been there and who else had been there at the same time.

" And now," he said when that was finished, " let's get back to the brief case."

" Let me say something else first," Sarah said. Her nervousness had been growing all the time that she had had to delay the start of what she considered the important part of her story. " I can't explain about the brief case without telling you something else. It's something that happened last week and it explains why I'm here and why Mr. Auty gave me the brief case."

" All right," he said. " Begin where you like."

" Well, it was last Wednesday—I mean Wednesday a week ago, and it was about half-past ten in the evening. I was walking home from the Underground and I saw a motor accident. A man was killed. Later on I heard that his name was Darnborough and that he was a private detective and that he was working for Mr. Auty——"

" Wait a minute," the inspector said. " Who told you that ? "

" Mr. Auty told me. He told me last night. That's to say, he told me about this man working for him. I knew his name already and that he was a private detective, because the police had questioned me about the accident and had told me that much. And you'll find, if you ask those police about me, that I told them something . . . It sounded fantastic at the time and they wouldn't listen to me, but perhaps you will, now that this other awful thing's happened. You see, I said that I was sure that it hadn't been an accident, but that the driver of the car had run this man down on purpose. And I said that if I ever saw the driver again I'd recognise him. But I couldn't describe him. You can understand that, can't you ? I just said he had a thin, dark face. And I knew that that was nothing for the police to go on and I thought the whole incident was closed as far as I was concerned, and then I came down here and one of the first people I met was the driver of the car. You've just been talking to him. It was Mr. Nock."

Hughes moved his chair sharply so that its legs scraped the polished floor.

" A remarkable coincidence," he said, " or wasn't it ? "

" It wasn't." Then, thinking over the tone in which he had spoken, she said, " Don't you believe me ? "

" We'll come to that later—probably much later," he said.

" But if it wasn't a coincidence, what was it ? "

" Well, I've got to go back to that Wednesday again," she said. " You see, just after seeing that accident, I ran slap into Mr. Auty—I mean literally. We bumped into each other at the corner of the street. He saw that I'd had a bad shock and he saw me home. I told him all about the accident, and about my being sure it wasn't an accident and about my knowing that if ever I saw the driver of the car again I'd recognise him. Mr. Auty didn't seem to believe me at the time. He was very nice to me but I thought he'd decided I was in a hysterical state and was doing his best to calm me down. Then, just before he left, he asked me to come to this party. He said he wanted someone along whom he could trust. It didn't make sense to me at all, but—well, it isn't often one gets such an opportunity, besides, he'd been so nice to me. So I accepted. I got here yesterday. And as I told you, one of the first people I met was that man Nock."

" Just a minute," Hughes said. The man who had gone to fetch the brief case had just returned. " Well ? "

" There's no brief case on the wardrobe or anywhere else in Miss Wing's room," the man said. " There are two suit-cases, but that's all."

" Search the rest of the house."

The man went out again. Hughes turned back to Sarah.

" No brief case. What do you think about that ? " he asked.

There had been some change in his manner.

Leaping to the conclusion that he had considerable doubts of the existence of the brief case, Sarah said hesitatingly, " I don't know. It must be somewhere."

" Presumably," he agreed.

" I told you the truth about it," she said. " Mr. Auty gave it to me and asked me to give it to Miss Barbosa this evening and I put it on top of the wardrobe in my room. . . . Oh wait ! " She snatched up her handbag. " He gave me the key of the brief case. Here it is." Taking the key out of her bag, she handed it to Hughes.

" Well, let's have the rest of the story," he said.

" Where was I ? "

" You'd just seen Pete Nock."

" Oh yes. So of course, as soon as I could, I got hold of Mr. Auty and told him that this man I'd just seen was the one who'd driven the car and killed the detective. And he wasn't at all surprised. He said he'd just wanted to be sure and he pointed out that there were three thin, dark men staying in the house, and that from my description it could have been any of them. Then he told me that it hadn't been a coincidence, his being almost on the scene of the accident, because the detective had been working for him and he'd been on his way to meet him. That was all he told me then. I wanted him to explain more and he said he'd tell me the rest of the story when he'd had a talk with Miss Barbosa."

" You'd still no reluctance about going to Nice ? " Hughes asked.

" Well, I had," Sarah said. " I was very inclined to go straight home. But Mr. Auty seemed so anxious that I should go to Nice and he seemed so worried and scared. . . . Next day he told me more about that, when he knew that he couldn't fly with the rest of us. I showed him that I didn't like the idea of going without knowing a little more about what I was in for, so he explained to me what this party was really for. And then he gave me the brief case."

" So we're going to get an explanation of this party, are we ? " Hughes said. " I've been waiting for that."

" It's a rather queer explanation," she said. " I wasn't altogether sure that I believed it until Mr. Auty was killed. You see, what he told me was that there'd already been three attempts on his life. That was what Darnborough was working on. And Mr. Auty seemed to think it quite likely that the person who'd actually made the attempts was Nock, but that it was at someone else's orders, because Nock had no reason for wanting him out of the way. So Mr. Auty had collected here all the people who had something against him, not his friends at all, but his enemies, and . . ."

She paused there. Fixing her attention carefully on the inspector, she tried to guess how he was taking her story. But there was not much to be read on his reddish, freckled face or in his serious eyes.

With more hesitations between her words, she continued, " You see, this villa of Miss Barbosa's isn't actually in Nice. It's in the mountains and very isolated. Mr. Auty's plan was to get all these people there and then force out of them which one had been trying to get him killed. He wanted me there, he said, because he wanted someone who could help Miss Barbosa if things went wrong . . ."

Again she stopped. More and more clearly, as she had been telling the story, she had been realising how utterly fantastic it sounded. Besides, it seemed to her that unless the brief-case could be found, there was no way whatever of verifying the fact that Auty had told her this story and that it had not all been invented by her.

" That's all," she said abruptly.

" Well, Miss Barbosa will be arriving to-morrow," Hughes said, " and no doubt she'll tell us the rest."

Sarah started. She had forgotten that Anna Maria Dolores was a party to Auty's scheme and would be able to corroborate all that Sarah had said. The thought of that made her feel better.

" Everything I've told you is true," she said.

" It's a remarkable story," Hughes replied without any sound of irony. " It may simplify things for us that at least one person here was in Auty's confidence. Thank you, Miss Wing."

She rose. " The brief-case——"

" When it's found, I'll let you know. I'd like you to be there when we open it."

She turned and went out. As she went she was repeating in her head the words that Hughes had just used about her being in Auty's confidence. Had there been sarcasm in his tone ? Had he disbelieved the whole story and had he reminded her of Miss Barbosa's part in it as a warning rather than as a reassurance ? And what was she to do if Miss Barbosa refused to corroborate the story ?

But there was no conceivable reason why Miss Barbosa should do that. Thoughts of that kind, Sarah told herself, sprang from the atmosphere of nightmare that had been deepening around her since that night when she had seen the man killed in the street. She would have to be careful not to let them overpower her.

She went out into the garden. The group under the copper beech was the same, except that Mrs. Kenny had rejoined it. Hector was still weeding. Alec Marriner was still walking up and down the sunlit lawn.

Seeing him, Sarah stood still and frowned. She had done it again. She had again kept to herself the conversation that she had overheard the evening before in the garden.

She had also said nothing about the revolver in the flower bed.

CHAPTER XII

WHEN MARRINER saw her, he stopped his pacing and came towards her. Sarah acted as if she had not seen him and walked along the path towards the orchard. She did not think that he would follow her when she so pointedly avoided him. Going to the bench where she had sat the evening before, she dropped on to it exhaustedly and buried her face in her hands.

She felt as if she were about to start crying, yet the tears did not come. It would have been easier for her if they had come, for they might have brought with them the emotion that was supposed to cause them, grief. This seemed to have been shocked out of her. She felt hardly any grief for Mark Auty, but only an indignant horror which sharpened into a feeling painful to bear whenever the image of him, lying on the floor, the knife in his back, and the bottle and the empty glass on the floor near him, reappeared to her mind's eye. She wanted revenge for his death on one of those people sitting on the lawn, yet she felt no sorrow for him.

A step on the path near her made her look up. Marriner, after all, had followed her. Sitting down on the bench beside her, he said abruptly, " I'm going to tell you something."

She drew away from him.

" Don't tell me anything you haven't got to," she said in a low voice. After a quick glance at him, she had looked down at the grass, but she could feel his strange, bright, eager eyes on her face. " I won't promise to keep anything to myself—anything at all." She said it all the more definitely because of the secret that she had already kept for him unasked.

" I haven't said I wanted you to, have I ? " he said. " I just want you to listen and get rid of that look on your face."

" What look ? "

" That look of misery. That look of something unspeakably frightful having happened. It hasn't, you know."

95

She turned towards him. " Isn't murder frightful ? "

" Yes and no. There are worse things." He paused and corrected himself. " Worse things than some murders."

" If the rest of what you want to tell me is on the same lines as that," she said, " I don't particularly want to hear it."

" Please listen, all the same. You didn't really care much for Auty, did you ? "

" I've told you about that already," she said.

" I know. But I want to be sure. Because if you were in love with him, or anything like that——"

" In love ! " she exclaimed. " I hardly knew him."

" You see, if you were in love with him, you'd either not believe what I'm going to tell you, or you'd be so hurt by it that I don't suppose I could go on and tell it."

She was looking at him steadily now. " Perhaps I'm not going to believe it anyway."

" That's possible too, of course. But it needn't stop me trying. You see, he wasn't worth being miserable about. He wasn't worth one single tear from someone like you. He wasn't exactly a nice person. In fact, he was something pretty bad. In fact, he was just about the vilest creature that it's ever been my bad fortune to meet."

" So vile that you came here to kill him, didn't you ? "

He did not seem much surprised at her saying that. Frowning so that his heavy, straight brows drew together, he said sombrely, " That's true, of course. I'd hardly thought of anything else from the time that I knew I was coming back to England. But I didn't know you could tell that by just seeing me. Or was it the way I talked this morning ? "

" I was sitting here yesterday evening when you and Mr. Auty were talking together on the lawn," she said.

" Oh. Then you'll know why . . ." He stopped, seeming to be trying to recall just what had passed between himself and Auty. As an afterthought, he added, " And so I suppose the police have heard about that already. Thanks for letting me know. I might have made some effort to suppress my reason for coming, but I won't make that mistake now."

" As a matter of fact, I didn't say anything about it. There was such a lot I had to tell them that—that I just forgot it, I suppose," she said.

For a moment he said nothing. Then he said with an odd abruptness, " I see. Thank you. It was nice of you."

" I meant to tell them, but I just forgot," she said.

" Yes, of course. Well, they'll probably find it out anyway. In fact, I shall probably tell them. You see, I'll have to tell them what I know about Auty, for the sake of whoever it was who did the murder. Though a knife in the back isn't my idea of how to kill a man. Incidentally, there's something I can't understand about that old woman's story of what she saw."

" You mean that she saw so much and yet didn't see the murderer ? "

" No-o," he said uncertainly. " Not that exactly. I believe the police have been testing that out and it's quite true that if the murderer stood where she says he did, she wouldn't have seen him. All the same, I wonder how good her eyesight is. She's pretty old, isn't she ? "

Sarah was beginning to feel that he was trying to edge away from the subject that he himself had started.

" You've still not told me what you had against Mr. Auty," she said.

" But I thought you heard all that last night."

" Not that part of it. I heard you threaten to kill him, but I didn't hear why."

" Oh." He had a habit of saying that one syllable, then stopping to think. When he spoke again, it was in a quick little spurt of words. " He was a murderer himself, that was why."

" I don't believe you ! "

The anger in her voice roused some anger in him. He spoke on a rougher note.

" He'd murdered twelve men and got away with it."

" Twelve men—what nonsense ! " But the number struck some chord of memory. " What twelve men ? "

" Men who escaped from a prison camp and were shot down as they came out of the tunnel they'd made."

" Oh no ! "

" Yes."

" But how d'you know ? How d'you know it was Mr. Auty who gave them away ? " With all her strength she was ready to resist any belief in what he had to say.

" I know," he replied, " because, in his own way, he rather liked me and took the trouble to save my life."

" D'you mean he actually *told* you he'd given them away ? "

" No. But you see, there were to have been fourteen of us. He and I were to have been in the party and helped make the tunnel. Then the day before it was ready, he did a very queer thing. He picked a quarrel with me. That wasn't like him at all, you know. He was always good-humoured. He'd take anything you said with a laugh and apparently forget about it. But that day he suddenly went raving mad at some silly thing I did and turned on me and beat me up. He was a great deal bigger and stronger than I was and of course he could do what he liked with me. The guards dragged him off and he disappeared, as we thought, to solitary confinement. I wasn't badly hurt, but enough to make me a danger to the others if I went with them. So I stayed behind. That's how I'm here now. We heard the shots in the darkness. . . . And a few weeks later Auty turned up again, and from then on the guards always treated him extraordinarily well. People got a bit suspicious about it, but he laughed it off, saying that all you had to do to make the guards treat you decently was show that you weren't afraid of them. At first I stood up for him. I thought his losing his temper with me had been genuine and that it had happened because his nerves were at the stretch because of what was coming off next day. But one day he said something to me about having saved my life. He said it jokingly, but suddenly I saw something in his face and realised what he meant. I don't mean I really grasped it straight away, but I've had a lot of time since to think it over and to get over my first feeling that someone who seemed such a pleasant, normal person could really have done a thing like that. I began to remember all sorts of details that fitted in——"

Sarah broke in fiercely, " And d'you mean you're going to condemn a man as a mass murderer just because of a look you saw on his . . . ? " Her voice faded. The words, as soon as she had spoken them, had reminded her that it was only because of the look on the face of the man driving a car that she had decided that Henry Darnborough had been murdered.

" But even if—if he did give something away," she said, " it must have been got from him by torture. I'd never condemn anyone for what they gave away under torture."

" Nor would I. But he hadn't been tortured. When he came back into the camp, he looked like a man who'd been for a rest-cure."

" But why should I believe any of this story at all ? "

He stood up and walked a few steps away down the path, then turned back and faced her again.

" There's no reason why you should. But it's true."

That sounded very like what she herself had said not long ago to Inspector Hughes.

" And you came here, meaning to kill him because of this ? " she said.

" I thought I meant to," Marriner answered. " I'd thought for a long time that that was a job I'd got to do. I thought I owed it to the others because of having had my life saved by the swine. But when I got here . . ." He stopped, looking hopelessly confused. " Something seemed all wrong about the idea. Probably I'm just a coward— that's something I've always suspected about myself. But anyway, last night I realised I'd never actually do it and it was just deceiving myself to go on pretending I was going to. So I chucked my gun away and decided to clear out of here this morning."

" *You* threw your gun away ? " Sarah said excitedly. " When ? Where did you throw it ? "

" It was some time in the middle of the night," he said. " I threw it out of my window. I should think it must have landed in that flower bed where Hector's been busy weeding."

She nodded. " Hector found it."

" I thought he must have. And he'll have turned it in to the police and I'll have a lot of explaining to do. But I knew I'd have to do that, anyway."

She nodded again, rather absently. She was struggling against belief in his story, thinking that, after all, there was no reason on earth why she should believe any of it.

" Why have you told me all this ? " she asked at length.

He sat down again beside her. " Because I wanted to make sure you knew a little about the kind of man that Auty was. I don't know what your connection with him was and I don't know why you're here, but I've had a feeling all along that you could afford to know a little more about him than you did. I've had a feeling that you might have walked into something that you didn't understand——"

" I've done that all right," she said. " But perhaps you have too. Tell me, why did you change your mind about going back to London this morning ? Why didn't you go ? "

" Because as soon as I heard about the telephone call from the mysterious Uncle Gilberto, I decided that there was something queer on foot and that I'd better stay and find out what it was. Obviously Auty was playing some peculiar game. I didn't believe in Uncle Gilberto for a minute. Did you ? "

From the gap in the yew hedge another voice answered, " If you don't mind my joining you and speaking for myself, no."

It was Hector. Wiping the sweat off the top of his bald head, he came trotting along the path towards them. They made room for him on the bench and he sat down between them.

" D'you know, the existence of Uncle Gilberto seems to be regarded with as much scepticism hereabouts as that of an unpopular deity," he said. " Yet the interesting thing is, that he exists. He not only exists, but he is due to arrive in London one day soon, as Auty told us. The police have found a letter to that effect in our friend's desk. But now, before I forget, Miss Wing, there's something I want to ask you. You remember what I found in the flower bed this morning ? "

" You needn't be afraid of mentioning it in front of Mr. Marriner," she said. " It belongs to him. It was he who thought that the flower bed was a good place for it."

" As I dare say it was," Hector said, " only you ought to have taken the trouble to bury it, Mr. Marriner. Well, Miss Wing, I just wanted to ask you if you've got it or if you know what's happened to it ? "

" No," she said. " Don't you ? "

" No. It was criminally careless of me to forget about it when I heard those screams, but that's what I did, and when I returned, the thing had gone. I was hoping you'd got it. But I thought I'd make sure about that before the police have me in for questioning. I rather think my turn will be next. Incidentally, I've got something else to show them that I found in the flower bed."

He held out his hand. On its palm lay a key.

Marriner stretched out his hand to take it, then withdrew it.

" You found that in the flower bed just now ? " he asked.

" Yes."

" Is it the key of Auty's room ? "

" I rather expect to find that's what it is, though I'm leaving it to the police to find out."

" How did it get into the flower bed ? "

" Any one of us could have dropped it there without being noticed."

" Any one of *us*, but no stranger."

" Just so."

Sarah asked, " But why should anyone throw it into the flower bed ? "

" Why should anyone throw a revolver into the flower bed ? "

" To stop himself using it, apparently."

" Well, there you have your answer, then. To stop the key being used—for the time being."

Marriner stood up. His face was angry and he looked as if he meant to say something. But changing his mind, he walked away towards the house. Then he changed his mind again and came back.

" I haven't got that revolver," he said. " I gave up the idea of using it for good, not only for the time being."

Again he turned and this time did go away.

Hector sighed and said, " Oh dear, these highly strung people. . . . I'm sure I never meant . . ."

" Only you did, didn't you ? " Sarah said.

" Dear me, no, I'm not so subtle. But please tell me, Miss Wing, did that quite pleasant-looking young man really come here with the idea of using that revolver on someone ? "

" So he says."

" Good gracious. I wonder how many more murderous types we have about. What about you ? Did you come here with the idea of killing anyone ? "

Sarah heard herself laughing. The sound shocked her and died.

Hector said heavily, " No, I agree with you, one shouldn't make jokes at the moment. But has it struck you how fortunate you and I are, that we have unbreakable alibis ? It may save us a lot of awkwardness and worry."

" You and I and Mr. Nock," Sarah said.

" Oh yes, Nock. I'm rather sorry about that——" Hector stopped, looking towards the yew hedge. A step had sounded beyond it and an instant later Lorna Carver appeared in the gap.

Plainly she had not come there looking for them but to walk by herself for a little while and think. She was looking very worried and she was tearing a damp handkerchief to pieces with savage fingers. When she saw them she gave them first a blank stare, as if she did not recognise them, then she frowned.

" Sorry, am I busting in on something ? " she asked.

" Not in the least," Hector said. " Won't you come and join us ? "

She came towards them with dragging feet and sat down on the bench.

" And to think that the whole bloody business is my fault," she said drearily.

She looked a different person from the one she had been at breakfast. All her brittle vitality had gone. She was sagging and subdued. Her eyes were red and filled with terrified desperation.

Hector seemed moved. " That's rather a lot to take on yourself," he said. " This is going to turn out to be one of those crimes that have rather more to them than meets the eye. At least, that's my guess."

" But you don't know," she said. " It was all my fault that we came. Tim didn't want to. He said from the first that there was something queer about it. But I thought how wonderful it all sounded and I turned really nasty till he gave in. Tim snarls at me a lot, but he always gives in in the end. And now look what's happened."

" Are you implying, Mrs. Carver," Hector said cautiously,
" that your husband is responsible for this murder ? "

" No," she said with weary impatience. " Whatever d'you
take me for ? "

" But you said——"

" I said it's all my fault we're here, didn't I ? "

" Oh, I see. That's all you said ? "

" Look here, what are you getting at ? " she asked. " Are
you trying to say I said Tim did it ? Because that's a lie
and Miss Wing here can back me up that I never said
anything of the kind. Tim didn't do it. But he's going to
be arrested for it. And that's why I'm going mad thinking
about its being my fault we're here. If only I'd listened
to Tim ! "

Hector nodded understandingly.

" I imagine we're all saying, if only we'd stayed at home,"
he said. " But we didn't, and that's that."

" Yes, but you've got an alibi," she said accusingly, as if
this deprived him of any right to speak. " You and Miss
Wing and that creeping creature Nock are all out of it.
Unless . . ." Her eyes moved calculatingly from Hector's
face to Sarah's. " Unless you're all in it together."

" But your husband isn't the only one who hasn't an
alibi," Hector said.

" Maybe not," she replied. " But he's the only damn'
fool who's gone and left his finger-prints on the glass on
the desk in Mr. Auty's study."

This silenced Hector. He looked ready to admit now
that she had something to worry about. He started tapping
his plump chin with the key which he had found in the
flower bed and humming softly and abstractedly under his
breath.

" Talking of finger-prints," Sarah said, " what about
that key."

He made no reply, so Sarah repeated the question. He
gave a start and replied, " Too late to worry. I'd got mine
all over it before I realised what I'd picked up. Mrs.
Carver . . ."

" Look," she started again without giving him time to
go on, " Tim didn't do this murder. Tim didn't like Mr.
Auty—I don't know why, but he didn't. But he didn't

murder him. He went down this morning to have a talk with him and while he was in that study place, Mr. Auty gave him a drink. And Tim put the glass down on the desk. And it's still there. So Tim can't say he didn't go into the room this morning and he can't say someone saw him come out long before the murder happened, because nobody did see him. He came out and he went up to our bedroom and I was there waiting for him and so I can say that that was ages before the murder. But who's going to believe me ? Who's going to believe the loving wife of the silly bloody fool ? " She was near tears.

" You know, it takes more than the lack of an alibi to convict anyone of a murder," Hector said. " There's the question of motive, for instance, and the ownership of the weapon and all sorts of other things, no doubt. You really mustn't be so distressed, Mrs. Carver."

" Tim hadn't any motive for killing Mr. Auty," she said between sobs. " He didn't like him, but he'd nothing against him. He said Mr. Auty had something against him and that's why Tim didn't want to come, because he thought there was something queer about Mr. Auty inviting him when he'd something against him. But I don't think Mr. Auty really had anything against him, because he helped us buy our hotel after the war, just because he and Tim had been friends in the army, and Mr. Auty was ever so nice to me yesterday. . . ." Her voice died away miserably.

" Well, well," Hector said thoughtfully. " Well, well." He went on tapping his chin with the key. " You know, this is probably going to be the most upsetting week-end that any of us has ever spent. D'you know where your husband is at the moment, Mrs. Carver ? "

" He's in with the inspector, probably making a fool of himself," Lorna replied.

" Will he tell them about the wine-glass ? "

" God knows. I told him to. I told him to keep nothing back. ' It's much the best thing to do,' I said, ' when you've nothing on your conscience.' But he said, ' You're a stupid fool, you never know what you're talking about.' But that doesn't mean anything special. He always talks like that. . . . Oh God, what's happened now ? "

This was because a policeman had just appeared through the arch in the yew hedge.

He advanced towards them and Sarah could see Lorna bracing herself to hear what he had to say. But it was to Sarah that he spoke.

"A brief case has been found, Miss Wing, and the inspector would like you to say whether or not you can identify it as the one that disappeared from your room."

CHAPTER XIII

SARAH GOT UP quickly and went with him to the house. They went into the sitting-room. The brief-case was on a table in front of Inspector Hughes. He gestured towards it. "Well ?"

She looked at the brief-case without touching it.

"It's been forced open," she said.

"Yes. But is it the case that Mr. Auty gave you ? "

"Oh yes."

"Sure ? "

"Yes, I remember that stain on the leather. Where did you find it ? "

"In a cupboard on the upper landing, behind a lot of junk. Look inside it, will you ? "

Sarah opened the case. There were some papers in it, but these were crumpled and pushed to one side. The rest of the case was full of cotton wool.

She looked up, puzzled.

"I don't understand. How did this stuff get in here ? "

"Don't you think it was probably there all the time ? "

"But Mr. Auty showed me . . ." She stopped. She realised that all that she had seen when Auty opened the case had been a layer of papers. "You mean that the papers I saw had just been put in to cover up this cotton wool ? "

"It looks like it, doesn't it ? "

She frowned unhappily. "Then he was lying to me."

"It looks like that too, I'm afraid."

"But it doesn't make sense. I mean, suppose the case had been opened in the customs. I'd have found out then what was in it."

" Yes, there's that. Though he may have decided to chance your getting through without having to open it."

" But what was in it, anyway, that he couldn't tell me about ? "

Hughes shrugged. " Whatever it was, it isn't there now."

" There's nothing there but cotton wool ? "

" That's all."

She looked up into his serious, unrevealing face.

" I wonder how many other lies he told me," she said, " and why he should have bothered to lie at all."

She was feeling hurt and angry. Remembering how readily Auty had deceived her after the accident to Darnborough, she realised that although he might have decided that she could be a useful tool in some scheme he had had on foot, he had never, in fact, dreamt of giving her his confidence.

" What sort of thing d'you think it was that was really packed up in here ? " she asked.

" Something breakable, I suppose," Hughes said.

" And valuable."

" That seems probable, though things can be valuable in various ways."

" And something that he wanted taken out of the country, but was afraid to take out himself."

" That's going rather fast," he said. " As you pointed out, there was no guarantee that you wouldn't have to open the case in the customs."

" Yes. It's hard to understand, isn't it ? "

He smiled fleetingly. " Not just the easiest thing in the world. Now you'd better go and get some lunch, Miss Wing. I believe it's been taken out to the garden."

She turned towards the door. But she was still thinking of what could have been packed up in the cotton wool and she had no desire for lunch.

" It must have been something he thought I'd have refused to carry for him if I'd known what it was," she said, " yet something which it isn't illegal to take out of the country and which isn't dutiable in France. What answers to that description ? "

He did not reply.

In the doorway she turned, asking another question. " I

suppose the murderer must have been one of us—one of us in this house ? "

" That seems almost certain," he said.

" And Mrs. Kenny, Mr. Kenny, Mr. Nock and I are out of it. What about the servants ? What about that little man in the white coat ? "

" The servants were all together, having some mid-morning tea in the kitchen."

" Which leaves the Carvers and the Pointings."

" And Mr. Marriner."

" Yes, Mr. Marriner. . . . And I suppose it's certain that the murder and the theft of this thing that I was to carry to France are connected ? "

" Murder and theft are different crimes. They don't have to be connected."

" But it's probable, isn't it ? "

" As a matter of fact," he said, " that's one of those things on which I'd far sooner keep an open mind."

" I was just thinking . . ." But she found, when she tried to find words for it, that what she was thinking was only half-formed, and as Hughes now plainly wanted to get rid of her, she stopped her sentence with a worried shake of her head and went out.

She went out to the garden and found that a table had been brought on to the lawn and a cold meal laid there.

No one, with the exception of Hector, was eating with any enthusiasm. Again with the exception of Hector, who was disposing with pleasure of a bottle of claret and whose cheeks had grown rosy from the wine, the faces of all of them had the pallid, empty look that comes from strain. So far as they showed any expression at all, it was simply of dislike for one another's company. Each seemed to be blaming the rest for his situation and now and again open suspicion flared in the glance that one turned on one another.

The questioning went on through most of the afternoon, but the police did not trouble Sarah again. As soon as she could she fetched a book from the house and returned to the orchard. This time nobody followed her and settling herself there, she opened the book and for a while pretended to herself that she was actually going to read. But at last, laying the book aside, she sat staring before her, trying to put into words a thought that at one moment seemed perfectly clear and reasonable and at the next moment to mean nothing.

In the end she made this much sense out of it. Auty had believed that one of a certain group of people had been attempting to have him killed. He had believed also that, whichever of the group this would-be murderer might be, a certain article in Auty's possession was of interest to him. This article was fragile, probably not highly valuable and not dutiable. Yet it was of a nature which, if she had known that she was carrying it, might have alarmed Sarah. The murderer was not to know that she was carrying it, but had received a hint that it might be waiting for him in the villa in Nice. The mysterious object, in fact, was the bait that Auty had intended to use in his trap to catch a murderer. Arrived at the villa, he would have let everyone have a glimpse of this thing, which would then have been put in a place of not too complete safety. The murderer then would have attempted to steal it and Auty would have pounced on him.

The sky, during the afternoon, gradually became overcast. Presently a chilly little breeze sprang up, which whipped a light drizzle through the air and drove Sarah indoors again. She found that the party had now assembled in the drawing-room, and that Hughes had apparently left the house. Seeing her pass the window, Hector called out to her to join them and as she went into the room, he came to meet her. He was in a cheerful but controlled state of drunkenness, with his face red and shiny, while he swayed a little on his feet. His speech, however, was quite normal.

" Come and sit down with us and listen to what I'm going to say, Miss Wing," he said. " I'm just going to make a little speech. Nobody wants to hear it, but I've been telling them that they've got to listen whether they want to or not. And I want you to listen too. I want everybody to listen. So come and get yourself a glass of sherry and sit down. Mr. Marriner, please give Miss Wing a glass of sherry."

Sarah looked round the room and saw a group of glum faces turned uninterestedly in her direction. Only Mrs. Kenny, taking her usual pride in any performance of Hector's, smiled at her and gestured to the chair at her side.

"There," Hector said happily as Sarah sat down by his mother, "that's fine. That's everybody. That's just what I want. And you needn't be afraid I'm going to bore you, because as soon as I get started on my little speech, you're all going to sit up like anything."

"Well, I wish you'd sit down," Tim Carver said. "Watching you swaying about is beginning to make me feel seasick."

"I am not swaying," Hector said. "I am absolutely steady on my feet." He gave a lurch towards a chair. "And my mind, let me assure you, is perfectly clear, perfectly lucid. In fact, at the moment I think I can claim to see certain things with a peculiar clarity. They stare me in the face." He paused. "*I* stare *them* in the face." He paused again and seemed to be listening to the echo of the two sentences to see which of them he preferred. Then he smiled at the company and said, "Have it your own way."

"All we want is to get out of here," Carver said. "If you've nothing to say, don't try to say it."

"I have a great deal to say," Hector said. "I had a great deal to say to the police and now I'm going to say it all to you. If you only knew, that's very nice of me. I might let the police surprise you with it. But I don't think that would be kind. Also I think it would be a waste of an opportunity, because here we are, all of us, stuck here for we don't know how long and all except one of us wanting this little matter of our friend's death solved as quickly as possible, so why shouldn't we get to work together on it? Why shouldn't we pool our knowledge of one another and our host and then see how things look? Has anyone got anything against that?"

There was silence. It might have been bored silence, for there was no sign of interest in Hector's little speech. Yet the tension in the air had increased while he was speaking. Sarah was not sure what made her aware of it, yet she knew that it had happened.

"Well, to begin with," Hector went on, "I want to explain that I don't take any pleasure in dragging anyone's secrets into the light. However, that will happen to you all at the inquest, so a little rehearsal now may help you rather than otherwise. And I'll begin with my own secrets—my own and my mother's."

" Mine ? " Mrs. Kenny said in a startled voice.

" Only," Hector said, " those that concern this man whom we've all been calling Mark Auty."

The Pointings looked at one another. There was a flash of panic in the woman's eyes and the beginning of a movement as if she were about to rush from the room. But her husband gave a slight shake of his head.

" I'm beginning with the Kenny family," Hector went on, " because in point of time we come first and because I think my mother was responsible for the first really important step in the man's career. It's that that I'm going to talk about. Any questions ? "

" Get on, get on," Lorna Carver said shrilly. " Get on or shut up."

" I'll get on," Hector replied gravely. " And if there's anything you don't understand, just stop me. Stop me and buy one ! "

In a tone of sharp disgust, Nock muttered, " Christ, how I hate a drunk ! "

Mrs. Kenny's eyes blazed with rage. " You prefer drug-addicts, no doubt."

" Now, now, darling," Hector said pacifically, " though there's many a true word spoken in jest. Now listen to me, all of you. Talking of Auty, or Ardwell, which was his real name——" A rasping intake of breath from Mrs. Pointing checked him for a moment, but he went on at once. " Yes, about twenty years or so ago, his name was Mark Ardwell and he worked in the Kenny mill in Bradford. A very taking young fellow he was too, big and fair and good-tempered, just the kind my mother admires. He was very intelligent too—that goes without saying. So it seemed a shame to leave him just tending a piece of machinery and much better to have him short taughthand—taught short-hand—and all that, and then to promote him a bit more and a bit more, till he was practically my mother's private secretary. And that wouldn't have been the end of it either, that's quite obvious, if he hadn't thought it a good idea to write my mother's name on a few cheques that she knew nothing about."

Behind his glasses, Hector's eyes took on a look of owlish severity.

"Not a good idea really. Or was it? If he'd struck to the straight and narrow path——"

"Cut that out," Carver said, "and get on with the facts."

"Oh yes, certainly. Get on. Where was I? Oh yes, forgery. . . . Well, that's a crime, of course, and naturally it was I who found out about it and my mother was very annoyed with me for finding out about it. Still, she agreed with me you couldn't have that sort of thing in an efficiently conducted business, so she told Ardwell that it wouldn't do at all and that she was going to call the police. Only, of course, she never did call the police. She gave Ardwell a chance to talk first and he persuaded her not to call the police on condition that he went straight off and joined the army. That was nineteen thirty-nine, you see, a time when a deal of that sort seemed to make good sense. So off he went, and a year later we heard of his death in an air raid. And that was that, so far as the Kenny part of the story goes —until quite recently, when photographs of our old friend started appearing from time to time in the newspapers. Then one day he wrote to my mother. He said he wanted to express his gratitude to her for having given him a chance to redeem himself, explained that he'd changed his name to help him start a new life, that all his success was due to her and so on. Very proper, very touching. And then, a few weeks later, came the invitation to this party." He stopped abruptly and turned to Mrs. Pointing. "The next bit of the story's yours," he said. "Will you tell it yourself, or shall I go on?"

She gazed at him in horrified silence.

Her husband put a hand over one of hers.

"Go on, Vi—tell it yourself," he said. "Hector's quite right, it'll all have to come out anyway."

She shuddered and looked down at their two hands, joined together.

"Yes," she said huskily. "I see that. All right, I'll go on. You see, Mark Ardwell was—is—was my husband. We got married while he was working for Mrs. Kenny. We kept it very quiet, because Mark had an idea that she wouldn't like to think of him getting married and I went on working——"

She paused as, with a violent little movement, Mrs. Kenny

stubbed out a cigarette in the over-filled ash-tray near her. For once the old woman went on grinding the cigarette against the side of the ash-tray until its glow was quite extinguished.

" I was working as a mannequin in a Bradford store," Mrs. Pointing went on. " I'd regretted my marriage fairly soon, because I'd had a few glimpses of Mark's dishonesty, but I knew he'd had a bad home and a bad start in life and I thought that perhaps if he had some help now . . . Well, that doesn't matter. Anyway, one day he came home and said he was fed up with Mrs. Kenny and with me and with Bradford and that there was a war coming anyway and that he was going off to join the army. I think I knew then that I shouldn't see any more of him and really I was glad to be let off so lightly. And a year later I heard of his death in an air-raid. I wrote to Mrs. Kenny then and told her about it and she came to see me. She was very kind to me and offered to help me. I didn't know the story of the forged cheques and she didn't tell me. That was very kind."

The two women looked at one another for an instant, then Mrs. Kenny's hand reached for another cigarette.

Mrs. Pointing went on, " About two years later, I met Denis and we got married. It was bigamy, of course, but I—I didn't know that. I went to quite a new life with him and I've been very happy. Then one day, like Mrs. Kenny, I saw Mark's photograph in a newspaper. You can imagine what that meant to me. I'm not a brave or unconventional woman. My position and my name mean a great deal to me, I hate the thought of scandal and having my life smeared over the Sunday papers—and that's what I thought would happen if it came out that a man like Mark Auty had a wife who had bigamously married another man. I didn't know what to do. I was tempted to keep silence. But then I told Denis and on talking it over together, we decided that I should write to Mark and tell him that I had recognised him and ask him if there was no way that an annulment of our marriage could be arranged. His reply was an invitation to this party. He wrote that he was as anxious as I to clear things up, since he himself wished to get married, and that the first thing was for us all to discuss the matter fully together. He said that we should have the chance to do this in peace at Miss Barbosa's villa. I didn't like the sound of that at all, but we accepted the invitation, thinking that perhaps we could have the discussion here and then go home again. But it was clear that Mark didn't intend to fall in with any such plan. Yesterday he carefully avoided having any time with me alone, so there was nothing to be done but go on to Nice as we'd agreed. I'm not sure—perhaps at the last moment we shouldn't have gone after all. I'm not sure . . ."

Her voice faded. She sat gazing before her, not panic-stricken any more but with a look of weary discouragement on her face. The look said that it had cost her a great effort to expose herself and that the worst pain for her now would be sympathy.

Her husband spoke before anyone could make the blunder of offering it. " Neither of us had any idea what scheme Auty had in mind. But I had a scheme. It was quite simple. It was to tell him that Vi would proceed with a divorce action on the grounds of desertion. Really nothing else was ever possible. I had no intention whatever of going to Nice with him. If he hadn't been killed before I had a chance to talk to him, I should have told him so this morning, then my wife and I would have gone home."

" Are you sure he was killed *before* you'd a chance to talk to him ? " The question came from Tim Carver.

Hector held up his hand. " One thing at a time, please. That sort of thing can come later. At the minute we're busy with the past. And your past, Mr. Carver, comes next. Suppose you tell us about it now."

" I'm not telling anyone about anything," Carver said. " I mind my own business."

" Won't you tell us about your old friendship with Ardwell, or Auty, as he was calling himself by the time you met him ? " Hector said. " Your old army friendship."

" I tell you, I'm not telling——" Carver was interrupted there by an attack of sneezing.

His wife said nervously, " He's got nothing to tell. They were friends, that's all. There's nothing much you can say about that, is there ? "

" Sometimes there is, sometimes there isn't," Hector said.

" Would you prefer that I do your talking for you, Mr. Carver ? "

The sneezing stopped. " You can say anything you damn' well like," Carver said. " All I'm saying in advance is that it isn't true. You're drunk and it's only fools who'll listen to you."

" I am not drunk," Hector said. " I am never drunk. However, I haven't really a great deal to say about Mr. Carver, except that he and Ardwell—only let's call him Auty now—he and Auty were in the army together in Cairo and Carver taught Auty all he knew, as the saying goes, about the army. And what Carver knew about the army was the way to make a lot more money than his pay by selling army petrol, tyres and so on to the Egyptians."

" That's a lie," Carver said and began sneezing again.

Hector took no notice. " They were both corporals at the time and for a few months they were inseparable. But Auty was on the way up and Carver got left behind. He resented it and told one or two people some things that he knew about Auty. One of them was that Auty hadn't stopped at petrol and tyres. He'd got to know some things about the trade in drugs in the near East, made some useful connections in it and laid the foundations of a nice little business for himself later on. Isn't that so, Carver ? "

" You're a drunken liar," Carver managed to splutter, before burying his face in his handkerchief again. " All right, we may have flogged a few tyres now and then—who didn't ? It was my own sergeant who put me up to it. But the rest's all lies. Auty was sent out on desert patrol and then he got a commission and that was the last I heard of him for years. I heard later on he'd been taken prisoner. And then one day, when the war'd been over about eighteen months, I ran into him by accident in London. He was doing all right then, he said, and when I said I wanted the chance to buy a pub somewhere, he offered to lend me some money for old time's sake. But it wasn't charity, you can bet your life. I've paid interest on it and paid it promptly too."

" Have you got the receipts ? " Hector asked.

" Of course. What d'you take me for ? "

Hector sighed. " A careful man, in your way. Well now,

let's go on to the next instalment and that's the prison-camp. Marriner, are you telling your own story or shall I save you the trouble ? "

" I think I'd like you to tell it," Marriner said. " I'd like to find out what you know."

" Well, a good deal of it's inference," Hector said, " but of course, being Auty, it's another success-story. He was the man whom the Germans got to love—the German guards at the camp, you know. From small beginnings, he became the man for whom they'd do anything. That was after someone had betrayed·to them the existence of a tunnel, through which twelve men one night attempted to escape. All twelve were killed." He paused and cocked an eyebrow at Marriner. " That's really all I know. I don't know that Auty betrayed them. If there was any evidence of that, I imagine he'd have died long ago. But as these various stories begin to build up Auty's real character for us, I must say I feel it's not impossible that Auty traded those twelve lives for his own comfort."

Marriner was looking at him steadily. " What interests me," he said, " is how you got hold of all these stories about all of us."

" Yes ! " Mrs. Kenny exclaimed, mangling the cigarette she was smoking. " Hector, you amaze me. You've never told me a word of all this."

" I try to save you what worries I can, darling," he answered complacently. " Now let's have the two remaining stories. I'm not sure which order they should come in, because the fact is, there's one person here about whom I know very little. Indeed, I don't know at all where she fits in. So we'll leave her to the last—shall we, Miss Wing ? Let's go on to Mr. Nock's story now. Mr. Nock, will you talk or shall I ? "

" It seems a pity to stop you when you're doing so nicely," Nock replied. He said it as if he were humouring Hector's intoxication and as if the matter had very little interest for himself.

" Very well," Hector said. " I rather like it that way. It makes me feel important. Well, as you may all know, Mr. Nock is the proprietor of a club called the Songbird, a rather shady place of the kind that gets closed by the police every little while and opens up again under a new name. Only he isn't—or wasn't—the actual proprietor. The man behind it and behind a few other ventures of Mr. Nock's—and you see, that's where those Egyptian connections came in so useful—was our friend Auty. Isn't that so, Mr. Nock? Haven't you and Auty been business partners now for a number of years, and wasn't it Auty who usually had the more profitable ideas?"

Nock's thin, dark face remained unresponsive. "You're telling the story, not me," he said. "But if you repeat that I use my club for peddling drugs, I'll sue you for slander."

He got up and walked to the window, standing there with his back to the room and his hands in his pockets.

Hector turned to Sarah. "And now you, Miss Wing."

She was feeling cold all over from the shock of what she had been hearing.

She could not have answered at once even if she had been sure of what she wanted to say and she was not at all sure of what she did want to say. Though she had told her story without hesitation to the police, she was far from certain that she wanted to tell it to the people in this room. To some of them she would have spoken readily, but the sight of Nock's thin, well-dressed figure outlined against the window was enough to make her think very carefully before she spoke.

The thought of Auty himself almost eluded her. It was as if, during the recitals she had just heard, he had ceased to have any existence. When she tried to remember him as he had been that evening in her room, and then tried to fit the good-humoured, sensible, sympathetic personality on to the doings of a conscienceless pirate called Ardwell, nothing resulted. The two images would not fuse, but only blotted each other out, so that nothing was left but a blank.

But Nock, at the window, was not a blank.

"Well, Miss Wing, haven't you anything to add to this attractive picture of our dead host?" Hector said. "Don't disappoint us."

"I've very little to tell," she said.

As she said it, Nock turned round to face the room again.

Without looking towards him, Sarah went on, "I was in the A.T.S. during the war and after it, for a short time, in

116

Germany. During that time I was Mr. Auty's driver for a few weeks. I didn't know much about him except that he was very easy to get along with. Then last week I met him quite by chance and he asked me to come to this party."

" Is that all ? " Hector asked. " Is that really all, Miss Wing ? "

" That's all."

" I wish I believed you," he said. " I would like to believe you. And that isn't only because you're the one person here on whom I've no information."

" But, Hector," Mrs. Kenny broke in, in a tone unusually uncertain and querulous, " I simply do not understand. I do not understand how you've succeeded in collecting all this astonishing information about these complete strangers. And you've never even been away from Bradford to do it. I insist on being told how you did it—because I gather, from the absence of convincing denials, that at least some of it all is true."

" Yes, I think a good deal of it is true," he said. " But there's no miracle about it. You see, darling, when Mark Ardwell turned up again in our lives and I saw how the thought of him attracted you again, just as he had in the old days, I decided to take steps to protect you against yourself. In other words, I hired a private detective to find out all he could about Ardwell's past. I felt fairly sure it wouldn't be quite the creditable story that he wanted you to believe. Well, I was right, wasn't I ? Unfortunately this detective, Darnborough, was killed in a motor accident in London last week, so some of the final story may be missing. But I'd had several reports from him already and it's the fruits of those that you've just heard."

Sarah gripped the arms of her chair and leant stiffly forward.

" *You* hired Darnborough ? " she said. " Darnborough was working for *you* ? "

" Yes, for me," Hector said.

One of his very rare smiles touched Nock's tight lips.

" Interesting, isn't it, Miss Wing ? " he said.

CHAPTER XIV

LATER THAT EVENING Nock approached Sarah and said,
" Would you care for a stroll in the garden ? "

Nothing could have attracted Sarah less and the look on
her face made that plain. Yet she put down her coffee-cup,
got up from her chair and went out with him.

The drizzle of the late afternoon had stopped, but the sky
was still cloudy. The slight breeze felt damp and cool. The
grass glistened with moisture, but the rain had been too light
to soften the earth that had been baked by the morning's sun.

" And to think," Nock said, when they had been walking
along side by side for a minute or two, " that we might have
been in Nice by now."

" I'm glad we aren't," Sarah said.

" Oh, so am I. My idea now is to get home as quickly as
I can. I like peace and quiet." He waited for a moment
for her to make some comment, then added, " You don't
believe that, do you ? "

" No," she said.

" Yet you could be wrong," he said. " You were wrong
about Auty, weren't you ? "

She did not answer.

" Lots of people have been wrong about that one," he
said. " A clever man. But I could have told you about
him."

" No doubt."

" Meaning you wouldn't have believed me ? "

She stood still. They had just turned and were retracing
their steps along the lawn.

" Listen, Mr. Nock, you know what I think of you," she
said. " I told you. I told you what I'd seen you do. Now
what do you want to talk to me about ? Let's get it over
quickly."

He laughed without any sound of annoyance. " You never
saw me do anything, you know. On the night you mean, I
was in my club. I don't doubt you saw someone who looked
reasonably like me. I'm quite an ordinary-looking man."

118

She asserted positively, " I saw you."

" Not possible. I understand your being so sure, of course. You'd had a very nasty experience and you've had it so much on your mind ever since that seeing someone who looks moderately like the driver of that car, you can't persuade yourself you aren't seeing the same person. Common trick of the subconscious mind."

She smiled briefly. " Just how d'you know what experience I'd had, Mr. Nock ? "

" You told me yourself," he said.

" No, I didn't. I told you I'd seen you on a certain night in a street where an accident happened. And I never said anything about your having been the driver of the car."

If he was taken aback, he did not show it.

" Didn't you really ? " he said. " Then it must have been Auty who said it. He did say something about it when you bolted out of the room the moment you saw me. Something about your having seen an accident and having made up your mind it was a murder and being in a state where you thought every dark-haired man you met was the one you'd seen."

" I don't believe you," she said.

" Then ask the old lady," he said. " She was in the room too. I shouldn't wonder, as a matter of fact, if it wasn't that little speech of Auty's that's made her look at me as if I'd got the plague coming out on me."

" I still don't believe you."

" All right, my dear, I've never cared for argument. I like peace and quiet."

" Don't keep on saying that," she said in futile irritation.

" It's true."

" Look," she said, standing still again, " will you tell me what you wanted to say to me ? I don't want to prolong this walk any more than I must."

" Well, I just wanted to ask you a question, a simple question," he said.

" Then please go on."

" Whom did you think Darnborough was working for ? "

" Why d'you want to know that ? "

For the first time he spoke with some violence. " Because I want to know all I can. Because I want to get out of this mess we're all in and get home. D'you think I like it here ?

D'you think I like the company ? D'you think I like the
police coming nosing into my affairs ? I want to get the
whole thing cleared up and get off home."

" I don't imagine my thoughts will be much help to you."

" Your thoughts, as you call them, possibly not," he said
savagely. " But your mistakes, my dear, your mistakes may
tell me a lot of things. Go on—whom did you think Darnborough was working for ? When Kenny said he'd been
working for him, you yelped at him as if you'd been shot.
So what did you think ? Was it Auty ? Did you think he'd
been working for Auty ? "

She nodded reluctantly, feeling that probably it would
have been wisest to give no answer at all, yet just then not
caring very much what the result might be.

Nock laughed.

" That man ! " he said admiringly. " He'd say anything,
and he'd get away with it, nine times out of ten. A wonderful
gift. If only I had it, what couldn't I do ? But people
suspect me even when I haven't spoken one single word
that isn't the truth. It's something born in you, something
you can't help. Darnborough was working for Auty and got
killed by Auty's enemies, was that it ? Only now you know
who really killed Darnborough, don't you ? "

She raised her eyes to look at him squarely.

He said, " Leaving me out, if you don't mind."

" Mr. Auty wasn't the man who drove that car," Sarah
said.

" All right, he wasn't. Someone else did the actual dirty
work for him, but it was he who fixed it. He led Darnborough down there and at the right moment the other man
with the car did the job. And then—and then Auty ran into
you." He slipped an arm inside hers. " And that's the other
thing I want to know about."

She jerked her arm away from him, but found it held.

" You're the one person here I want to know about," he
said. " Why did Auty bring you ? What use were you to
him ? And what d'you know about this whole crazy party
of his ? If there's anyone here who knows what it was all
about, it's you. Well, what was it ? What had he told you ? "

His hand had tightened on her arm, but suddenly, at
something in her face, he let it go, saying in exasperation,

" All right, all right, no one's going to hurt you. I just want the answer to those few questions—but I want them honest."

" I've given my answers to the police," she said. " I don't feel like repeating them to you, of all people."

" Why not to me of all people ? D'you think I don't mean it when I say that all I want is to get home ? It may be— I don't say it is, but it may be—that I've even more reason than most of you for not caring particularly for having the police hanging around me. So I've even more reason than the rest of you for wanting things here cleared up. You know yourself I didn't have anything to do with Auty's murder, so why be a fool about the whole business ? Why not tell me what you know ? "

" I'll tell you one thing." They had gone round the corner of the house and were continuing slowly along the lawn in front of it. " Mr. Auty told me that three attempts had been made on his life. He thought it was quite likely that you were the person who'd made them. But he thought it was at someone else's orders, not for reasons of your own. I don't know anything about that. I saw you driving the car that killed Darnborough and also I know that you didn't kill Mr. Auty. So it looks to me as if Mr. Auty may have been right, only for some reason the final attack on him wasn't carried out by you, but by this other person who's been giving you orders. There are two of you in it and you know who the other person is."

Nock responded with a shout of laughter. It was the thin, shrill laughter of a person who is never at any time able to let his laughter out of him freely. It ended abruptly.

" There's only one person from whom I've taken orders for quite a while," he said, " and that's Auty himself. What d'you make of that ? Was he his own executioner ? "

He started laughing again.

" I didn't expect you to admit you knew who'd killed him," Sarah said, " but I think you do."

Taking his lace handkerchief from his pocket, he dabbed with it at his eyes.

" Let me give you a piece of advice," he said. " I've got nothing against you, so I'll give it free. Stop and think. Just stop and think. You know by now that Auty was a liar on the grand scale. He lied to everyone. He lied about everything. So why should you decide to believe one single thing he's said ? "

This was so true that Sarah winced. She knew now, looking back over her recent conversations with Auty, that there was not one statement, uncorroborated by other people, which she could dare to take hold of and say, " This is true." But it was horrible to have to agree with anything said by Nock.

" If there's nothing else you have to say," she said, " I'll go in now."

They turned their steps again. But immediately he said, " There's one thing I wish I could make sense of. I'd like to know what the old lady really saw."

" D'you mean when she screamed ? "

" Of course. Because she didn't see what she said she did."

" I don't understand."

" Just think it out. Whatever Auty was doing when he was stooping over the table, it wasn't pouring out a drink. Probably it isn't important what he was doing ; all the same I'd like to know what it was. What could he have been doing, stooping like that ? Writing something ? Looking at something ? "

Sarah remembered vaguely that Alec Marriner had said something like that too.

" But why couldn't he have been pouring out a drink ? " she asked.

Nock did not seem to hear her. " She's old," he said. " Her eyes won't be too good. She could easily get mixed up. I wonder if it *is* important."

They had just come level with the window of Auty's study and Sarah was looking towards it. She tried to imagine what Mrs. Kenny had seen and what there had been in the room after the murder that had told both Nock and Marriner that she had misinterpreted that action of Auty's as he stooped over the low round table. Not that Sarah could see how it could be important.

The room was dark. In the garden the dusk had scarcely begun, but behind the glass of the window there was deep shadow.

Then something moved in the shadow.

Nock saw it at the same time as she did. He took it casually, strolling to the window and peering in.

"What a fool you are, Carver," he said softly. "You're really out for trouble, aren't you?"

To her surprise, Sarah saw that the window was open. Going nearer, she noticed that one of the small, leaded panes had been broken. Nock pointed at it disdainfully.

"The door's locked, so he broke in here." He looked into the shadowy room again. "Well, are you coming out, Carver, or do I call the police?"

Carver came closer to the window.

"Mind your own business," he said.

"Like you're minding yours?" Nock said. "What d'you expect to find in there?"

"I said, mind your own damned business."

"If it's the thing that's missing from the brief-case, you haven't chosen the best place to look," Nock went on jeeringly. "The police have been over every inch of this room."

"It's my own business what I'm looking for."

Nock looked round at Sarah with a smile. "Repeats himself, doesn't he? A man of few words."

By putting her face close to the glass, she found she could see clearly into the room. All the drawers of the desk were open, with papers spilled out of them on to the floor. Carver was standing with his arms hanging loosely at his sides, but from the way that the fingers of one hand were flexed, it looked as if he were considering aiming a blow at Nock's face.

Nock went on in the same jeering tone, "They're smart, you know, the police. They'll have taken what you're after."

"You don't know what I'm after," Carver said.

"That's right, I don't know a thing," Nock said, grinning more widely. "Not a single thing, except that you're messing up evidence and the police are going to hear all about that."

"Go away!" Carver said furiously, moving a step nearer to Nock.

"Any time you say, so long as you come along too," Nock replied. "I'm on the side of the law, Timmy, and I'm taking no chances. The way the evidence is now, I like it. I want it to stay that way. No messing about with it, no tampering."

" I've not been tampering with any damned evidence," Carver said. " I've been looking for something that belongs to me, that's all. Now get out of my way."

He approached the window. Nock stood aside and Carver swung himself out and walked off round the house without another look at Nock or Sarah.

Nock stood looking at the broken window.

" No way of fixing it," he said. " I'll ring the inspector right away."

" What d'you think he was looking for ? " Sarah asked.

" Your guess is as good as mine."

" Somehow I don't think so," she said thoughtfully. " You sounded just now as if you knew a good deal about it."

" Just an act, to rattle him. He's the kind that rattles easily. And it's true, what I said to him. I like the evidence as it is. It leaves me in the clear. But there are several people here who'd like to pin this thing on me, and you never can tell what might happen once bright boys like Timmy start tampering."

" I don't see how any tampering in this room can affect the fact that you were on the lawn with me when the murder was committed," Sarah said.

" Take no risks, that's my motto," he answered. " A lot hangs on that old woman's word. And she didn't see what she said she saw. Not quite. And once she starts to alter her evidence at all, you never can tell where it'll end up. There isn't a person here who wouldn't be relieved to see me arrested. So I'm taking no chances, none at all. And I'm going right along now to telephone the inspector."

He walked off briskly.

More slowly, Sarah followed him along the path round the house. If she had not met Alec Marriner, she would have gone indoors and straight up to her bedroom, but seeing the young man walking towards her along the lawn, she stopped short and said, " I want to ask you something."

He nodded and stood still, facing her.

" It's about Mrs. Kenny," she said. " Both you and that man Nock say that she couldn't have been speaking the truth about what she saw in that room. I want to know what you mean."

" Isn't it obvious ? "

" Not to me."

" Well, it's because of that glass . . ." He stopped and took a look round as if he did not want to be heard.

" What glass ? " she asked.

" The one on the floor."

" At the foot of the bookcase ? "

" Yes. But d'you mean Nock's been saying the same thing to you ? Has he been saying that Mrs. Kenny was lying ? "

" Not exactly. But he says she couldn't have seen what she thought she saw. He thinks perhaps it's her eyesight, because she's old, and he says he wonders what Mr. Auty was really doing when he bent over the table, because he couldn't have been pouring out a drink."

" Yes, that's the point," Marriner said, " except that I should have guessed he *was* pouring out a drink but *wasn't* bending over the table. You see, if you bend over a low table to pour out a drink, it means that the glass you're filling is standing on the table. So if someone happens to stab you in the back while you're doing that, there's no reason why the glass you were filling should get up and roll across the floor to the bottom of the bookcase. It would just go on standing on the table."

" Unless you knocked against the table," Sarah suggested.

" In that case, other things besides the one glass would be upset."

" Yes—and nothing else was upset in there, was it ? "

" Nothing. But imagine it the other way round. Imagine that you've picked up a glass from the table and are standing upright, the glass in one hand, the decanter in the other, and you're pouring out a drink. Then someone stabs you and down you go. The decanter and the glass both go down with you and the glass rolls across the floor and hits the bookcase. Doesn't that fit the scene we found far better than what Mrs. Kenny said she saw ? "

They had reached the orchard, but instead of sitting down on the bench, they went on walking up and down.

" But that does mean that Mrs. Kenny was lying about what she saw," Sarah said.

" Or that she was mistaken."

" No, she might easily have made a mistake about what Mr. Auty was actually doing while he was bending over the table, but to make a mistake about whether he was standing upright or bending down would be much more difficult. And she's been absolutely positive that he was bending."

" Then perhaps she is lying," Marriner said.

" But why ? "

" That's beyond me."

" D'you think she would lie to protect the murderer ? " Sarah asked.

" If there was the remotest possibility that the murderer was little Hector—yes, without an instant's hesitation. But it wasn't Hector."

" And anyhow, how could that particular lie protect anyone from anything ? What difference could it make whether Mr. Auty was standing up or stooping ? "

" That's beyond me too."

" I wonder if she'd protect anyone else besides Hector. I wonder . . ."

" Yes ? "

She was wondering if it was conceivable that it could have been Mrs. Kenny who had been behind the three attempts that had been made on Auty's life.

But then she remembered what Nock had said, that there was no proof that any attempts had ever been made on Auty's life. Auty had lied in everything else he had told her, so probably he had lied about these too.

" I was wondering," she said, altering what she had been about to say, " if Mrs. Kenny herself could have any motive for wanting Mr. Auty killed."

" I think almost anyone might have had a motive for that," Marriner said, " but I don't think any motive in particular has appeared in her case. In Hector's, yes, but not in Mrs. Kenny's."

" In Hector's ? "

" Going by what he says himself," Marriner said, " he was nervous of Auty regaining his influence over his mother. That was why he hired the detective, wasn't it ? "

" You mean he was afraid that she might change her will ? "

" Of course. After all, he's only an adopted son."

" But it couldn't have been Hector who did the murder. He was out in the garden."

" No, it couldn't have been Hector."

" Then why should she lie—and why just that lie, that lie that doesn't seem to make any difference to anybody ? "

" Suppose," Marriner said, swinging round on the path, " we go and ask her."

CHAPTER XV

BUT WHEN they reached the house, they found that Mrs. Kenny had already gone up to bed.

Hector, as usual, had gone upstairs with her and lingered in her room to say good night. His face was flushed, his eyes were red and he was having a good deal of difficulty with the pitching of the deck under his feet, but his thoughts continued lucid, or nearly so.

" Darling, I hope you aren't very angry with me," he said, watching his adopted mother a little anxiously as she started walking up and down the room, whistling to herself.

She went on whistling for a moment before she answered, then she said abruptly, " I'm amazed. Perfectly amazed."

" At me ? "

" Of course. You're really an extraordinarily gifted boy, Hector. I ought to be aware of that fact by now, but again and again you take me by surprise."

" And you aren't angry with me ? "

" I'm extremely grateful to you. And so should the police be too. Your insight into the unspeakable Ardwell must have saved them a great deal of work. I'm only distressed at one thing."

Hector nodded his head heavily. " I know. I know just what you're going to say, darling. We always understand each other so well."

" It's about that detective——"

" I know. But if I'd told you about him, you'd have insisted on my dismissing him. Wouldn't you now ? "

" I should not ! " she exclaimed. " I should have been fascinated. I should have been enthralled. It's never occurred to me in my life to employ a detective. I can't think why, because now I see plainly what a wonderful idea it was. But you shouldn't have kept it to yourself, boy. That was selfish. I lead a very dull life. There aren't many excitements available to an old woman of eighty-three——"

"Eighty-three? Come, come," Hector said. "You've celebrated your eighty-third birthday at least four times to my knowledge."

She seemed not to hear him. "You don't seem to realise, you young people, that one needs interests, even at my age. I know you think excitement's bad for me, but that's a mistake. I need it, I thrive on it. Look at me now. This week-end has turned out far more interesting than I ever anticipated, and as a result, I'm feeling younger and more vigorous than I have for years."

Hector groaned. "Think of to-morrow."

"I never think of to-morrow."

"I know, darling. But I do, and I'll tell you just what's going to happen. You won't sleep to-night and to-morrow your head will be splitting, your back will be aching, your heart will be fluttering and your temper will reduce everyone who comes within ten yards of you to hopeless misery and dejection."

"Nonsense, I can always control my temper. But *your* head will be splitting and *your* temper will be dreadful— I'm quite prepared for that. But do I try to limit your pleasures, just because I have to suffer slight inconvenience from their after-effects ? Do I ? "

"Never," Hector said. "You're very wonderful to me."

"Well then, another time don't keep things secret from me that would bring a little interest into my life. It's not that I want to control everything you do or deny you a life of your own, but it's just that I think it's selfish of you to leave me out of things that I should find so fascinating."

"Yes, darling, I see. I'm so sorry."

"Another time——"

"Pray God there won't be another time. There can't be two Ardwells."

"I imagine there are a great many Ardwells. And no doubt there's still time for me to meet them, old as I am. But Hector——"

"Yes, darling ? "

" You didn't really imagine that he could supplant you in my affections, did you ? "

Hector scratched his bald head.

" No—no, I suppose not. But after all, you're quite right, your life must be dull with just me around. I'm not very bright or entertaining and my drinking must be rather boring for you—because I do drink a bit more than I should sometimes, I know that. And Auty—Ardwell was a clever devil and handsome and all that—and you're a woman."

She gave a delighted cackle of laughter.

" Boy, you're ten times cleverer than he was, and you know it. Even when you're drunk you know the things to say to please me. And you know that you're the one person I've known in all my life for whom I'd do anything— anything at all."

" Except let me have my own private detective all to myself—poor fellow."

" Oh that—that's different. Now go along to bed. I'm afraid you won't be feeling at all well to-morrow. All this excitement will over-strain you. I think probably you ought to spend the morning in bed. So good night, dear. Sleep well." She smiled at him tenderly.

" Good night, darling," Hector said. He sighed deeply.

Tim and Lorna Carver, in their room, were both in a state of sultry rage. They were not speaking to one another, but they made the exaggerated, noisy gestures of angry people, and from time to time, as they prepared for bed, their eyes met and remained fixed for a moment in a burning stare, as if they were welded together by their hatred.

They had been in bed, lying stiffly side by side in the darkness, for about a quarter of an hour, before either spoke. It was Tim who broke down then.

" Go on, go on—say it ! For God's sake go on and say what you're thinking ! Say I did it ! Say that's what you're going to tell the police to keep yourself in the clear. Don't think I don't know what sort you are. Stick by a man when he's in real trouble, eh ? I can just see it ! "

Lorna's response was to burst into noisy tears.

Tim lay and listened to it, then repeated, " Go on— say it ! "

" All right then, I will," Lorna said wildly through her sobs. " You're beginning to make me think you must have done it. This morning I wouldn't have believed it, not if you'd told me yourself. But now the way you're acting, I'm ready to think anything."

" That's what I thought. Hit a man when he's down, that's your sort. I'm in trouble, so you turn on me and call me a murderer. And it was you that made us come. Did I want to ? Didn't I say all along I didn't like the look of things ? "

" I know, I know," Lorna wailed. " I know it's my fault we came. Haven't I said so a dozen times to-day? But you're such a fool. If only you'd trust me and tell me the trouble you're in, I wouldn't get thinking things all by myself. What is your trouble, Tim ? Why don't you tell me ? "

" And have you tell it all to the first person who asks you ? Not much."

" I wouldn't tell a soul."

" You'd tell everyone. Haven't you been all round, telling everyone I was the last person to see Auty alive ? "

" I have not ! I told them you'd had a drink with him this morning, because you know yourself your finger-prints were on that glass on the desk, so it was much cleverer to tell everyone than to try to make a mystery of it. That's what innocent people do, they tell all they can. But I haven't said a thing to do you any harm, so why can't you trust me ? Why can't you tell me what you were doing in that room to-night ? "

" I have told you. I've told you I was looking for something that belonged to me."

" The thing that was in that brief case ? "

" No ! "

" What d'you think was in that brief case, Tim ? "

" I don't know any more than you do."

" And you really weren't looking for it ? "

" How could I be looking for it, when I don't know what it was ? "

" Well, what were you looking for then ? "

Tim swore violently, after which there was another silence. This time it was Lorna who broke it. " Tim, I know you aren't a murderer. If I've said anything to make you think

I thought so, it's only because you've been making me so unhappy, acting almost as if you thought I'd planned the whole thing, bringing you here and getting you mixed up in a murder and all. But I didn't. All I wanted was a bit of fun, Tim. I thought that was all it was going to be."

"All right, all right. I dare say I've said some things too I didn't mean," he said. "But that doesn't help much now."

"If only I knew what your trouble was . . ."

"Listen, the less you know, the better for you, see ?"

"Then you do know something about this murder ! "

He drew a sharp breath, seeming for once to be making an effort to control his temper. "If I knew a thing about it," he said, "I'd have told it all to the police and no maybe about it. It'd help me quite a bit if I could do that. If you help the police over a thing like murder, they don't worry so much about anything else you've done."

"But what *have* you done, Tim ? "

"God Almighty, can't you leave me alone ? "

"You're not worrying about that bit of black market stuff we've been doing down at the pub ? " she said. "Everyone else does it. Everyone knows you can't run a decent hotel these days without going a bit on the black market. You're not worrying about that, Tim ? "

His breathing sounded deep and rapid beside her and he did not answer except to mutter something inaudible to himself.

"Tim . . ." she said uncertainly.

Suddenly he started to talk, his hand gripping her bare elbow. "Listen, you little fool. You're always talking about the way my old pal Auty helped me buy the pub because we'd been friends in the army. Well, you didn't really believe that, did you ? You didn't think he'd have raised a finger to help me if I hadn't had a gun to point at his head ? I knew a thing or two about him and that's why we got the pub. And I haven't been paying him any interest on the money. He's been sending me receipts every quarter because that was the way I told him I wanted it. I didn't mean to push him too hard, see ? Just the down payment and then the receipts to remind him I'd got him where I wanted him and could ask for a bit more if the feeling should take me. But I didn't mean to do that.

Enough's enough. You're a fool to press a man till he gets desperate."

" Blackmail ! "

He seemed to miss the note of horror in her voice and went on, " If you'd listened to what that little drunk was getting at this afternoon, I shouldn't have had to tell you all this. He'd got hold of it all. But still, even he could see it means I'd no motive to kill Auty. When you've got a rich man where you want him, you don't murder him. He may think of murdering you, but you aren't going to murder him."

" And so that was why you didn't want to come—you thought he might be planning something against you ! "

" Well, I didn't think he'd asked me here for the sake of my blue eyes," Carver said.

" Then why didn't you go on refusing to come ? " she cried shrilly. " Oh God, why didn't you ? "

" Because there was one thing Auty had on me and I thought I might have a chance to get the thing. I'd made one mistake, see ? There was one thing I'd put on paper. I hadn't realised what I was doing when I did it, but Auty did and he let me know he'd kept it, so he could prove, if I pushed him too hard, that I'd done a bit of blackmail."

" So that was why you gave in about coming. It wasn't to please me."

" What d'you think ? " he said.

" And it was that thing you were looking for in that room this evening ? "

" Yes."

" And you didn't find it ? "

" I told you I didn't."

" And so maybe, after all, you did have a motive for killing Auty," Lorna said thoughtfully. " When the worm turns, you tread on it, in case it turns out to be a snake."

" He was a snake all right," Tim said, " but I didn't kill him."

" I wonder . . ."

" What's that ? " he asked quickly.

" Nothing. Good night, Tim."

" Good night. I—I didn't mean to tell you all this, Lorna, but you asked for it."

" That's right," she said. She was silent for some time, then whispered into the darkness, " I asked for it."

Vitamin pills, some liquid paraffin, some breathing exercises, and Peter Nock was ready for bed. Taking *The Ghost of Greystone Manor* out of his suitcase, he arranged his pillows comfortably behind him and settled down to read. The ghost in the story was walking very actively now, generally in the shape of a cloud with a peculiar and revolting animal odour, but occasionally solidifying, or rather, almost solidifying, into something more like a jelly that had not quite set. In this form it left drops of itself about the place, and these, when submitted to laboratory tests, turned out to be human blood.

The evening before, all this would have roused in Nock a state of exquisite terror. But this evening he actually skipped several passages and the look that developed on his thin, sallow face as he read, suggested that he thought the author was making rather a fool of himself.

After a while, he tossed the book aside and switched out the light. However, he did not sleep. Lying on his back with his hands clasped under his head, he peered up into the darkness. It seemed almost that he had no particular desire for sleep, for he did not reach for the bottle of sleeping-pills. It appeared that his own quiet thoughts were sufficient for Peter Nock that night.

Denis and Violet Pointing talked for a long time in whispers. They talked of the past when she had been the wife of Mark Ardwell. She talked with more freedom than she ever had before, her confession downstairs before so many strangers having broken down the restraint that she had insisted on imposing on herself, even, to some extent, with her husband.

She talked of all the suspicions that had wrecked that early marriage.

" I never knew anything for certain about his dishonesties," she said, " except of course in small things. I knew he never returned money he borrowed. I knew he'd never pay a bill if he thought he could get away with it. I knew he boasted about all sorts of things that weren't true; for instance, making out that his position with the Kennys was much better than it actually was. But I suspected other things too. I suspected that he was cheating Mrs. Kenny. I didn't admit that this evening, because, for one thing, I didn't see how it would help. I didn't know how he was cheating her. I didn't know about the forgeries. But I knew that sometimes we had money that hadn't been come by honestly and he'd laugh about it and say that I'd better not make any fuss because everyone would be sure that I was mixed up in it too. . . . . I haven't much courage, have I, Denis? That's been my trouble all along. I've always worried much too much over what people would think."

"Even over what I might think," he said.

His tone made her turn her head quickly, to look at him with startled eyes.

He was lighting a cigarette and went on watching the flame of the match, letting it burn almost down to his fingers, instead of blowing it out.

"I only realised this evening, while you were talking," he said, "that you always suspected he wasn't dead."

A dark flush mounted in her cheeks.

The match went out. He looked up at her.

"It was so, wasn't it?"

She met his look with one of great pain. "Yes. But I didn't *know*. It was like in the old days, always suspecting, never knowing anything for sure, not knowing how to start finding things out for sure without going through awful things oneself."

"Silly girl," he said.

"Yes." She smiled uncertainly. "But really I didn't *know*, Denis."

"Why did you suspect it, then?"

"I think it was mostly because I'd got into the habit of suspecting everything connected with Mark, so I couldn't take even the news of his death at its face value. Apart from that, the man who was killed in the blitz was a civilian and I felt fairly sure that Mark really had joined the army. He'd seemed to think it might turn out a good racket and whenever he talked on those lines, I did believe him."

"Anyway, he's dead now."

" Yes, really dead this time."

" But still leaving trouble behind him. However, I suppose it's natural enough that a man like him shouldn't die in his bed."

" D'you think they'll keep us here long ? "

" I don't know at all."

" Fortunately they can't seriously suspect either of us. We've no motive for murder, because it was Mark, not I, who was in a weak position. It's true I was terrified of the publicity if the truth came out, but publicity is just what we've got now, without limit."

He knocked some ash into an ash-tray. " Yes," he said.

" Don't you think so ? " she asked anxiously. " Don't you think that's how they'll reason ? "

" As a matter of fact, I was thinking of something else," he said. " I was wondering how much they believe Mrs. Kenny's description of what she saw. Because if they don't believe it . . ."

" Why shouldn't they ? Why should Mrs. Kenny lie ? "

" I don't know. She might not even know that she was lying."

" What d'you mean, Denis ? "

" I don't know exactly. I haven't worked it out. But when I was in that room with Nock, before the police came, I saw something. . . . But probably it didn't mean anything."

" What was it ? "

He ran a finger round inside his collar, moving his head uneasily. " It didn't mean anything," he said. " I'm sure it didn't mean anything. But tell me something, Vi . . ."

As he paused, a look of alarm deepened in her eys. The fingers of one of her large hands began to pluck at her skirt.

" You know when Hector came into the house, crying murder, and I went downstairs ? " he went on.

" Yes."

" How long before that d'you think you and I had been sitting in here together before that happened ? "

" Half an hour at least, perhaps longer. Perhaps as much as three-quarters of an hour."

" But you left the room during that time."

" Oh that—but that was just to go to the bathroom."

" I know. . . . You haven't mentioned it to the police, have you ? "

" No."

" Well, don't. And I won't either."

" Very well. But why ? "

" Just a precaution," he said, " in case Mrs. Kenny should decide to change her story."

" I don't understand," she said. " Why should she ? "

" Never mind. Just do as I say, will you ? "

She nodded, then stood up and started to unhook her dress.

" But if Mrs. Kenny is lying," she said, " it's to protect Hector, not any one else. And as things are, that doesn't make sense. There's no possibility at all that Hector committed this murder."

" None," he agreed. But he gave her a lingering and uncertain look as he did so.

Alec Marriner, alone in his bedroom, spent some time making a series of experiments which concerned a small, low table that he had moved to the centre of the room. There was nothing on the table, but from the pantomime that he went through, it was plain that his imagination had covered it with bottles and glasses. That these were not there in reality was fortunate, for his experiments took the form of a number of falls, all when he was standing near or bending over the table and on several occasions there would have been terrible havoc with the glassware.

Once the table went right over with a crash. A few minutes after this had happened there was a tap on the door and the manservant's voice inquired, " Are you all right, sir ? "

Marriner stayed sitting on the floor, rubbing an elbow.

" Quite all right, thanks," he called out.

Footsteps withdrew along the corridor.

When they had faded, Marriner got up, muttering, " I'm a fool. What does the damned thing matter, anyway ? "

Inspector Hughes reached his lodgings at about ten-thirty that evening. His sergeant was with him and was invited in for a drink. Both men were tired and had they been asked their opinions on the Auty murder, would have been inclined to make the same remark as Alec Marriner had made when he fell and hurt his elbow in the cause of detection.

Making themselves comfortable with their glasses of beer, they sat facing one another on either side of an empty fireplace that was concealed by a firescreen, embroidered by the inspector's landlady with a design of young ladies in crinolines. The light that shone on the two men, from a table-lamp at the Inspector's elbow, was contained in a strange, pagoda-like construction made of parchment and silk fringes and painted with elves and toadstools. The arm-chairs were covered in shiny, imitation leather, cold to the touch. Hughes had lived contentedly in this room for ten years.

For some minutes they sipped their beer and smoked in silence.

Then the sergeant said, " It's like I told you, my straw-berries aren't any good this year. I thought with all the dung I gave 'em, they couldn't fail. But they're no good. No good at all."

" Perhaps it's the plants," Hughes suggested.

" That's right. It must be the plants, I reckon," the sergeant said.

" You need some new stock, I dare say."

" Dare say I do."

Another silence followed.

Then the sergeant said, " Martin says it's the frost got the blossom. That late frost."

" Could have been that, I suppose."

" I don't reckon so. If it was the frost killed the blossom, we'd have a small crop. Stands to reason."

" Haven't you a small crop ? "

" Plants are loaded with fruit. Loaded. But no quality to it. No flavour."

" Pity."

" That's right."

Again there was silence.

It was a longer silence than before and this time it was broken by Hughes. Speaking at the ceiling, and in a half-muffled tone, as if he had forgotten the sergeant's presence, he said, " It's Questions A and B still. A—why did Auty ever give that preposterous party ? B—why did the old woman say she saw what she couldn't have seen ? Just answer me those two questions and we'll have the whole thing."

The sergeant sighed, leaving his strawberries to take care of themselves.

" I wouldn't mind knowing why Pete Nock's being so bloody co-operative," he said. " That seems to me as queer as anything."

" He's frightened," Hughes said.

" But why, when he, Kenny and the girl are all safely out of it ? "

" Unless Mrs. Kenny didn't see the murder at all. Suppose it was something else she saw, or suppose she was telling a downright lie. Then the murder could have happened a bit earlier, when Nock was still in the house."

" But that would mean she's been deliberately protecting him. What reason could she have for that ? "

" I don't know the answer any more than you do."

" How much d'you believe of the girl's story of the attempts on Auty's life ? "

" Not much. But I'm inclined to think they were Auty's lies, not hers."

" What did he pull her into this business for, anyway ? All the others had something on him—the idea for this party must have had something to do with that. But she seems just to be a nice girl, who thought he was a nice man."

" She'd seen a murder, hadn't she—and then found Auty on the spot ? I'd call that having something on him."

" Darnborough was murdered then ? "

Hughes emptied his glass and refilled it.

" Nock's alibi at the Songbird doesn't mean a thing," he said. " That woman of his would swear to anything. So would the barman. I'm inclined to believe the girl. I think she did see a murder. But that still doesn't tell us what Auty meant to do with all these people once he'd got them to Nice."

" Drown them in the sea, maybe," the sergeant said, and laughed. " It wouldn't have been a bad idea, at that.

Anyway, I'm looking forward to meeting Miss Anna Maria Dolores Barbosa."

" Me too." But as Hughes said it, his expression changed. He stared hard but unseeingly at the sergeant, who, after a moment, shifted uncomfortably and stood up.

" Well, good night," he said. " See you in the morning." Hughes did not reply.

As the door closed on the sergeant, Hughes muttered to himself in awestruck tones, harsh with incredulity, " Good God. . . . Is that the answer ? Good God. . . ."

CHAPTER XVI

MISS BARBOSA arrived on the following morning.

In herself she was the exposure of another of Mark Auty's lies. She was not the young and beautiful girl of his descriptions. She was a small, dark woman of about thirty-five, with an intense manner and stupid, anxious eyes. Expensively but not smartly dressed, there was something heavy and clumsy about her, which went with an air of nervousness and querulous insecurity.

Alec Marriner, catching a glimpse of her, as, accompanied by Hughes, she entered the house, muttered to Sarah, " Well, she's well out of it, at any rate. So far as she's concerned, somebody murdered Auty just in time."

Sarah had to admit that, from the look of things, Auty could have wanted Miss Barbosa for her money only.

" Though you never can be sure who'll seem attractive to another person." She said this, feeling that in some way she owed it to that dowdy, stumpy figure to say something in defence of the feelings that the dead man had had for her. With a frown, she added, " I suppose she'll have to be told what kind of man he really was. But it seems a pity that they had to drag her into it."

" I imagine it couldn't be helped. They probably think she can tell them something about the real reason why Auty collected us all."

" Now that I've seen her," Sarah said, " it would surprise me very much indeed if she could."

They went out together into the garden, where they felt

less enclosed with the crime and with the unpleasant mystery of the man Auty.

Miss Barbosa spent some time talking to the inspector in the sitting-room. Once or twice her voice, shrilly raised, reached Sarah and Marriner as they sat in the garden. But they could not hear what she said.

Some time later she emerged into the garden. Giving Sarah and Marriner a brief glance, she went and sat by herself, at some distance from them, carefully turning her chair so that its back was towards them.

She was still wearing her hat and coat, from which it appeared that she could have no intention of staying for long. Sitting slumped forward, she supported her head on her heavily ringed hands and remained like that, motionless, for several minutes.

" Ought one to go and talk to her ? " Sarah asked Marriner uncertainly.

" It doesn't look as if she wants it," he replied.

" Yet she might. Perhaps I ought to have a try."

But while she was still hesitating, Mrs. Kenny came out of the house and walked over to Miss Barbosa.

Sitting down near her, Mrs. Kenny held out her cigarette-case. Miss Barbosa made no move to take a cigarette. Mrs. Kenny helped herself, closed the case with a snap and leaning towards the other woman, began to talk in a low voice. She talked for a long time before she received any reply from Miss Barbosa.

Then all of a sudden a stream of speech burst from the small Brazilian woman. The ringed hands began to gesticulate. Sitting back, Mrs. Kenny listened and watched her thoughtfully.

The two women talked for some time. Miss Barbosa's voice was quiet, yet now and again it went loud and shrill, as it had when she had been talking to Hughes in the sitting-room. These outbursts usually ended in sobs.

After one of these occasions she jumped up, and with her handkerchief held to her eyes, plunged into the house. For a minute or two Mrs. Kenny remained where she was, then she got up and walked towards Sarah and Marriner.

" Poor thing," she said. " Poor, silly thing. I must say, I feel most sorry for her. She doesn't know which to grieve over at the moment, that man's death or her own disillusionment. They're both dreadful things for her to face. Unfortunately, I don't think she's going to face the disillusionment. I think she's preparing herself to blame everyone else and keep his memory sacred for ever. Ah, well."

She leant back in her chair, gazing rather vacantly before her.

She was looking very tired this morning. Her eyes seemed to have sunk back into her head, peering out at the world from bony sockets. Her mouth and chin trembled a little.

" Have the police told her everything ? "' Sarah asked.

" Oh yes. They appear to have told her some surprising things that they haven't told the rest of us. For instance, that there had been several other attacks on Ardwell's life." The deep-sunken eyes moved so that they met Sarah's. " It was you who told them that, I believe, Miss Wing."

" Yes," Sarah said.

Marriner exclaimed something, then was quiet.

" For your information," Mrs. Kenny said, " Miss Barbosa claims that there's no truth in the whole story. At any rate, Auty had never said anything about it to her. And she insists that he had no peculiar motive in giving this party. She says he merely wanted to introduce some of his old friends to her and that it was just like him to have such a noble and beautiful idea. The worst shock for her, the thing she can't get over, she says, is that one of his old friends is his undivorced wife. A divorced wife would have been bad enough, since Miss Barbosa's a Catholic, but the existing situation is quite beyond her comprehension. Now, Miss Wing, would you please be so good as to tell me this interesting story that you've told the police ? "

There was a sternness in her voice as she made this request that made her formidable.

Sarah saw no reason now why she should not reply. If the police had told everything to Miss Barbosa, there could be no objection to others knowing the story as well. So she told Mrs. Kenny and Marriner all that Auty had told her about his reasons for giving the party.

When she had finished, there was a moment of silence, then Mrs. Kenny said, " And you believed this extraordinary nonsense ? " She was looking at Sarah with unmistakable suspicion.

" I didn't know whether to believe it or not," Sarah said. " It sounded very convincing when he was actually talking to me. He *was* so convincing, you know. And then when he actually got killed, I thought . . ."

" Good gracious me, I never heard such nonsense ! " Mrs. Kenny said disdainfully.

" I wonder," Marriner said.

Mrs. Kenny turned her suspicious glance to him. " Come now, Mr. Marriner, I've taken you for an intelligent young man. The one thing you can be absolutely certain of is that whatever that man told any of us was untrue. In fact, I should say that the mere fact that he told Miss Wing this story is enough to eliminate that possible explanation of why he collected us all together."

" Then why do you think he collected us together, Mrs. Kenny ? " Marriner asked.

She stirred irritably. " I have no idea. And personally, I don't think we ever shall find out. The purposes of a brain like that are quite beyond the grasp of any ordinary mind."

Sarah was looking curiously at Marriner.

" Do you believe that story ? " she asked.

" Not exactly," he said. " All the same, one always has to come back to the fact that he collected here a number of his enemies and then that one of them killed him. And the story Auty himself told of why he did it, fits those circumstances as well as any I can think of."

" But we know now that one part of it, at least, is quite untrue," Sarah said. " That's his saying that Miss Barbosa was co-operating very actively in his scheme."

" Unless she's lying herself," Marriner said.

Mrs. Kenny shook her head decidedly. " Not on that point—no. She's just had the shock of her life, and if she'd had the faintest idea that one of the people she was to entertain was Mrs. Pointing, she wouldn't have co-operated with Auty even as far as she did. In fact, she would at once have broken off the engagement."

" Which is interesting in itself," Marriner said, " because it suggests that Auty can't have intended Miss Barbosa to meet any of us at all."

'He can't have intended her to meet Mrs. Pointing," Mrs. Kenny said. " That's certain. Miss Barbosa would have had nothing against the rest of us, unless we'd insisted on talking about Auty more than I think any of us would have done. The question is, what did he intend to do with Mrs. Pointing ? "

" Perhaps," Sarah said, " so far as she's concerned also, he was murdered just in time."

She was not quite prepared for what her words did to her two hearers. She had spoken almost idly, vaguely re-echoing what Marriner had said on seeing Miss Barbosa, when he had implied that Auty's death had saved her just in time from being married for her money. Sarah was not expecting the expressions of shock and then of startled interest that came to the faces of the old woman and the young man.

But Mrs. Kenny's face immediately became stern and suspicious again.

" It appears, Miss Wing, that you have a very lurid imagination," she said. " Incidentally, I wonder how much of this story that you told the police about the attempts on that man's life was his invention and how much your own."

Standing up, she dropped her cigarette stub on the grass, set her foot on it and ground it out with the look of stamping out something that she did not like. Then she walked away to the house, as erect as ever and as brisk in her walk, but stumbling once as she went, recovering herself with a little cry.

Looking after her, Marriner said, " That shook her. Why ? "

" It's shaken me," Sarah said. " I wasn't really thinking what I was saying. It just seemed to follow from what Mrs. Kenny said about Mrs. Pointing."

" Yet there could be something in it."

At that moment Sarah felt the same impulse as Mrs. Kenny, to stamp on the idea before it could grow.

" In that case, what use were the rest of us to him ? " she asked.

Marriner's eyes had the nervous glitter that Sarah had noticed at her first meeting with him.

" Of some use, that's certain," he said. " Perhaps one of us, or more than one of us, was going to take the blame for him."

" But there'd have been no motive. None of us had ever met Mrs. Pointing before."

" Oh yes, we had. That's to say, one of us had."

" Mrs. Kenny ! "

Marriner nodded. The excitement in his manner was increasing. " And now perhaps we've seen why Mrs. Kenny so disliked what you said. She may have thought all this out for herself. She may even have known something about Auty's plan. She, or, of course, Hector, may have overheard something, or come on some piece of evidence that gave the whole idea away."

" And then she murdered Auty herself ? "

Marriner gave a laugh and relaxed. " No, that isn't physically possible. Not at eighty-three, or whatever she is. And Hector has the completest alibi of anyone in the house except you. I'm afraid I was going a bit fast. All the same . . ."

" Yes ? "

" There's something in the idea that Auty couldn't ever have intended Mrs. Pointing to meet Miss Barbosa. And he *was* a murderer."

" Of those twelve men ? "

" Yes. Do you believe me now about that or not ? "

" I think I believe you." Yet it was not of the twelve men that Sarah was thinking, but of Henry Darnborough.

With a new jerkiness in his tone, he went on, " I'd like to know what you believe about something else. You realise I'm the one person in this house who hasn't any sort of an alibi ? The Pointings say they were together and the Carvers say they were together and you, Nock and Hector were all together out here. Well, what do you really think about that ? "

While he was speaking, Sarah's thoughts had been moving off down a trail of their own. She had been thinking about Mrs. Pointing and the state of fear that she had so plainly been in when she arrived at the house. That had seemed to be explained by her confession, under pressure from Hector, of her relationship with Auty. Yet it could be that there had been more to it than that. It could be that she had guessed that in coming to this house she had been taking her life in her hands.

At that point Sarah realised that Marriner had just asked her if she thought that he had murdered Auty.

" I—I think one of the others must be lying," she said. " I mean two of the others. The Pointings or the Carvers."

Instead of looking pleased, he frowned, and it was almost angrily that he said, " You've no reason for thinking that. You've no evidence."

" No," she agreed.

" That means that you could easily change your mind about it."

" It's you that's always changing your mind."

" Suppose some evidence turned up, something that made it look as if it was I who was doing the lying, what would you think then ? "

" D'you think there is some evidence of that sort ? "

" I didn't say there was. I only asked what you'd think if it turned up."

" Why, I'd believe it, I suppose."

" Yes, that's what I thought." But as he said it, he laughed ruefully. " Of course you would. You ought to. I'm an ass to hope that you might not. Oh well, I suppose the whole thing will be cleared up sometime. But it's very nerve-racking to come to a place breathing fire and slaughter against someone, and then, just when you've realised what a childish fantasy your idea of murder was, that person actually gets murdered and you find that you qualify perfectly as chief suspect."

" Excuse me." It was spoken just behind them by someone whom they had not heard approach.

They both looked round, and saw Miss Barbosa. As they got to their feet, Miss Barbosa plumped down in one of the chairs near them.

" You are Miss Wing ? " she said to Sarah.

Her voice was quiet but savage, while her dark eyes, which were small and round, had a timid sort of ferocity in them. Her face was puffy and white. She had just powdered it heavily to conceal the marks of tears, and the effect had been to draw attention to her blotchy pallor. Her lips were colourless.

Sarah sat down again. " Yes," she said.

Miss Barbosa did not even look at Marriner.

" You have told the police an extraordinary story about my fiancé and me," she said. " Let me tell you, it is all lies. All of it, lies."

" I'm sorry," Sarah said helplessly. " I only repeated what Mr. Auty had said to me."

" But why should he tell you such a story ? "

" I don't know, if it isn't true."

" I tell you, it is not true."

" None of it ? " Marriner asked.

" Not one word." Miss Barbosa's plump white hands, lying in her lap, clenched into fists. The sunlight glittered on her rings. " This villa in the mountains, there is no such place. My parents' villa is in Nice, close to the sea. And this brief case, with something in it that you were to give to me, I know nothing about that. And my fiancé's wish that you should be there to help me if anything happened to him, this is absurd. I do not know you. I know nothing about you."

" All the same, truly, it's what Mr. Auty said to me." Sarah had no idea how she ought to speak to the scared, angry, suffering woman, and thought that the less she said, the better it would probably be.

" And my Uncle Gilberto," Miss Barbosa went on, " he has been in London for the last week. It is true I spoke of him yesterday on the telephone, but only to ask after his health."

" I wish I could explain it to you " Sarah said, " but I don't understand it myself."

" But I—I understand it very well," Miss Barbosa retorted.

" I thought——" Sarah began, then something in the little, round, dark eyes stopped her.

" I know what you thought," Miss Barbosa said. " You thought, she is a fool, this foreign woman who is loved by Mark Auty. You thought, they will not listen to her because she is foreign. You thought, you can say what you like, they will believe you. But this shows how foolish you are, because I can prove all the things I say and you cannot."

" Of course you can," Sarah agreed. " And the only thing I can prove is that there was a brief case and that there was something in it which Mr. Auty told me nothing about."

" No, you cannot prove even that," Miss Barbosa said. " How can you prove what he told you ? Perhaps he told you that there was something in the brief-case for me, some gift, perhaps something valuable. Then how can you prove that it was not you who broke open the case and took what was in it ? "

Sarah thought it over, trying not to feel too scared or too angry at the question.

" I don't suppose I can," she said after a moment, " until they find out what really was in the case and who really took it."

Miss Barbosa nodded her head several times. " Yes, you understand I am not making any accusations except that you have told lies, lies, lies. I do not say you are a thief or a murderess."

" Thank you," Sarah said, a little bleakly.

Diffidently, Marriner joined in the conversation. " But what reason could there be, Miss Barbosa, for these lies that you believe Miss Wing has been telling ? "

She did not look towards him, but she answered promptly, " That is plain enough. I have been listening carefully to all that the police have had to say to me and I have been using my eyes, and I, I know who the murderer is and why Miss Wing is telling lies to protect him."

" To protect the murderer ? " Sarah exclaimed. " But *I* don't know who he is, even if you do."

Miss Barbosa made a scornful sound.

" Did not my fiancé go to your flat last week ? " she said. " Did he not stay late ? Did he not make love to you ? And then did you not come here with your lover, this man here, who has learnt of this—oh yes, I have been watching you both, I know you are lovers—and then did not your lover, in his rage and his jealousy, stab my fiancé in the back ? " She turned suddenly on Marriner, lifting her hands as if she were ready to claw at his face. " You are the murderer," she said, " you who have no alibi and you have spoken openly to all of your hatred of Mark Auty. And this girl has been telling her fantastic lies to draw attention away from the simple and obvious fact that this was a crime of vengeance on account of her infidelity to you."

CHAPTER XVII

SARAH COULD feel the colour mounting in her cheeks. She hardly dared glance towards Marriner. When she did, it was with relief that she saw that he was as red in the face as she was.

" Go slow," he muttered to her, trying to return Miss Barbosa's fiery look as if he were not in an agony of embarrassment. " Remember that you're dealing with a Latin mind."

In a tone of triumph, Miss Barbosa went on, " Yes, now I know that I was right. I can see the guilt in both your faces." She stood up. " I shall now go and tell this to the police." She walked off hurriedly, a heavy, clumsy, agitated and determined figure.

Sarah put her hands to her hot cheeks.

" There's nothing like not being guilty of anything at all for making one behave like a bloody fool, is there ? " she said.

Marriner laughed. " You needn't worry. That story won't stick."

" I suppose she had to make up something to keep her mind off Mrs. Pointing," Sarah said. " But perhaps she isn't really wise to talk too much about jealousy as the obvious motive."

" Only I imagine her own alibi is cast-iron. But that reminds me . . ."

They were both speaking rather rapidly, with a lightness that they had not troubled to assume earlier.

" Of what ? " Sarah asked.

" Uncle Gilberto. You weren't the only one who heard Auty's story about him."

" Anyway, I'm glad she went in," Sarah said. " Conversation with her was rather a strain—particularly as I feel horribly sorry for her and don't want to hit back at her, if I can restrain myself."

" Quite a character, she made you out," Marriner said. " The only thing is, she got me all wrong."

" Only you ? "

At that moment a window of the sitting-room was opened and Hector leant out.

" Hey, you two, I want someone to drink with," he called. " Come in and join me. The police have just cleared out of here."

A little relieved at the interruption, they got up and went in.

Hector was alone in the sitting-room, busy with a tray of drinks. He looked as if he had something on his mind that he was in a hurry to talk about and that it was for that reason that he had called them in, rather than for the one he had given.

" I've just acquired a most interesting piece of information," he said excitedly. " By great guile I wrung it out of the inspector, who wasn't at all eager to part with it. What d'you think about it ?—Auty died intestate."

Marriner had just sat down. Though he did not say anything, he immediately jerked himself forward so that he was sitting on the extreme edge of his chair.

Sarah said, " But can they be certain of that already ? "

" You mean a will might turn yet up somewhere? Of course that's possible," Hector said. " But it doesn't look likely, because apparently the subject of a will was under discussion between Auty and his lawyer. Auty had told his lawyer that as soon as he was married, he was going to leave everything he had to his wife. His wife was going to make a will, leaving everything to him. The lawyer had never heard of the existence of any previous will of Auty's."

Marriner slid back in his chair again and looked pensively at the ceiling.

" I wonder how long Miss Barbosa would have lived after her marriage," he said.

" Who inherits his money now ? " Sarah asked.

" That's the interesting part of it," Hector said. " I can't say I know anything about the laws governing intestacy, but at a guess, I should say his wife, wouldn't you ? "

" Mrs. Pointing ! " Sarah exclaimed.

Hector nodded impressively.

" I can't say I see her taking it," Marriner said.

" Ah, that's a thing you never can be sure about," Hector said. " Sometimes people have an impulse to refuse tainted money, but more often than not, they get over the feeling that it's tainted as soon as it gets into their own hands."

" Had he a lot of money to leave ? " Sarah asked.

Hector gestured at the room. " This house was his and he seems to have been able to keep it up well and live in it fairly luxuriously. That takes a lot of money nowadays."

" And what about the Pointings ? " she went on. " D'you think they need money ? "

" Everyone needs money."

" I don't believe it," Marriner said. " I can't see those two taking anything at all from Auty."

" Except his life, except his life," a voice said from the doorway.

It was Nock. He came in and sat down in a chair near the window, fiddling for a moment with the lace handkerchief in his pocket, arranging it more to his liking.

The friendly expression froze on Hector's face.

" You should be careful about saying things like that," he said. " It's going too far."

" I've told you," Nock said, " I was on the stage once. A rotten life. I left it without regrets. But now and again I catch myself quoting, or almost. There's no need to take any notice of me on those occasions."

" You didn't mean what you said ? " Hector asked.

" I meant it about as much as you meant what you were saying," Nock said. " And weren't you saying just what I said ? "

Turning away, Hector refilled his glass. The tips of his ears had reddened.

" I don't suppose you want a drink," he muttered to Nock.

" No thanks."

" I wasn't accusing the Pointings of murder," Hector went on uneasily, " which you were. The only person here whom I want to accuse of that is you, and I can't do that without accusing my own mother of telling lies and keeping bad company."

" Your adopted mother," Nock said.

Hector's face flushed an even deeper shade than his ears, the ears that Mrs. Kenny had claimed were a clue to his character. " What's that got to do with it ? "

Nock gave a pat to his lace handkerchief and looked up

with a smile on his lips. But there was no trace of a smile in his eyes.

"I like things to be accurate, that's all," he said. "I like the truth."

"I wonder if you can even spell the word," Hector said.

"Listen." Nock's cold stare settled disdainfully on the glass in Hector's hand. "I know how you'd like to fix things. I know everyone in this house would like to pin this thing on me. I'm not under any illusion that I'm among friends. But I'm not going to oblige in any way. The truth suits me and I'm not going to let you forget it."

Sarah was looking in a puzzled way at the two men.

"Why are you both trying to pick a quarrel?" she said. "I don't see that that's going to help either of you."

"I'm not picking a quarrel," Nock said. "I don't pick quarrels. I just like things to be accurate."

For a moment it looked as if Hector were going to retort to this with something even angrier than he had said before. Then, passing a hand over his bald head, he turned to Sarah, smiled and said, "Thank you, Miss Wing, that was just the right thing to say. I was letting my nerves get on top of me. The fact is, this man gives me shivers up and down my spine. I can't bear to see him sitting there, refusing a drink when no decent man would, and making me forget too what I was going to say when he came in."

"I know what you were going to say," Nock said. "You weren't going to accuse those Pointing people of murder, but you were going to say that you've only to look at them to see that things are pretty tight for them and that if Auty's money should happen to come their way, through their own efforts or anyone else's, you don't see them saying no to it more than once or twice, and never on paper."

Hector gestured helplessly. He went on addressing Sarah. "I hate to agree with a single thing that man says, but there you have it—that was just about what I was going to say. But I stick to it that that is not an accusation of murder. It's merely adding to the facts we possess already, something that we didn't know before, which is that the Pointings had a possible motive for wanting Auty's death."

"Only," Marriner said, "if they knew that he hadn't made any will. And how could they have known that? No, if either of the Pointings killed Auty . . ." He stopped, because at that moment Inspector Hughes appeared at the door and told Sarah that he wanted to speak with her.

As she followed him out, she felt fairly sure what it had been in Marriner's mind to say. He had been about to say that if either of the Pointings had killed Auty, it had not been because of his money, but because they had discovered something of Auty's intentions concerning Violet Pointing.

Sarah now felt certain that Auty could never have intended that Mrs. Pointing and Anna Maria Dolores Barbosa should ever come face to face, and that he must have had some plot prepared for getting rid of his wife before the two women could meet. But she hoped that Marriner would not offer this theory to Nock, or even to Hector, for if anyone was to hear of it, it ought to be the inspector.

Hughes took her into the dining-room. The door beside the fireplace, leading into Auty's study, was now open, but he did not approach it.

" I saw you talking to Miss Barbosa just now," he said abruptly. " I imagine she's told you that the whole story you told us was untrue."

" It wasn't untrue," Sarah said.

" I haven't said it was, have I? I've only said that Miss Barbaso says it is."

" It's the story that Mr. Auty told me," Sarah said. " The lies, if they are lies, were his, not mine."

" All right." He was leaning against the table with his arms folded, looking as if he meant to keep her there only for a moment. He was more tense this morning, more restless. Sarah felt that something must have happened that had changed his attitude to the job in hand.

" Miss Wing, did you ever have the feeling that Auty had anything against you? " he asked.

" No, he was very nice to me," she said.

" You never had the feeling that he had a grudge against you, or was afraid of you? "

" Good heavens, no. How could he have been? "

" It never occurred to you that you had some knowledge about him which he might consider dangerous? "

She hesitated. " No—that's to say, not till last night. Last night I did begin to wonder. . . ."

" Why last night ? "

" It was after a talk I'd had with Mr. Nock," she said. " I'd heard just before it that Darnborough had actually been working for Mr. Kenny, not for Mr. Auty, and I'd begun to realise how many lies Mr. Auty must have told me. And then Mr. Nock suggested that it had been Mr. Auty who'd been responsible for Darnborough's death." She smiled uncertainly. " Coming from that man, I didn't know what to make of the suggestion. I've told you, I *know* he was the driver of the car. So I didn't feel inclined to believe anything he might say about what happened that evening. Yet, in a way, his idea seemed to fit with the facts, and if it did . . ."

" If it did, it occurred to you, you'd been a witness to the fact that Auty had been very near to the scene of the accident. And you'd made up your mind that it had not been an accident, but murder." He was speaking quickly, with repressed excitement in his voice. " Well, go on. Did nothing else strike you ? "

" Of course it made me wonder more than ever why Mr. Auty really asked me here," she said. " If all the things he'd told me were lies and if in fact he didn't trust me at all but was afraid of me, it didn't make sense at all, his asking me here, where I'd actually meet Mr. Nock and realise that he had some connection with Mr. Auty."

" Didn't it ? " He was staring at her hard, challenging her to make sense of the puzzle, to see something that he had seen, to make some guess that he had made.

" No," she said after a moment. " Not to me. After all, I'd never dreamt of connecting Mr. Auty with the accident. And when I'd told the police that I was sure it had really been murder, they weren't even interested. The whole incident was closed, as far as I was concerned."

" But suppose something had happened to re-open it. Suppose some days later you'd read in the papers about another accident with which Auty had unquestionably been connected. Mightn't that have started you thinking along a new line ? "

" An accident—some days later ! " Now, she thought, she saw where his questions were tending, and before she had had time to think out whether or not she really wanted to ask it, the question slipped out, " You mean to Mrs. Pointing ? "

" All right, let's say to Mrs. Pointing," he said.

" Well, I might have thought it curious," she said. " All the same, things like that happen without there being anything sinister in it. Some people do seem to be in accidents, or on the scenes of accidents, again and again for no particular reason."

" That's true. But I think Auty might not have felt sure that that would be how you'd reason about it."

" But in that case . . ."

" Yes ? " he said.

She was suddenly feeling cold again, though her mind was not really conscious yet of shock.

" In that case, he must have meant me to be in the accident too," she said, hearing the words come out of her as if they had been spoken by another person.

" Yes, Miss Wing," Hughes said. " I think, as far as you were concerned, Auty was murdered just in time. But I'd hoped you were going to say something more. I've got an idea now about this party which is so horrible and sounds so preposterous that I've been hoping someone else would get the same idea, to convince me that I've not lost my reason. However, let's skip that. You realise now, don't you, that you yourself may have been in considerable danger from Auty ? Recognising that, are you still quite sure that you have no knowledge of the contents of that brief case."

" None at all," she said. " I saw the papers on top, but I never looked under them."

He made an impatient gesture, as if he had suddenly decided to give up some quest.

" Very well, then," he said briskly. " We'll proceed. That thing, whatever it was, has got to be found. I'm having the whole house searched again and all the people in it searched. There's a matron upstairs in your own room. Will you please go to her now ? After that, please go to the sitting-room and stay there."

Before she had any time to answer, either in acquiescence or protest, he walked out.

CHAPTER XVIII

When Sarah returned to the sitting-room, after the police matron had searched her, she found a very silent party gathered there. As she came into the room, Pointing went out and Sarah took the chair that he had left. She wondered what Hughes had said to produce the silence. But when she thought of asking what it had been, the silence itself checked her.

They were all there except Pointing, who had gone, she supposed, to be searched. Miss Barbosa was there, sitting stiffly in a high-backed chair near to the empty fireplace. It occurred to Sarah as possible that it was the presence of the little dark woman and not anything said by the inspector that had dried up the speech in everyone else. Yet she was aware of a feeling of shock in the room. Every face showed it, particularly that of Miss Barbosa herself. All had the stiff, mask-like quality that faces have when they cover a turmoil too great to be expressed, not a wilful concealment of thoughts, but a sheer helplessness to reveal them. It was an eerie feeling, sitting there, looking round and for some reason, not daring to ask what had happened.

Suddenly, in the silence, Lorna Carver began to laugh. It was hysteria, but for a moment no one did anything to stop it.

Half-laughing, half-sobbing, Lorna pointed a red-nailed finger at everyone in turn, all except Miss Barbosa. "Mrs. Kenny—Hector—Mrs. Pointing—Mr. Marriner—Miss Wing—Mr. Nock—Tim—me—and Mr. Pointing!" Her small body rocked in her chair. "Nine of us! God, isn't that funny? Isn't that a joke? Why don't you all laugh?"

She pressed her clenched fists to her temples and screamed with laughter.

Tim Carver looked round apprehensively. Mrs. Kenny frowned. No one else stirred.

"Nine!" Lorna Carver screamed. "*Murder in time saves nine!* And here we all are, all nine of us, trying to catch out the one who saved us. What are we doing it for ? Why don't we shake him by the hand and thank him ? Wouldn't we all have been blown to pieces in that beastly plane if he hadn't done it ? "

It ended in more wild peals of laughter.

Mrs. Kenny got up, crossed to Lorna's chair and hit her hard in the face.

The response was an even louder scream than before, then a collapse into subdued sobbing.

Mrs. Kenny returned to her chair.

" It's a long time since I've heard anyone having real hysterics," she said. " They seem to have gone out of fashion."

" All the same, it's true what she said," Tim Carver muttered. " Whoever murdered Auty did save us all."

" Including the pilot and crew, don't forget," Hector said, " which brings the total well above the nine that Mrs. Carver finds so dramatic."

Sarah found her voice. " Will someone explain this to me ? "

" Ah yes, you missed it, didn't you ? " Hector said. " Well the inspector, jolly fellow, has just been giving us his theory of the crime—that's to say, of the motive for crime. It seems that last night he and the sergeant were having a chat over their beer about the day's work, and the sergeant made a facetious suggestion that Auty's purpose in taking us all to Nice was to drown us in the sea. From that it was only a step for the nimble wits of the inspector to arrive at the conclusion that what Auty really intended to do with us was to have us all blown to bits in mid-air by a bomb, which he had given to you to carry, Miss Wing, in the mysterious brief case."

In a flat, quiet voice, which brought all eyes on to her, Miss Barbosa said, " It is not true."

" I'm afraid it is, you know," Hector said.

Sarah began to say, " So that was what he meant . . ."

Mrs. Kenny spoke coldly. " I assure you, Miss Wing, we all realise that you had no knowledge of the contents of the brief case."

" I should think we do ! " Marriner said hotly. " Wasn't she going to get it, like the rest of us ? "

" Maybe she was," Nock said. " On the other hand, maybe she was going to be saved at the last minute by some Uncle Gilberto."

Marriner jumped to his feet. " You damned swine ! "

A little surprised at the violence of his feelings on the point, Sarah said to him, " Do sit down again and keep quiet. A row of any sort now would be the last straw."

" Thank you, Miss Wing," Mrs. Kenny said. " I agree with you. Mr. Nock, please refrain from behaving any more revoltingly than you can help. And Mr. Marriner, please don't brawl. The nerves of all of us must be at breaking point."

Marriner sat down, muttering to himself.

Nock caught Sarah's eye and deliberately flickered one eyelid at her.

" Miss Wing and I have the same sort of sense of humour," he said. " We can each take a joke."

Sarah shuddered.

" But has the inspector said why we were all to be blown to bits ? " she asked. " I can see why he might want to get rid of one or two of us, but why all the rest ? What had he against Mr. Nock, for instance ? I should have thought they were the most excellent friends."

" We were Auty's disreputable past," Hector said. " We were the people who knew how he'd got to where he was. But he'd reached the point where it was going to pay him to be relatively honest. He'd got a position and—forgive me, Miss Barbosa—he was about to marry a very rich wife. So he decided on a clean sweep of all the people who had knowledge of him that he thought dangerous. A conception rather on the grand scale, but perhaps not so tremendous to someone who, as Marriner can tell you, had already arranged the deaths of twelve men, merely for his own comfort."

" It is all, all untrue," Miss Barbosa said drearily.

Sarah supposed that she would go on saying that for a long time. She would not explain it, she would not embroider it, she would merely let the bald statement block her mind until forgetfulness had become effective in doing the work for her.

Hector was continuing, " I imagine we're all inclined to

echo Mrs. Carver and say that whoever got rid of Auty for us, we'd like to thank him and join together to pay his passage to any country that hasn't got extradition laws. But there's one serious side to all this that we haven't considered. It will be apparent to the police now that every single one of us had a motive for the murder of Auty."

" Well, you needn't worry," Nock said. " You're out of it."

Hector took no notice of him. " The question is, however, who had a chance to know that Auty had put Miss Wing in charge of a brief-case with a bomb in it ? Miss Wing, can't you tell us anything about that ? "

She had no answer ready for this. But even if she had had one, it would have been interrupted by a burst of sneezing from Carver.

As it was stopping, he spluttered, " You're all talking too damned much. You said yourself, you'd like to thank the man, whoever he was. Why not leave it at that then ? Give a vote of thanks and shut up."

" Even though," Hector said, " all of us, or rather, most of us, including you, Carver, are now in the same danger as we were in from Auty. And personally, if I had to choose between death by hanging or death by a sudden explosion, I'd prefer the explosion. It's true it'll only be one of us, not the whole nine, but still, that leaves eight who have a certain interest in arriving at the truth. Miss Wing——"

Sarah had been fidgeting uneasily in her chair. She could tell them now, if she wanted to, two things about the time that the brief-case had been in her possession. She could tell them about the door in the upper corridor that she had heard softly close as she went to her room, and she could tell them about her meeting with Alec Marriner in the corridor just outside her door. Yet what was the use of saying anything ? Most of the party had their rooms along that corridor. It might have been any of them. And as for mentioning her meeting with Marriner . . .

Suddenly she exclaimed something. While she had been hesitating, her fidgeting hands had touched an object that had been pushed down into the depths of the chair.

As she dragged it out, Miss Barbosa screamed and put her hands over her eyes.

"Don't! Don't!" she shrieked.

Carver jumped to his feet.

Nock muttered, "What the hell?"

Dazedly, Sarah looked at what she was holding. It was the revolver that had vanished from the garden at the time when Mrs. Kenny's screams had taken Sarah, Hector and Nock, running, to the other side of the house.

Realising that she was pointing it directly at Miss Barbosa, Sarah apologised hurriedly and laid it down gingerly on a small table near her.

"I just found it in here," she said, pointing down into the chair.

There was a moment's silence, then Nock went off into a burst of his thin, uneasy laughter. He laughed and laughed as if he had just been told the best joke in the world.

In the midst of it, Pointing returned to the sitting-room.

Looking up at him and speaking in a voice still sodden with tears, Lorna Carver said, "Mr. Pointing was sitting in that chair!"

Hughes was behind Denis Pointing. Pausing just inside the door, he looked questioningly at Sarah, while Pointing's gaze, after one quick look at the revolver, went straight to his wife. Then he turned his head to look at Hughes.

"Yes, I was sitting in that chair," he said.

"And the revolver?" Hughes asked.

"Mine," Marriner answered.

"How did it get into the chair?" Hughes asked.

Pointing walked farther into the room and sat down on the arm of his wife's chair.

"I pushed it down there when I heard that I was going to be searched," he said.

Hughes crossed to the table where Sarah had laid the revolver. He picked it up.

"Unloaded," he said, "and apparently of no importance in the case. Why were you afraid of having it found on you, Mr. Pointing?"

"I suppose because it wasn't mine," Pointing said, "and because it would have been a little difficult for me to explain why I was carrying it around."

"And why were you?"

" Well, there's a killer in this house, isn't there ? And you aren't always on hand, Inspector."

" You thought it might come in useful, even if it was unloaded."

" Exactly."

" Did you know whom it belonged to ? "

" Not till just now, when Marriner said it was his."

" And how did you get hold of it ? "

This time Pointing did not answer. He had thrust his hands into his pockets and was swinging one foot to and fro. His ruddy, pleasant face had tightened into something hard and secretive. His wife's, on the other hand, had gone pale and flabby, as if life had drained out of it.

" How did you get hold of it ? " Hughes repeated.

" You know, I don't think I'm going to answer that question," Pointing said, " until I've consulted my lawyer."

" In that case," Hughes said, " I can tell you how you got it. There was only one time when it could have happened. That was between the time when Mrs. Kenny started scream-ing and the time when Miss Wing and Mrs. Kenny returned to the chairs on the lawn. It was during that short time that the revolver vanished."

As he paused, Pointing said, " I see the implication. You mean that if I took the revolver then, I must have been downstairs at a time when I've claimed to have been upstairs with my wife in our bedroom."

Carver broke in, " And at the time when the murder was being committed."

Hughes turned on Carver, furious at the interruption, telling him to keep quiet.

Pointing went on, " You see, Inspector ? You see why I don't intend to say any more until I've consulted my lawyer ? And I imagine that if you intend to ask me any more questions, you'll have to give me the official warning. Now have I your permission to use the telephone ? "

" Certainly," Hughes said stiffly.

Pointing got up and went out.

After a moment's hesitation, Hughes went out too.

When he had gone, Tim Carver stood up, stretched and said, " Well, that's that. I reckon it won't be long now before we're all on our way home."

" And just what do you mean by that ? " Mrs. Kenny asked sharply.

Carver's sullen, handsome face was lit up by a mocking smile.

" I don't want to put it into words with Mrs. Pointing in the room," he said. " I'm very sorry for her and I'd like to say I stand by what I said earlier, that I think we ought to be offering a vote of thanks to whoever killed Auty, not helping the police put a rope round his neck. But I dare say it won't get to that, anyway. No one ought to be hanged for putting an end to a mad dog."

" Be quiet, you devil," Mrs. Kenny said furiously. " Are you completely without decent feelings ? And don't imagine for a moment that the police have forgotten that it was your finger-prints that were on the glass on the desk."

" Oh, but that was from earlier," Carver said easily. He was looking more cheerful than he had looked ever since his arrival in the house.

" Can you prove it ? " Mrs. Kenny asked. She turned to Mrs. Pointing. " Take no notice of him, my dear, and don't worry on account of your husband. That policeman is any-thing but a fool and I'm sure the whole thing can be explained."

Mrs. Pointing showed no sign of having heard either her or Carver. She was leaning back in her chair, her face still with the drained, flaccid, vacant look that had come to it while her husband had been talking to the inspector.

Mrs. Kenny went on, " You really have no cause to worry. That policeman's obviously quite wrong in saying that that was the only time when your husband could have got hold of the revolver. Someone else could have got hold of it then and later left it where it was found by your husband."

" If that's so," Carver said, " why didn't he say so when he was asked ? "

" I've no doubt he was very wise in refusing to answer all further questions," Mrs. Kenny said. Her face had flushed with agitation and she was looking at the other woman in real distress. " Mrs. Pointing, I assure you, I can't believe anything bad of your husband and I feel absolutely certain that the circumstances will clear him as soon as they're fully explained. And I feel sure that no one else in this room believes——"

" Ah, but she does herself ! " Miss Barbosa exclaimed, pointing a plump finger at Mrs. Pointing.

To this Mrs. Pointing showed some response. She lifted her head to meet the eyes of the speaker and the two women exchanged a long, strange, somehow intimate stare.

Seeing it, Mrs. Kenny seemed to become even more agitated than before. It was as if a deep indignation were boiling up in her, coming to the point of exploding over everyone in the room. Hector, who was watching her intently, stirred uneasily, then abruptly got up, went round behind her and laid his hands on her shoulders.

" Take it easy, darling," he said, bending over her. " It isn't your job to handle this."

" Leave me alone," Mrs. Kenny said impatiently.

" But really. You oughtn't to be here at all. You ought to be resting."

" *You* ought to be resting," she said sternly. " You've had much too much excitement during the last few days. You know you always suffer for it."

" But won't you please go and rest," he said. " Just go and lie down until lunch-time."

" Certainly not. I never felt better."

If anything, Hector's attempt to calm her had made the colour grow darker in Mrs. Kenny's cheeks. " As the oldest person present," she said, " who has undoubtedly seen most of life, I should be failing in my responsibilities if I disappeared from the scene. I feel that if I go, everyone will turn on this poor woman and tell her that her husband is a murderer. I don't intend to allow that."

Miss Barbosa had a fierce, glittering little smile on her face.

" It is that she herself believes that he is a murderer that is important," she said. " Look at her. Tell me she does not believe it."

" No," Mrs. Pointing said, low-voiced.

" Yes, yes, she believes it," Miss Barbosa said. " Now you all begin to understand, now you see the truth. All this talk of bombs and aeroplanes and devilry unbelievable, all this is nonsense. It is the so-called husband of this woman who has done the murder. And why? That is very simple. She was once Mr. Auty's wife, it seems. But she left him, she abandoned him, she let him think that she was dead, so that she could marry, if you can use that word, this other man who was richer then than her true husband. He was only a poor man, he was no use to her. But many years later she learns that he is now a rich man, much richer than this one with whom she has been living in a sinful union and so she begins to remember whose wife she really is. She learns too that this real husband of hers has made no will and that if he dies, she will inherit the fortune he has built up alone, with his own brains and enterprise and no help from her——"

" Be quiet, you silly creature!" Mrs. Kenny said, almost purple now with anger.

" Darling——" Hector said imploringly.

" Hector, I beg you not to interfere with me!" Mrs. Kenny exclaimed, turning her wrath on him. " Can't you see what this sort of talk is doing to poor Mrs. Pointing and how absolutely unforgivable it is. I will not allow it to continue."

" It's all right, Mrs. Kenny." Mrs. Pointing's voice was soft and dead. She stood up, her tall, heavy figure, that had been so limp a moment before, developing dignity and self-assurance as she stood there. " Of course none of these things are true. But you yourself said something that is true and now that I've thought it over——"

" Don't!" Mrs. Kenny said. " Don't say another word! I won't let you. I forbid you."

" But I want to," Mrs. Pointing said. " I've thought it over and I see it's the only thing to do. You see, it *was* someone else who took that revolver from the lawn and gave it to Denis. It was I."

Mrs. Kenny's voice rose almost to a scream.

" No, you are not to go on! I absolutely forbid you. You must do what your husband is doing, refuse to answer questions until you have consulted your lawyer. You have a perfect right to do so. No one can force you to say anything at all."

A shade of irritation crossed Mrs. Pointing's face.

" I've said I want to speak," she said. " And I want to

say the rest of it. It's—it's quite simple what I have to say. It was I who killed Mark Ardwell."

" No, no, no ! " cried Mrs. Kenny and hid her face in her hands.

CHAPTER XIX

WITH A QUICK, silent movement, Nock came up out of his chair and stood over Mrs. Kenny.

" So you knew all along who did it ? " he said. His fine voice was quiet and deadly.

Sarah realised that Mrs. Kenny was trembling. When the old woman raised her head from her hands, the colour had gone from her face.

" No," she said. " I didn't. There's some mistake."

He bent a little over her. Hector, standing behind Mrs. Kenny, stood watching her with a look of dazed amazement.

" You knew all along," Nock said. " You saw her."

" No."

" But you were waiting, weren't you, until you could pass it on to me ? "

" No, no, I saw nobody—I saw an arm," Mrs. Kenny said. " I didn't see Mrs. Pointing. I'm sure there's some mistake."

" D'you know what I'd have done to you if you'd tried to implicate me ? " Nock said.

The challenge in that helped Mrs. Kenny to recover herself. She drew herself up. But she was still shaking.

" Knifed me, shot me, or run over me in your car, no doubt," she said. " But how could I have implicated you, when my son, whose word I'm accustomed to accept, tells me that you were with him at the time of the murder ? "

" But you'd have thought something up if you could, wouldn't you ? " Nock said. " And that's why we haven't been told the truth about what you saw through the window."

" I have told the truth."

" Oh, no. Oh, no."

While the two were speaking, Mrs. Pointing, standing in the middle of the room, was almost ignored.

Nock went on, " Are you going to tell the truth now, Mrs. Kenny ? "

" I shall stick to what I've said all along," she answered.

" That's foolish of you. There's at least one thing you'd better alter."

" I don't know what you're talking about. I did *not* see Mrs. Pointing."

" You understand, I'm not trying to make trouble for Mrs. Pointing," he said. " I join with Carver in saying that Auty's gone where he belongs. But if you try to shield her at someone else's expense and that someone turns out to be me—because that's how you'd like it—you needn't think I'll sit and suffer like a little gentleman."

" That I should not have expected," Mrs. Kenny said, much calmer now. Yet she seemed unable to withdraw her eyes from his.

" All right," he said, " all right. Just so that you understand." He turned to Mrs. Pointing, " If I were you, I'd withdraw that confession. That's my advice for what it's worth."

He walked out of the room.

Mrs. Kenny had put her hands over her eyes while he said the last few words, but when he had gone she looked up at Mrs. Pointing.

" Do as he said, Mrs. Pointing," she said. " Withdraw that confession."

With a tired shake of her head, Violet Pointing answered, " I can't. It's true."

" Please, please," Mrs. Kenny said. " I implore you ! "

The other woman began to look puzzled. " But why ? What is it to you ? And why should that man, of all people, tell me to withdraw ? "

" I don't know," Mrs. Kenny said. " But I think you can be sure he knows what he's talking about."

Still looking deeply bewildered, Mrs. Pointing went on slowly, " He was so contradictory. First he attacked you for protecting me, then he told me to withdraw, as if he were trying to protect me too."

" I wasn't protecting you," Mrs. Kenny said. " I didn't see who did the murder."

" I don't want to withdraw," Mrs. Pointing said. " I want to speak to the inspector."

" He won't believe you," Mrs. Kenny said, " any more than any of the rest of us do."

" Speak for yourself," Carver said. " I'm quite ready to hear what she's got to say. You aren't the boss here, you know, Mrs. Kenny, whatever you may be at home."

Mrs. Kenny glowered at him.

" D'you know, I believe I find you an almost more detestable character than that Nock creature," she said. " He, at least, has intelligence."

With a laugh, Carver answered, " I don't see anything intelligent about telling a person to withdraw a confession that no one forced them to give."

" Oh, you don't ? " There was angry scorn in Mrs. Kenny's voice. " Mrs. Pointing, let me ask you once more —please, please withdraw. I may be wrong—perhaps you will be believed, perhaps you did do the murder, but whatever the truth of that may be, do listen to me when I assure you that it won't be for the best if you insist on making this confession."

" I don't understand," Mrs. Pointing said helplessly.

" Then do what I say."

" No, I can't ! "

Mrs. Kenny raised her hands and dropped them again in a gesture of desperation. As Pointing came into the room, she said to him, " Mr. Pointing, I wish you would take your wife into the garden and reason with her quietly. It seems to be beyond me, so I think I shall go upstairs and lie down." Yet she did not move.

A shadow falling across the window made Sarah glance towards it. Nock was standing outside, looking in. As he saw her looking at him, he turned away in a leisurely way, lighting a cigarette and walking on.

Pointing had said to his wife, " What is it, Vi ? "

She raised her voice deliberately. " I've just told them that it was I who killed Mark Ardwell. Now I want to tell them how it happened."

"Good God, are you mad ? " Pointing cried, striding forward.

From behind him Hughes said, " Just a moment, Mr. Pointing. Mrs. Pointing, I have to warn you——"

She interrupted him impatiently, so that the rest of what he said was almost lost, " I want to speak ! You can listen or not as you choose, Inspector. Afterwards I'll make a formal statement of it and sign it, or anything else you want. But now, please listen."

She did not look at her husband and as he advanced, she moved farther away from him.

" You know of my relationship with Mark Ardwell," she said, still speaking loudly to emphasise the fact that she was making a public statement. " I told you all about that yesterday. So I needn't go into that now. You know that I came here hoping that some way could be found of dissolving our marriage without scandal. I never had the slightest intention of going to Nice. I simply wanted to have a talk with Mark. Well, he evaded me. He kept saying that we'd talk when we got to Nice. And time was passing. In another hour or so, we'd have been on our way. I was sitting upstairs with my husband and suddenly I felt that the whole situation was so intolerable that I'd got to do something—at once. Without giving Denis any explanation, I left the room and went downstairs. Mark was in his study. He was alone. I went in and shut the door. I told him that I must speak to him immediately as I didn't intend to go to Nice at all. He got angry at once and said that for my husband's sake—for Denis's sake, I mean—I'd better go. I didn't understand him, but he said that if I didn't do as he wanted, he'd set to work to ruin Denis completely and that he could do it. I didn't know what he meant, but I could tell from his tone that he was serious. When he'd said it, he stooped over the table where the drinks were and began to pour himself out a drink . . ."

She paused and Hughes, with an odd gleam in his eyes, said, " Ah ! And then, Mrs. Pointing ? "

" I don't remember it very clearly," she said. " I lost my head. I know there was a knife lying on the desk. I picked it up and struck him. Then I ran. And as I went, I heard screams in the garden. For some reason, I ran straight out of the house, to the garden at the back. I suppose I was thinking of running away altogether. There was nobody there, but there was a revolver lying on the grass. I stopped to pick it up and while I was doing that I began to recover my wits a little and I went very quickly upstairs. When I saw Denis, I said something about having been to the bathroom and I slipped the revolver into my suitcase. I'm sure he didn't see me do that, but I suppose he found it there sometime later. That's all."

She drew a long breath and now at last looked at her husband. It was a long look, straight into his eyes and full of intense emotion.

" So now we've had two descriptions of the murder," Hughes remarked. " Interesting, isn't it, that the two people from whom we've had them should have decided to tell the same lie about it ? "

Mrs. Pointing might not have heard him. Her husband had gone to her and put an arm round her shoulders, drawing her against him.

It was Mrs. Kenny who replied. " I've told no lies, Inspector. I told you what I saw. This poor woman, I agree, is obviously lying, for reasons we can easily guess, but what I told you was the exact truth about what I saw."

" No, Mrs. Kenny," Hughes said. " You couldn't have seen what you said you did. If you had, the glasses and bottles on the table would have been all over the floor, instead of there being just one glass on the floor, at some distance from the table. Auty was stabbed while he was standing upright, a decanter in one hand, a glass in the other. Why you've chosen to lie on that point I still don't know, or whether, indeed, it's possible that you made some kind of honest mistake. The reason for Mrs. Pointing's lie, of course, is obvious. Accepting your description of the murder, she merely repeated it—a sign, I should say, of her complete innocence or else of very deep cunning."

" Inspector," Pointing interrupted.

" One moment, please, Mr. Pointing," Mrs. Kenny said. " May I reply first to these insinuations. I'm aware, Inspector, that I'm an old woman and that my eyesight is not as good as it once was. As you say, I may have made a mistake. I won't attempt to dispute the possibility, for mistakes are possible to everyone. But I object strongly to the suggestion that I lied deliberately. I consider you have no right to make such a suggestion at all when you can't advance any reason why I should have lied. I can't myself see that the point is important. Standing or stooping, Mark Auty is dead and that's that. Now, if you will allow me, I'm going upstairs to lie down. The strain of things has really been too much for me and I'm not feeling at all well."

She got to her feet. Hector offered her his arm and she took it.

As they were leaving the room together, Hughes said, " And now, Mr. Pointing, perhaps what your wife has just said may make you feel like telling the truth about how that revolver got into your hands."

" I believe I'm not compelled to give any evidence that may tend to incriminate me," Pointing said.

" But how can that incriminate you, if what you said to me out there a few minutes ago is true ? " Hughes asked.

Mrs. Pointing looked questioningly at her husband.

Hughes explained. " A few minutes ago, Mr. Pointing gave me an interesting piece of information. It was that when he was called down to the room where the murder had been committed and climbed in through the window, there were signs that some of the blood from the wound was already beginning to clot. Well, Mr. Pointing ? "

" Yes," Pointing said, " I did say that."

" But that means——" Mrs. Pointing began.

" It means," Marriner said eagerly, " that the murder may have been committed earlier than we've all believed."

" But then what *did* Mrs. Kenny see ? " Sarah asked.

" What it means," Carver said belligerently, " is simply that Pointing's lying. It's become important to him to prove that the murder happened earlier than it did and so he suddenly remembers that Auty's blood was beginning to clot. Well, it would have been a whole lot more convincing if he'd remembered that before any of us had found out that either he or his wife was downstairs at the time of the murder."

" It was I who came down, it was not my wife," Pointing said. " She told her story simply to take suspicion from me. I should have thought that was plain enough to everyone."

169

" So you admit that you came down and took the revolver from where it lay on the lawn ? " Hughes asked.

" Yes," Pointing said, with more exasperation than fear in his voice. " I did. But I did not murder Auty."

" Let's stick to the revolver," Hughes said. " What brought you down ? "

" I came down because I'd seen something rather odd from the window," Pointing said. " I'd seen Mr. Kenny and Miss Wing examining a revolver. Then I saw Mr. Kenny wrap it up in his blazer and put it down and go back to his gardening. I didn't understand the situation at all and it made me feel exceedingly curious, so when a little while later I looked out of the window again and saw everyone on the lawn suddenly go rushing off, I nipped down quickly, took the revolver and got back again to my room as fast as I could. By chance this was at a time when my wife was out of the room. A few minutes later we heard of the death of Auty. . . . I never told my wife anything about the revolver, but last night I advised her to say nothing about having gone out of the room at all. This was because I saw how serious the consequences for me might be if it was discovered that I'd been downstairs just at the time I had."

" This was before you'd thought up the story of the blood having started to clot," Carver said derisively. " Where's Nock ? He'll tell us whether or not it was clotting."

From the chair where she had been sitting limply, apparently hardly conscious of what was going on around her, Lorna Carver suddenly sprang up and planted herself in front of her husband. Her make-up was in streaks and her blonde knot of hair was coming undone. Her reddened eyes blazed with a look of hatred.

" And what difference does it make to you ? " she cried. " Why should it matter to you if the murder happened a a bit earlier than we thought it did ? It's true you were downstairs yourself a bit earlier—we all know that. You were downstairs with Mr. Auty, having a drink and trying to make him part with the evidence he'd got that you'd been blackmailing him. But it wasn't you that did the murder, was it ? *Was it ?* So what does it matter if the blood was clotting or not ? "

Carver's expression was one of the deepest amazement. He was so startled by his wife's words that it was a moment before he remembered to be even as angry as he usually was when she spoke. Even when he did, there was a lameness about it when he said, " You've gone out of your mind. You don't know what you're talking about."

" Oh yes, I do," she said. " I know that I've been living for years in a place I thought we'd come by honestly with money we'd a right to. But that isn't so and you've made me be your partner in something criminal and horrible. And I hate you for it ! I hate you ! "

" Frightened, aren't you ? " he said. " Frightened you may have to suffer for it yourself in some way. A wonderful wife."

" I'm not your wife any more," she said. " I've finished with you."

" Fine, fine ! " he said violently. " That's what I was wanting to hear. And now will you tell me why, if I murdered Auty, that old woman upstairs went to a lot of trouble to lie on my account ? Can you see her doing that ? Can you see anyone of her sort worrying for a minute over what might happen to someone like me or you ? "

" Maybe it wasn't to protect you she was lying," Lorna said. " Maybe she had her own reasons."

" For instance ? "

" Well, she might have thought it wasn't you she saw. She might have thought it was Nock or Marriner."

" See her lying to protect Nock ? Oh, my lord ! " Carver burst into nervous laughter.

" Well, Marriner then."

" Maybe, if she thought she saw Marriner, she did see Marriner. But I don't see her lying for his sake either. Why should she ? She's not daft. She'd have nothing to lose by sticking to the truth. No, you take it from me, there's only one person she'd lie to protect and that's her darling Hector. And he's out of it. You can't tie him up with this, however you try. What I believe is that she isn't lying at all. Maybe Auty wasn't stooping when she said he was. But what does that amount to ? Only that she was excited when she first told the story and didn't know properly what she was saying, and then, being old and stubborn, went on and stuck to it. That's what I believe and that the only person who's lying now is Pointing, when he tries to put it over on us all that the blood was clotting."

" That's an explanation of the situation," Hughes said, " that had occurred to me. Yes, Mr. Kenny ? " For Hector had just returned to the sitting-room and was standing at the inspector's elbow, trying to catch his attention.

" My mother wants me to give you a message," Hector said. " She'll come down herself in a few minutes to confirm it, but she asks you to give her just a little time to rest. She's very upset and she's lying down. The message is that you should on no account consider arresting either Mr. or Mrs. Pointing for the murder of Ardwell. Neither of them had anything to do with it. She says that she can tell you who the real murderer was, even though she didn't see him. She's decided to do this, I believe, because she's realised what a danger her silence can be to innocent people, though she'd been hoping that Ardwell's murder could go unpunished. Now, if you'll excuse me, I'll go back to her. I'll bring her down with me in a few minutes."

He turned and went out again.

This time the inspector followed him. In the sitting-room nobody moved or spoke.

Then Carver said, " She's an old fool. If she'd keep her mouth shut, there'd be no evidence against anybody——"

His words were drowned in the crash of an explosion.

The house shook with it, the windows clattered and somewhere somebody gave a terrible, shrill scream.

CHAPTER XX

WHEN THE BOMB exploded in Mrs. Kenny's room, it killed Hector outright. But his body partly shielded Mrs. Kenny from the force of the explosion and though she was unconscious when Hughes plunged into the room, to be met by a dark cloud of dust that rolled up at him like smoke from a fire, and though she was bleeding from a deep cut on her forehead, she was still breathing weakly.

The room was wrecked. Panelling and plaster had been

torn from the walls and ceiling. Furniture was split and overturned. The glass from the windows had been blown out into the garden, leaving only a few jagged fragments in the frames. In the midst of the wreck, the body of Hector Kenny was something at which it was best not to look. While Hughes stood there, a cupboard door that had been hanging at a strange angle on one hinge, fell with a crash.

There had been a rush of feet on the stairs, but the sergeant, who had been only just behind Hughes when he went into the room, turned everyone back. In silence the remainder of Mark Auty's guests went back to the sitting-room.

Except that Lorna Carver began to cry, the silence had them all by the throat. They might have been stricken dumb. While the voices of the inspector and the sergeant and of other policemen sounded up and down the staircase, while the clanging bell of an ambulance was heard approaching and the sound of hurrying footsteps grew in loudness in the corridors and in the rooms overhead, so that the house seemed to be all din and feverish haste, in the sitting-room nobody moved, nobody spoke. What might have been hours went by.

It was not really as long as that. Gradually the noise in the rest of the house grew less. The ambulance drove away again. The voices that had been shouting at one another dropped to undertones. The tramping about upstairs came to an end. Several men left the house and the sense of activity faded to nothing. It was as if the silence in the sitting-room had spread through the rest of the house and quietened everything.

Then a new voice sounded in the hall, an excited, protesting, foreign voice, and Miss Barbosa, exclaiming, " Uncle Gilberto ! " got up and stumbled out of the room. She was not seen there again.

About twenty minutes after that, Hughes reappeared. He stood in the doorway, an angry-looking, tired man with a bleak, strained face and his clothes smudged with dust.

" All right, you can all go home," he said.

No one moved or answered him.

" Go home ! " he said louder. " Go—the whole lot of you."

Pointing recovered himself first. " I think you should tell us what's happened," he said.

" They're both dead," Hughes answered.

" Mrs. Kenny and Hector ? "

" Yes. She lived a little while. It looks as if he tried to throw himself in front of her to save her, but he wasn't quick enough."

" Was it suicide ? " Pointing went on. " I mean, with her sending him down like that with that message about my wife and me, and probably not expecting him back quite so soon——"

" For God's sake ! " Hughes nearly shouted. He was like a man who had seen and felt too much during the last hour to be sure of what he was saying or doing. " Why else d'you think I'd be telling you to go home ? Now get your things together and go. That's what you want."

Nock rose to his feet. " It's what I want. Thank you, Inspector."

He went out briskly.

Marriner was frowning heavily, His eyebrows were drawn straight above the brightness of his eyes. " But why ? She couldn't have killed Auty. Nor could Hector."

" Couldn't he ? " Hughes said.

" Did she talk before she died ? " Carver asked.

" She talked a little."

" But——"

Hughes was almost snarling. " You know all you need to. You'll no doubt read the rest in the papers. Now go and pack. There's a train to London every hour. If I were you, I'd do my best to catch the next one."

Sarah stood up.

" That's what I'll try to do," she said, and, like Nock, went out.

She went to her room and packed as quickly as she could. If she had not needed to do that, if she could have gone straight out of the house, she would have done so. Everything about the house was touched with horror. The room, with its low, sloping ceiling and the dark age of its furniture, which had seemed to her charming and picturesque on her first evening there, now seemed to her to represent all that had been corrupt and dishonest in Auty and sinister about his end.

She could have packed more quickly if she had not been shivering. Her shaking hands were clumsy. She was forgetful, too, of where she had put the things that she had unpacked. Afraid of leaving things behind, she went through drawers and cupboards more than once, and then, because she had packed so badly, had difficulty in closing the cases that had closed easily when she had packed them before.

She had just finished and was standing in front of the mirror, hurriedly dabbing powder on to her face, when there was a knock on the door.

She did not call out, " Come in," but went to the door to see who it was.

It was Hughes.

He said, " I'd like to talk with you for a minute, Miss Wing. Mind if I come in ? "

She opened the door wider. He came in and closed it. Seeing her packed cases and her readiness to be gone, he said, " You aren't losing much time, are you ? "

" You told us to go," she said, standing in the middle of the room, her hat on, her bag and gloves in her hand.

" Oh yes. I spoke in recognition of your good sense, nothing else," he said. " Strangely enough, some of the others seem reluctant to go. They want to know more." He pulled a chair forward and sat down astride it. " Don't you ? "

" More than anything else, I want to get away," she said. " I've had enough. After all, I'm one death up on the others. I saw the end of Henry Darnborough."

" Ah yes. Darnborough. Well, I shan't keep you a moment. I just want to ask you something about Hector Kenny."

" I don't expect I can tell you anything that I haven't told you already."

" You're probably quite right. But I want to make sure about that. I want you to think carefully and then tell me if you're still absolutely certain that Hector Kenny never left the garden all the time that you were there on the morning of the murder."

" I'm quite certain," she said.

" There weren't even a few minutes when you were looking down at a book, perhaps——— ? "

" I wasn't reading."

" Or talking to someone else ? "

" I was talking to Mrs. Kenny some of the time and to Mr. Nock, but I know that Hector Kenny never left the garden. He was weeding the flower bed most of the time, though for a short while he sat and talked with me. That was when he was showing me the revolver."

He nodded. " Yes, that's what I thought. But I wanted to make sure that even now he's dead, you'd still say the same thing."

" Why should his being dead make any difference ? "

He stood up. " Miss Wing, I've been investigating the murder of Mark Auty. I've been doing my best to catch his murderer. But that doesn't mean I haven't realised that there was a lot to be said for the idea that Auty's better dead. If I'd happened to be on your side of the fence instead of mine, and if I'd known that a generally speaking decent little man like Hector Kenny had saved my life and the lives of several other people by murdering Auty, I won't swear that I wouldn't have been prepared to provide him with an impregnable alibi." His serious expression was relieved for a moment by an odd smile. " I'm speaking without witnesses, of course."

" But Hector couldn't have done it," she said. " Dead or alive, that's still the truth. He never left the garden."

" Well, that's that, then." He turned to the door.

She took a quick step towards him. " But *did* Hector do it ? Is that what you think."

" They'll decide that at the inquest," he said. " Thank God I haven't got to make their minds up for them."

" But what do you think yourself ? "

He paused with one hand on the door handle.

" Mrs. Kenny lied," he said. " She lied from start to finish."

" You mean that business about Auty stooping over the table when he couldn't have been ? "

" I mean about ever having seen the murder at all. She did the whole thing to provide the murderer with an alibi. In fact, the murder had happened some time before she went to post her letters. And Pointing guessed that when he saw that the blood from the wound was already beginning to clot by the time that he climbed into the room through the window."

" So that was true ? "

" Yes. But I don't think we'd ever have heard about it if Pointing hadn't suddenly discovered that he was in a certain amount of danger himself. He had no very violent feelings against Auty's murderer."

" Well, why did Mrs. Kenny make that blunder about Auty stooping, which made you suspicious that she was lying ? She didn't do it on purpose, did she ? "

" Oh, no. But just imagine how it could have happened. She and the murderer plan the affair. The murderer says, ' I'll arrange things so that it looks as if I'd killed him when he was pouring out a drink.' And that's what he does. He arranges things so that it looks as if Auty had been standing with a decanter in one hand and a glass in the other when he was stabbed. But Mrs. Kenny, going to the window of Auty's room and looking in, sees a low table covered with bottles and glasses. So what she visualises is Auty stooping over the table when he's killed and that's what she describes."

" But I still don't see how it could have been Hector ? " Sarah said stubbornly. " I know it's difficult to imagine her lying to save anyone else, but I saw him in the garden all the time—I saw him myself."

Hughes had opened the door and had taken a step through the doorway. Now he changed his mind, came back into the room and closed the door.

" Shall I tell you what Mrs. Kenny said before she died ? " he asked.

" What was it ? "

" She said only a few words, with breaks in between. She said, ' I did it . . . yes, I lied . . . to save my dear boy. . . . I knew, you see . . . ' "

" And that was all ? "

" Yes. But those were her exact words."

Sarah gestured helplessly. " She was mistaken, that's all. Or else . . ."

" Well ? "

" Or else, if you filled in the gaps between the words, you'd find they meant something different."

" Try and prove it," he said sombrely as he went out, " now that Mrs. Kenny's dead."

CHAPTER XXI

IN THE BIG stone house in a suburb of Bradford, a brother-in-law of Mrs. Kenny's, with whom she had always been on rather bad terms, walked from room to room with the small, anxious-looking man who for forty years had been Mrs. Kenny's lawyer. The housekeeper, who was still living in the house, let the two men in, then withdrew abruptly to the kitchen, muttering something about, " hardly cold in their graves."

The rooms were all in semi-darkness, for the blinds at the windows had been drawn in sign of mourning. The dim light touched the polished surfaces of great slabs of walnut and mahogany and the gilt frames of the pictures that almost entirely covered the walls of the high rooms. Thick carpets deadened the footsteps of the two men. They spoke in undertones.

" What will it fetch, this sort of thing, nowadays ? " the brother-in-law asked. " It's all good, solid stuff. My sister-in-law would never put up with anything gimcrack."

" Quite true, quite true," the lawyer said. " But it's hard to say. Before the war, of course, it would have gone for nothing. Too old-fashioned, you see, too big for small houses and so on. Then, after the war, you could have made a fortune by selling it. People would buy anything, sometimes just for the wood. After all, take a table like that, beautiful, seasoned walnut. I've sat at it many a time in the old days and as I remember it, when it's completely extended, it must measure at least seventeen feet. Well, you could practically furnish a whole room just with the wood from that table."

" But what would it fetch ? " the brother-in-law asked.

" Hard to say, hard to say. As I was telling you, just after the war, any price you liked to name. But now . . .

Well, prices are just as high, or higher, but people aren't buying like they were. In fact, you may not be able to sell half the things at all."

" What about the house itself ? "

" Ah, that's a problem too. Very unpredictable. In your place, I'd convert it into flats."

" Well, I've been thinking of that."

" It's what I advised Mrs. Kenny to do. Even she couldn't afford the staff of servants the place needed and really she'd been living in only three or four rooms for years, with that housekeeper you saw and a charwoman. And, of course, Hector. Hector looked after the garden. But she wouldn't listen to me about the flats, or anything else. A very independent woman, all her life."

The brother-in-law began to laugh, but hurriedly suppressed the sound, which echoed shockingly in the great, shadowy rooms.

" And everything would have been Hector's," he said. " And Hector would have sold it immediately and gone to live in the country, to garden and fish. Still, she wouldn't have known any more about that than she knows about what I'm going to do with it."

" I don't think, you know, that she'd have minded what Hector did with it, if it had made him happy," the lawyer said. His tone implied that he feared that the brother-in-law might not be as exempt as Hector from the criticism of Mrs. Kenny's ghost.

The two men walked on softly into the next room.

The brother-in-law was saying, " Talking of flats . . ."

In a bedroom of a hotel on the edge of Dartmoor, Lorna Carver was opening drawers and cupboards, tearing her clothes out of them and piling them on the bed. On the floor there were two or three open suitcases. With the tense, exaggerated gestures of someone who is fuming with rage, she folded and refolded her belongings, packed, unpacked and re-packed, talking to herself half the time, sometimes out loud, sometimes only with a quick, silent motion of her lips. Under her usual heavy make-up, her face was colourless, so that the patches of rouge on her cheekbones looked like postage stamps pasted there.

179

Once she caught a finger in the hinge of a cupboard and as the pain of it jabbed through her hand, tears filled her eyes. Thrusting the finger into her mouth, she sucked it, whilst the tears ran harder. For a minute or two it looked as if she might give way to them completely. But then, with a fierce shake of her head and without troubling to dry her eyes, she returned to her packing.

By the time that she had finished, a taxi had arrived and was waiting before the hotel entrance.

Going to the window, she beckoned to the driver and he came upstairs to help with her luggage. He took the two large suitcases, while Lorna followed with a hat-box and a small handbag. They met no one on the stairs or in the lobby, and though Lorna hesitated near the door that led to the bar, it was only for a moment. Going on again, she stepped into the taxi. The driver slammed the door on her and climbed into his own seat.

Only then, Tim Carver appeared in the doorway of the hotel. But he stayed slightly within it, the shadow from the doorway falling across his face. He stood with his feet apart and his hands in his pockets. When the taxi drove off, he did not wave or make any gesture, only when it was out of sight, he strolled back into the bar.

A farmer, who was standing by the counter with a mug of cider in front of him, said, "Wasn't that the missus, Tim ? "

" That's right," Tim said.

" Going on a holiday ? "

" That's right."

" Going for long ? "

Tim shrugged. " Long as she feels like."

" Ah, do her good, I reckon, after that do you've had. Bad shock for a girl like Lorna."

" That's right."

" Bit of a job for you, though, managing without her."

" Maybe. I've got a girl coming to help."

" Temporary like ? "

" Depends on the girl."

Something in his tone made the farmer look at Tim speculatively.

" That affair you got mixed up in, it's all over, I suppose."
He pushed his mug forward for more cider.

" No, I shouldn't say it was myself," Tim said. " ' Person
or persons unknown '—when that's the verdict, it can always
get opened up again."

" Yet the old lady practically accused her son, didn't she? "
the farmer said. " I don't see why that wasn't good enough
for them."

Tim did not answer. He busied himself polishing glasses.

" In my opinion," the farmer went on, " it won't never
be solved."

" Whose asking your opinion ? " Tim flared up. Then he
drew a deep breath, pressing the back of his wrist against
his sweating forehead. " Sorry, Ernie, I didn't mean to say
that. My nerves are all to bits. No offence."

" That's right, no offence," the farmer answered. "You've
had a bad time, I reckon. You need a holiday, like Lorna.
By the way, where's she gone ? To stay with her family ? "

" She hasn't any family that I know of."

" Gone to Torquay, maybe."

Tim shrugged again, then, as an afterthought, added,
" Oh yes, Torquay."

The farmer finished his cider, picked up his hat and stick
and turned to the door.

" Well, good-bye, Tim. See you to-morrow."

He went out.

In the road he met an acquaintance who was just about
to enter the bar.

" See Mrs. Tim go off in the taxi ? " the farmer said.

" Aye," the other replied.

" Going to Torquay for a holiday, Tim says."

" She'll have a long wait for the train then."

" That's what I thought. But she could catch the London
train just nicely. Well, good-day to you."

" Good day."

The two men parted.

In the white-panelled drawing-room of a house in an
Oxfordshire village, Denis and Violet Pointing sat drinking
tea out of their blue and gold Queen Charlotte cups before
going up to bed.

The faces of both were haggard with tiredness. They had been making a pretence for the evening of talking of other things than the murder of Mark Auty, but this had given the conversation of both of them the entirely artificial sound of people talking to an invalid, inexpertly trying to conceal from him the seriousness of his condition. They had agreed together that they would not go on talking about the murder, and both had loyally, stubbornly stuck to the agreement. But the strain on both had been great.

At last, with the long hours of the night ahead of her and many thoughts pressing on her mind, Mrs. Pointing gave way.

" Denis, if they never really find out who did it, it's going to cling to us all our lives, isn't it ? "

" They will find out," he said.

" I don't see how. Now that Mrs. Kenny's dead, I don't see how they can ever prove who did it, even if they're pretty sure who it was."

" I think they're quite sure who it was," Denis said.

" Perhaps. But all the same, how can they prove it ? Isn't it going to follow us now for the rest of our lives ? "

" Even after Mrs. Kenny's message that neither of us had had anything to do with it ? "

" But how do we know that that message came from her ? We only heard it from Hector. And then Mrs. Kenny said something incriminating Hector, which everyone could see didn't make sense. So I don't think that anything that Mrs. Kenny said will turn out to have much importance."

Denis turned this over in his mind for a moment. " Is this leading up to anything special, Vi ? "

" No," she said, " although I was wondering . . ."

" Well ? "

" I was wondering if our lives here were going to become impossible."

" Do you want to move ? "

" Oh no—no ! " she said passionately. " And it would be the same anywhere else, wouldn't it ? "

" I should think so. And you see, dear, I don't think the case is by any means closed. There are all kinds of things that may yet be found out. Where that knife came from, for instance."

She shook her head. " I don't see how they'll ever find out who it was. And because we have the motive of Mark's money, some suspicion will always stick to us. Even if we give every penny of it to charity, people will say that that's only because, after all, we were afraid to accept it."

" Then let them say it. Let them say anything they like."

She gave a smile which seemed only to deepen the lines about her tired mouth.

" Yes, I know that's the answer—the only answer," she said. " I'll try to live up to it."

" I don't think you'll have to for long," Denis said. " I don't believe for a minute that the man will get away with it. They'll get him somehow. Killing Mrs. Kenny may have saved him for the moment, but in the long run it'll be the finish of him."

" What I don't understand," she said, reaching for the teapot, " is why, with her last breath, she tried to save him."

" To save him ? " Pointing said in a puzzled tone.

" By accusing Hector. That's the only reason I can think of for her doing that. She was trying to save the murderer. She knew Hector was dead and couldn't suffer, so she accused him."

" But she didn't."

" She said——"

" Yes, yes, I know what she said. But there's more than one way of taking what she said."

It was Mrs. Pointing who was looking puzzled now.

He went on, " She was trying to tell us, while she was dying, why she had acted as the accomplice of a murderer. She lied, she was trying to say, to help the murderer who was going to save Hector from being blown up by Auty's bomb. She knew, she was trying to say, what Auty's plan was. As a matter of fact, Vi, it's my belief that it was Mrs. Kenny who planned that murder. She saw Sarah Wing with the brief-case, got suspicious, investigated, and not being inhibited, as the girl had been, and as Auty, of course, had known she would be, about prying under a layer of personal letters, found the bomb. At that point she decided that Auty had got to be killed. Someone else was her tool and someone would probably have been paid an executioner's fee——"

But then," Mrs. Pointing interrupted in excitement, " the real murderer was Mrs. Kenny."

" You can put it like that, if you like."

" That wonderful old lady ! "

" Wonderful old lady—she was vain, autocratic, self-indulgent, overbearing, ego-centric, probably cruel. But she was old, so everything was forgiven her. Age is one of the greatest charms in the world."

" Yet Hector did adore her, you know. He really did."

" Well, it isn't the only time in history that a good man has loved a bad woman."

" Yet she saved the lives of all of us."

" Granted. Yet if you or I had happened on that bomb, would we have murdered Auty ? "

" I don't know what I'd have done."

" I know what I'd have done," he said. " I'd have quietly ditched the bomb and let Miss Wing carry her perfectly harmless suitcase to Nice. Then she and Marriner and the Carvers and the Kennys could have had their happy week-end at the expense of Miss Barbosa and you and I could have come home."

" Don't you think, in that case, there'd have been another bomb for the return journey ? "

He put down his cup so abruptly that it clattered in the saucer.

" Yes," he said. " Yes, of course. So that was the reason . . ."

" Though she could have taken the bomb to the police."

" A bomb that she'd found in Miss Wing's possession ? " He picked up his tea-cup again, smiling ruefully across it at his wife. " Whatever she was, she could think fast, that old woman. I think I'd better take back the things I've been saying about her. And now there's something else we've got to think about. Isn't it time we fixed the date of our wedding ? "

Wearing a dinner-jacket, with a lace handkerchief jutting from the breast-pocket, with the scent of a fresh shave and hair-oil about him, Peter Nock strolled into the bar of the Songbird. The hour was early and not many people had arrived. Harry the barman was whistling through his teeth and looking bored. When he saw Nock, he twitched his eyebrows in surly greeting.

"Well, you look pleased with yourself all right," he grunted. "You didn't get to Nice, though, did you?"

Nock had glanced at the table in the corner. It was empty. "Where's Myra?" he asked.

"Gone to telephone her mother. You know Myra. Always telephoning her mother." There was a curious light in Harry's dull eyes.

"How long ago did she go?" Nock asked.

"Yesterday evening."

Nock swung round on him. "*Yesterday——?*"

A little, malicious smile tugged at the corners of Harry's mouth. "That's what I said."

Nock's hand slid towards his pocket, but then dropped to his side. He smiled too. Indifferently, as though the barman had merely made a bad joke, he asked, "What's the idea, Harry?"

"Just like I said," Harry answered. "She went to telephone her mother, never came back."

"Was she drunk?"

"Oh sure. And mad at you. Fit to be tied. Mind you . . ."

"Well?"

"I got the idea that girl never did care for getting mixed up with murder. I reckon her mother must have advised her against it."

Very softly, Nock said, "D'you ever wonder, Harry, if one day you'll say one thing too much? Could happen, you know. Could easily happen."

"Maybe I'm not the one who's said too much," Harry said. "Maybe that was Myra."

As if uncontrollably, one of Nock's thin hands moved towards his pocket again. Harry saw it and his smile grew wider.

"Not here I wouldn't, Pete," he said. "You got an audience."

He was looking over Nock's shoulder as he spoke. Nock jerked round. Two men had approached and were standing close behind him. They were both big, heavily built men. There was no mistaking what they were.

For an instant Nock looked wildly round. There was a door not a yard away. But one of the men was already between Nock and the door.

Harry picked up a bottle of whisky and poured himself a drink.

" Always said you liked peace and quiet, didn't you, Pete ? Well, this is where you start to get it."

At the same time one of the men was saying to Nock : " Peter Nock, I am a police-officer and I have here a warrant for your arrest for the murder of Henry Darnborough . . ."

After an uneventful day, Inspector Hughes and the sergeant had strolled back together to Hughes' lodgings and the sergeant had been invited in for a glass of beer before going on to his home.

" All the same," the sergeant was saying as they went into the house, " it could have been any of the others who killed Auty."

" No," the Inspector said, " it was Nock."

" Oh yes, I don't need any persuading—it was Nock," the sergeant said. " All the same, it could have been Carver or Marriner or Pointing or any of the women, come to that."

" No," Hughes said, as the two men settled themselves comfortably in the room lit by the lamp decorated with elves and toadstools. " There was only one person who was helped by the old woman's lies and that was Nock. Her story didn't give anyone else an alibi. Pointing was even endangered by it. But it placed Nock safely in the garden at the time of the murder. Only he hadn't been there long, like Miss Wing and Hector. He'd come straight out there after doing the murder and that was the signal for Mrs. Kenny to go and post her letters. That was all clear enough once it was clear that Mrs. Kenny had been lying about what she saw. The only trouble was to find any reason that could make a woman like Mrs. Kenny go into partnership to do murder with a man like Nock. She seemed to have nothing against Auty except that forgery years ago, which she'd already forgiven him once. But once we'd got on to what Auty had really brought those people together for, that was answered." As long as he lived, Auty would be a danger to all the people who knew anything about him."

" All the same, you'd never have got Nock convicted on that evidence."

" No, that's what he was counting on. It'd never worry Nock how much he was suspected of a thing if it couldn't be proved."

" D'you think he was meaning all along to do Mrs. Kenny in as well ? "

" I shouldn't think so. Alive, she'd have been a source of revenue. What he hadn't counted on was that a woman like Mrs. Kenny can't look on and let innocent people get into trouble. When she saw what her story was going to do to Pointing, she began to think she'd have to change it. First of all she implored Mrs. Pointing not to confess——"

" So did Nock."

" Oh yes. Disinterested Nock. Co-operative Nock. The first person to realise that Mrs. Kenny had spoilt the whole show by describing Auty as stooping over the table. Nock had the wit to draw other people's attention to that and try to make out that Auty must have been stooping, but for some reason that wasn't pouring out a drink."

" I wonder if Mrs. Kenny would actually have told us the truth or whether, upstairs in her room, she'd thought out another story."

" Who can tell with a woman like that ? But Nock was afraid she was going to tell the truth and as soon as he over-heard from the window that she was going upstairs to lie down, he got the bomb from where he'd hidden it in the garden, and when he was sure that she really meant to talk, he lobbed it in at her bedroom window."

" I'm glad we can get him for Darnborough," the sergeant said. " I'm glad for little Hector's sake."

" Oh, we'll get him all right. With that woman of his deciding to talk, and Miss Wing's identification of him, and the whole tie-up with Auty coming out, we'll get him. More beer ? "

" No thanks. Time I was getting home."

" Good night, then."

" Good night."

In a restaurant in Percy Street, Sarah Wing and Alec Marriner sat together at dinner. Sarah was wearing a dress that she had bought to take to Nice. They had cocktails and wine and spent more money than Marriner could afford, but he looked quite happy about it. They talked about East Africa. For several hours neither of them mentioned murder.

THE END

〉〉〉 If you've enjoyed this book and would like to discover more great vintage crime and thriller titles, as well as the most exciting crime and thriller authors writing today, visit: 〉〉〉

The Murder Room
Where Criminal Minds Meet

themurderroom.com